Mind Th

C000076567

KIM GUINAN

Copyright © 2019 Author Name

All rights reserved.

ISBN: 9781097842599

DEDICATION

I dedicate this book to my husband, children and grandchildren.

CHAPTER ONE

The day sweltering, the outside temperature tipping thirty degrees, Piccadilly tube station is hot, humid, and suffocating! My way ahead bloated with a stream of people dribbling out of every orifice, within seconds of stepping on to the underground platform, I am swallowed whole by a pressing crowd.

Carried forward, strangers invading my personal space, to add insult to injury, it is then that I find myself stood directly behind the most odious slug of a woman. My nose hovering within millimetres of her fetid hair, I try not to gag. Barely able to move and seething with irritation, I breathe shallowly and centre my thoughts. Battling for precious inches, I extend my rigid arms out and away from my sides, but it is no good. I am stuck!

A sudden, hot breath of wind puffing in from the left and the air around me tenses. The crowd heaving in response, behaving like a giant amoeba, it surges forward, taking me with it.

The edge of the platform in sight, without deliberation, I shove my foot, hard, into the back of the knee of the repulsive female blocking my way. An anticipatory tightening in my belly, a pulse throbbing in my temples, there is a shiver of excitement as I watch with a fascination bordering on the obsessive, the woman's not inconsiderable bulk collapse down and forward. She, falling heavily on to the person stood in front of her, who in turn topples just as awkwardly on to the unfortunate person standing in front of them, I feel an unexpected moment of anxiety, of being scared for a second or two. But then I knew, it was going to be all right. In the unfolding chaos, no one has noticed me, or my part in it.

And so it is, I find myself — well — revelling in the aftermath of my random act of violence.

Oh, come on, you sit there and dare judge me?

Having seen an opportunity, I simply seized it, that's all.

Wouldn't you, if you had been in my shoes?

In their confusion and horror, the populace panicking, scattering away from the ensuing pandemonium, like the pins from a bowling ball, I welcome an instant relief of pressure.

At the same time, I hear the sudden and piercing scream of a dying woman falling on to the electrified tracks. Her shriek a heady mixture of terror and pain, it is immediately followed by the high-pitched squeal of metal screeching against metal as the hurtling train, comes to a dead stop.

'Mind the gap!' booms out the automated announcement as the train arrives into the station.

CHAPTER TWO

Gemma Atkinson shouted up the stairs in a mounting frustration.

'Henry, Jessica, please… get a move on or we're going to be late!'

Pacing up and down the narrow and compact hallway of the too small house they all had to share, glancing at her watch, she sighed out heavily with irritation. At this rate, she was bound to be late for work again.

A Victorian end of a terrace, Gemma's home was located in Leyton, an east London suburb close to the green spaces of the Lea Valley, the Hackney Marshes, and the Olympic Park. Stratford International Station and the Westfield Shopping Centre also easily accessible by a short ten minute train journey, the area was convenient and supposedly smartening up its act. Mainly populated with families local to the area, although she could have done with a bigger house, it was a place Gemma felt comfortable with.

Because of their son — the house jointly owned but a divorce in the works — Gemma had been legally granted the right to stay in the property until Henry turned eighteen. In return, Gemma finding herself locked in to an awkward custody arrangement — Paul having his son to stay every other weekend and fifty percent of the school holidays — the irreparable breech between the marital pair had been wedged open even wider. Paul paying child maintenance and still part owner of the house, no matter what way Gemma dressed it up to herself, she still felt disagreeably obligated to Henry's father.

At last, his sturdy little legs and arms pumping, Gemma watched with a certain amount of trepidation as her seven year old son lunged down the staircase and flung himself toward her. Automatically shoving out a steadying hand, she hastily pushed it into Henry's chest to prevent him from barrelling into her.

'Whoa there, slow down young man.'

Henry threw his mother a puzzled look. 'But you said we had to hurry up?'

'I know, but there's no need to flatten your poor old mum in the process. Go on, quick. Go and grab your school bag,' she encouraged.

Fifteen year old Jessica idly followed in Henry's wake as though she had all the time in the world. Plugged into her mobile as usual, her face was wearing its customary look of petulance as she studied something of *vital* importance on the screen in front of her. Gemma, meanwhile, was totally blanked.

Ignoring an almost overwhelming urge to yell at the girl, to insist she put away the phone and scrub off the too heavy make-up her school had only last week, sent a scathing letter home about, Gemma turned smartly on her heel and headed for the front door. With any luck, this morning, she might be on time and right now, that was all she cared about.

Flinging open the front door, Gemma ushered out both of the children. The kids misplacing gym kit, homework, lunch boxes, whatever they hadn't sorted through the night before and having promised the opposite, every school morning it was the same. She forever nagging them to find their stuff, to get dressed, to eat their breakfast, to clean their teeth, to get a move on, no wonder Dave always left early, she thought as given the choice, so would she.

Stepping out over the front doorstep Gemma violently shivered as she shrank into her coat. Unseasonably cold for early October, frost laying in thin slivers of silver and platinum along the tops of fences, paths and car windscreens, Gemma hunched her shoulders against the frigid air. Her impractical high heels slip-sliding down the minuscule garden path, she suddenly realised, the damn car would need scraping.

The kids already at the car, Henry yelling for the doors to be unlocked, Gemma looked briefly toward the heavens as she cussed in a responsible silence.

Henry and Jessica dropped off at their respective schools, Gemma was sat at her desk pretending she had not arrived late, and that she really wanted to be there. Her computer humming, drowning her in emails, she was desperate for a restorative coffee but ignored the urge. Any minute now, her psycho boss was sure to be hounding her down.

Restlessly staying put — the story of her life — and feeling unexpectedly sorry for herself, Gemma gave in to a moment of weakness and began to question a few of her more recent life choices. Whatever happened to her taking her time, to proving to herself she had what it took, to go it alone? And what on earth made her think she would ever be any good as a pseudo step-mother to a highly temperamental teenager, when she was barely out of nappies herself? Talk about muddleheaded, she thought, with a decent amount of regret.

Feeling as though she had too many responsibilities, too little time and far too little sleep, for a very real moment, Gemma wished she could somehow wind back the clock and start all over again. She shook her head at herself, at her self-pity. What she really needed, she told herself, was a distraction, some unadulterated fun or an adventure. Something that would return her misplaced sense of humour before it became permanently lost.

Muffled footfalls.

Perhaps, she continued to berate herself, if she had put more effort into changing her job rather than her partner?

The footfalls sounding louder, getting closer as her boss bore down on her, Gemma shook away her misgivings. Now was not the time for brooding on her complicated life.

Hastily delving into her bag, Gemma grabbed amongst the debris of clutter for her pocket mirror, found it and sprung it open. Smoothing a hand over her chin length bob — a style the hairdresser kept cutting back in even though Gemma had been desperate to grow it out — she attempted to pat it into some semblance of order. Giving her lightly freckled, very ordinary apple-shaped face a cursory once-over, she sighed at her reflection. Pasty faced, dark circles under her eyes, she hated that her sleep deprived life made her look so frazzled.

Sweeping down the office corridor as though she owned the place, Katie Pride stopped directly in front of Gemma's desk. Her electric blue eyes were as icy as her smile was cold.

'So, you finally made it then?' said Katie, loudly enough for everyone in the open-plan office to hear.

Gemma's shoulders drooped.

'Traffic bad again, was it?' she chuckled.

Katie's voice high and squeaky, her laugh false, everything about the woman grated on Gemma's easily shredded nerves.

'Cat got your tongue?' Katie demanded to know.

With significant discomfort, Gemma looked up at the petite woman hovering above her. Taking in the lightly but perfectly made-up face, the bouncy blonde curls floating around a slender neck sitting casually atop ultra-slim shoulders, she tried not to be envious of the younger, prettier, much thinner woman.

'Morning Katie, I'll go get your coffee, shall I?' Gemma enquired with a false serenity. *She needs me far more than I need her,* she silently deluded herself.

Katie dropped a folder the size of house brick on the end of Gemma's desk, tapped her finger on it a couple of times.

'Yes, but make it snappy, we have a lot to get through today. And it's not like *you* have a lot of time to spare, is it?'

Katie never missing an opportunity to knock her part-time hours, along with the fact she was having to leave the office even earlier than usual today, Gemma gritted her teeth as she stood up from her chair. Her blouse immediately coming untucked from the waistband of her too tight skirt as her love-handles spilled over and pushed it out, Gemma bestowed an embarrassed smile on her skinny, perfectly dressed boss.

'Sure, I'll be back as soon as I've got your coffee.'

Watching Katie swish off in an exquisite set of clothes that probably cost more than her monthly mortgage repayment, Gemma could not help but feel yet another sudden and disruptive spark of jealousy toward her arrogant by name as well as by nature, boss. Guessing the pristinely dressed and perfectly timed Katie Pride, with her live-in nanny, housekeeper, gardener and chauffeur, had not wasted any precious minutes searching all over the house for *her* kids missing stuff, she sniffed dismissively. She also bet Katie had not missed out on her breakfast, or had to drink a cold mug of coffee that morning. Or that Katie's car, kept in its super-duper garage that was almost as big as a house, did not have to be scraped free of ice before she had been driven off to work that morning.

Loathing her boss as the beginnings of a headache tapped at her temples, there were days when Gemma dreamed about Katie Pride being killed off by some maniac — poisoned, shoved under a bus or train. Anything, really, that would rid her of the bloody woman.

Roll-on two-thirty, Gemma thought as weirdly, she began to look forward to a dentist's appointment that she had, up until that moment, been dreading.

CHAPTER THREE

Later that same day, Dave was attempting to gauge Gemma's mood as she entered the kitchen. His freshly showered partner looking a shade distracted, he was trying to work out if was he going to be able to open a beer and the start the evening early?

'Kid's OK?' he asked as Gemma stopped just in front of him.

Gemma saying nothing in reply, not a word, finding himself on the receiving end of one of those long steady looks that had the tendency to frighten children and strangers, but not him, he had to smile. Loving the very essence of her, there was nothing Gemma Atkinson could ever do, or say, he thought happily, that would ever scare him away.

Kissing Gemma on the top of her slightly damp head, her hair the colour of chestnuts and smelling of something fruity, Dave suddenly found himself wanting to bury his face into its depths. Then remembering he needed to get to the bottom of whatever her problem was, he curbed his desire and reluctantly pulled back from her.

'Something wrong? Do I need to go up there?' Dave asked bouncing his head toward the slightly peeling ceiling.

'No, no, it's all fine. Henry's in bed and she's...' Gemma paused to correct herself. 'Jessica is doing her homework.'

Gemma's usual speaking style quiet but firm, Dave knew she rarely spoke without thinking, but her voice sounding dejected in spite of the encouraging words, he could not lie to himself. Something was wrong, he knew it.

Not for the first time since moving in with Gemma, Dave asked himself if he had been clumsy? If he had not properly taken Gemma's feelings into account before pushing her into a full-on relationship? Meeting Gemma, falling so head-over-heels in love with her, for the first time in a long time, he had felt so confident and carefree, so unable to resist. Yet ever since they'd moved in together, become an *official* family in the eyes of their families and friends, there had been days when he worried he'd bulldozed Gemma into something she'd not been quite ready for.

Lifting Gemma's hand, Dave lightly kissed her palm. No longer able to ignore the droop in her shoulders as she took back her hand and moved firmly away from him, he forced out the words he had been so determined *not* to ask.

'Gemma, is it me? Have I done something to upset you?'

There was a beat of silence as Gemma blatantly avoided his gaze.

'Gemma?'

Gemma turning to face Dave as she leaned up against the side of the kitchen countertop, looking hesitant, she exhaled a heavy sigh.

'Of course you haven't. Stop worrying. Everything's fine, I'm fine. Just tired.'

'Tired?'

She nodded.

'Yeah, it's been a long day.'

'Go on,' Dave encouraged, keen to hear about anything that meant there was nothing terribly wrong with their relationship.

She dispatched a weary smile.

'Katie, she took umbrage at my leaving early. Reminded me that as I'm *only* part-time. That I should book my *personal* appointments *outside* of my normal working hours, not in them.'

'Surely she knows how difficult it is to get a dentist's appointment?'

'You're kidding me, right?'

He shook his head.

'Katie would never lower herself to use the NHS,' continued Gemma. '*She,* has a private dentist and a private doctor. Whatever, she hates me.'

'Oh, Gemma, come on,' Dave protested.

'It's true. She hates me. And she hates that I work part-time.'

Again, Dave shook his head. Gemma was overdramatising, surely?

'But didn't she hire you?'

'Yes.'

'For a part-time role?'

'Yes, but it wasn't by choice. Somehow, in her head, my being part-time demeans her status within the company. She has always wanted a *full-time* assistant. And she loathes the fact, she's not been allowed to have one.'

'But that's not your problem?'

'I know. But who else can she take it out on?'

Dave thought, shrugged. He was at a loss.

'*Her* manager, I don't think so,' said Gemma, answering her own question.

'Sounds like she's a right *bitch*,' Dave emphasised, feeling upset for Gemma. 'I don't know how you keep working for her?'

For the first time since Gemma entered the kitchen, Dave found himself on the end of a proper smile as she threw him a conspiratorial grin. He felt a great sense of relief wash over him. Her problem was not with him, or their relationship.

'You can say that again, the *bitch* part, I mean.'

Dave reciprocated Gemma's smile.

'Remind me, how long have you been working for her?'

'About two years, I got the job right after Paul left. Reasonable salary, great hours for Henry's school and desperate for money, I practically bit her hand off. If I had known then what I know now, I would have run a mile.'

Dave thought for a moment.

'Now we're living together, why don't you start looking for another job?'

Gemma sighed. She vigorously shook her head.

'How can I even think about changing my job, while yours is hanging in the balance?'

'My situation should not get in the way of *you* improving yours,' he shot out.

Stung into defensiveness, the hurtful truth in Gemma's words hitting home, Dave's words had been ejected rather more tartly than he had intended. Thinking on how uncertain his job was, how brutal the gossip was, how on edge it all left him, Dave's face clouded over with anger.

'Yeah, sure...' Gemma mumbled to herself, no longer looking him in the eye.

He pushed away his dark thoughts.

'Sorry, what did you say?'

'Nothing.'

Why does she do that, Dave asked himself impatiently? Why does she hide what she's really saying, what she's really thinking? Not something Sarah had ever struggled with, he thought, a tad bitterly. A feisty, second-generation Italian, Sarah had never been afraid to let him have it, both barrels.

'Don't lie to me, Gemma,' he accused, unable to stop himself.

Gemma's face tightened.

'Don't worry about it.'

Dave blew out a breath.

'I'm not worried about it. I just wish you would say what you really mean,' he snapped out.

Neither of them able to look each other in the eye, there was a tense and lengthening silence.

Really not wanting to fight, Dave shook off his frustration and changed the subject.

'Look, whilst you've been upstairs, I haven't exactly been idle,' he pointed out, keeping his voice determinedly upbeat as he threw his hands expansively round the room. 'I've tidied up the kitchen and the lounge. Got them both ready for later.'

Flicking her eyes rapidly round the room, if she ignored the messy back door groaning under the weight of coats and school bags hanging from hooks, Gemma had to admit, the kitchen looked uncommonly tidy and much cleaner than it had an hour ago. Knowing Dave's significant effort needed to be acknowledged, and wanting to, she hastily apologised.

'Sorry, Dave, I should have noticed. Looks great. Thank you.'

He gave her a crooked smile.

'Welcome.'

Dave threw Gemma a speculative look.

'Gemma, I have to ask… Jessica, you sure she was OK, earlier?'

Picking up a large metal spoon, Gemma stirred something hot and steaming in one of the two saucepans bubbling on the stove. Thinking on the unpleasantness of his daughter's reaction toward her, only a few minutes ago, Jessica nastily insisting she get out of *her* bedroom and all because she had dared to try and engage the ungrateful child in some pleasant chitchat about her day, she smarted all over again. What the hell was wrong with the girl? All she wanted was to get to know her better?

'She's fine, doing her homework,' she said carefully.

Gemma's heart heavy with the lie she had just told and the thought Dave's daughter might actually hate her, she was hoping he was none the wiser.

'Good'

'I suggested she might want to come down a little later,' she said lightly over her shoulder. 'To say hello.'

'You sure she can tear herself away from her phone for that long?' Dave teased, his voice heavy with a mock sarcasm.

'Yeah, minor miracle, eh,' Gemma agreed, being careful not to wipe the trusting and unsuspecting smile from Dave's face as she matched his irony with some of her own. 'She'll be down, I'm sure of it.'

'Great.'

'You know what I still can't believe,' said Gemma, 'is that we have company coming over tonight? Remind me again, whose bright idea was it to have guests over for dinner on a school night?'

Dave flashed Gemma a cheeky, boyish look as he walked toward her.

'Mine, of course. I thought it would be fun to punch a little excitement into our dreary suburban lives,' he quipped.

Dreary and suburban, is that what he really thought their life was all about, she could not help but wonder miserably? Uneasy over

Dave's choice of words and highly sensitive to everything at the moment, before she could stop herself, Gemma threw him a troubled look.

'Hey, stop looking so worried, I was only joking.' Dave reassured. 'And as for our guests, I simply took it for granted you wouldn't mind,' he explained.

'Well, I don't like being taken for granted,' said Gemma defensively.

Dave pulled Gemma away from the cooker and into an embrace.

'Don't be cross with me. I thought it would be good idea, that's all.'

'And after dinner? What are we supposed to do with them then, play Scrabble?'

'Scrabble, we're not dead yet, you know,' Dave whispered into Gemma's warm ear.

Nuzzling into Gemma's neck, Dave savoured the scent of her as he ran his mouth up and down the softness of her throat. With a pang of aching regret, he wished they had more time... before their guests arrived.

The tension of earlier inexorably melting away, Gemma slowly began to relax in Dave's arms as the sexual attraction that had been there from the beginning, stirred in her loins. Permitting herself to enjoy the warmth of his hot lips against her cool skin as he kissed her neck, her ears, the hollow in her throat, her mouth... Then all of a sudden, she was brought down to earth with a painful bump.

Wincing, Gemma pulled herself away from Dave. Putting a tentative hand up to the side of her face, she cupped her aching jaw.

'Ouch, that really hurt.'

Dave butterfly kissed the side of Gemma's jaw a couple of times.

'Sorry, sorry, I forgot all about the filling. Better now?' he asked.

Dave's eyes still devouring her even though he was visibly concerned, she had to smile.

'Mm, much better, thanks.'

Dave leering at Gemma as he came back in to cup her ample buttocks with both hands, to gaze down into her ample cleavage, she dispatched him a coy smile.

'Sorry about earlier, I was being a grouch. It'll be good to see your sister again.'

'Yeah, I haven't seen her in so long, I'm beginning to forget what she looks like,' Dave joked.

Gemma nodded.

'I'm intrigued to meet the new boyfriend. She's been so mysterious about this one. What about you?'

Dave let Gemma go. Striding over to the fridge, the door sucking open, he reached inside and got himself a beer.

'Whatever,' he shrugged dismissively. 'She's had so many of them over the years…'

Gemma nodded. Dave leaving the sentence hanging as he alluded to his sister's ever tumultuous love life, she could hardly disagree. At best a terrible flirt, at worst a devourer of men, it was hard to keep up with Carly's relationships. Yet Carly having confessed to being on a self-imposed break from the dating scene these last few months, curious, Gemma could not help but wonder if this one would be in the same vein as all the others — grungy, moody, unreliable and broke?

Gemma exclaimed with a keen pleasure as she opened the front door to Dave's baby sister.

'Hey you, long time no see.'

Dropping a kiss on to the side of Carly Roger's cold cheek, giving her a firm squeeze, Gemma quickly introduced herself to the new beau in her best friend's life, then ushered for the two of them to come into the warmth of the house.

'Come on, come on in, it's freezing out there.'

Steve Quinnell initially hanging back behind Carly before coming to the fore, he threw out his right hand for Gemma to shake. Fully suited and booted, wearing a white button-down shirt under his suit jacket, conservative tie, black leather shoes and a great-to-meet-you smile, she shook Steve's hand. Polite and well mannered, she thought, trying not to be surprised.

Pushing the front door closed with a snap, then hearing the sound of footsteps padding overhead and guessing Jessica was preparing to make her way down the stairs in order to greet her favourite aunt, Gemma hustled the couple in front of her to get a move on. There was no way she was up to running the risk of having to deal with any further toe curling awkwardness from Jessica, in front of her guests. Motioning for Carly and Steve to make their way down to the open plan kitchen-diner extension located at the opposite end of the narrow hallway, she too, got a wriggle on.

Dave greeting his sister just as enthusiastically as Gemma had, he delivered a quick handshake to the rather imposing man stood directly in front of him.

'Wow sis, where on earth did you dig this one up from?' he asked, making an exaggerated point of looking up at the intimidating frame towering over him.

'Sorry?' Steve queried, looking perplexed.

His cultured voice sounding uncommonly soft and smooth for a man of his stature, Gemma took a better look. Guessing he was somewhere in his early forties, tall and broad-shouldered, with a tapered waist, long arms and even longer legs, he oozed the confident air of a successful man, along with a concentrated gaze that made her face tingle.

Clean shaven, no glasses, classically good-looking with strong features — cool brown eyes, a long nose, a fleshy bow shaped mouth, and jet black hair with a featherlight touch of grey at either temple — barring movie stars, Steve was easily, Gemma judged, the best looking man she had seen for quite some time. His manner cool and calm, physically a completely different kettle of fish to Carly's usual dates, perhaps, she mused, there was hope for this one. Time would tell.

'Hey, stop being a jerk,' Carly enforced, before poking her tongue out at her older brother, like a naughty five-year old.

Dave responded with a hearty and unaffected laugh.

Watching Carly and Dave's antics, the good-natured sibling-rivalry being played out in front of her, Gemma smiled. It had been a while since Dave had seen his little sister and it was good to see the close-knit siblings enjoying each others company again.

'Don't mind Dave,' she interjected, grinning across the room at Steve as she sought to mitigate any potential discomfort their guest might be experiencing. 'As you can see, being a short-arse, he has a natural tendency to be jealous of anyone who stands even an inch taller than himself.'

'Short-arse? Who are you calling a short-arse?' Dave challenged tongue in cheek as he wittily made a show of pulling himself up to his maximum height of five-eight. 'And you have the cheek to call me rude,' he continued, boisterously pretending his male vanity had been affronted.

A broad grin settling on Dave's amused face, whilst two additional pairs of eyes — one mischievous, the other contemplative — also interestedly perused his slight form, Gemma gave herself a minute to deliberate on a suitable response.

Even though he had been a marathon runner up until he hit his late thirties, at forty-three, no longer lithe and sporting a little buddha belly, Dave was, Gemma mused fondly, a little rumpled around his age softened edges. His mouth thin, he had an aquiline nose, soft brown eyes and hollowed out cheekbones. His features all very unremarkable, they were set in a face that had exceptionally pale, almost translucent skin. His head displaying a stubble of carrot-red hair so curly and kept so short he appeared almost bald, *Jasper Carrot, eat your heart out,* Gemma thought with a wry smile as she thought through a suitable answer.

The kitchen door being suddenly thrown open with an almighty crash as it hit the wall behind it, Jessica bursting into the room as if she had been blown through it by a hurricane, all four of them jumped.

'Christ, Jessica, make an entrance why don't you,' Gemma voiced without thinking.

Dave threw Gemma a hard look. She looked away.

Ignoring Gemma's comment as well as her father's obvious displeasure, Jessica raced across the room like a small an overexcited two-year old.

'Aunty Carly,' she squealed, flinging her arms around a visibly startled Carly.

'Hey, Jess, how are you?' her aunt replied as she gently extracted herself from Jessica's overzealous clasp. 'God, it seems like ages since I last saw you. And look at you, I'm sure you've shot up again.'

Watching the aunt and her taller — by at least two or three inches — niece heartily embracing each other, Gemma pondered on Jessica's ever increasing height. Had Jessica, she wondered — as with the Italianate looks and the womanly figure — inherited her tall gene from her mother's side of the family? Only if not, it was certainly not from that of her father's side of the family.

'It's been ages,' Jessica complained with a childlike whine that instantly grated on Gemma's nerves. 'Why haven't you been to see me sooner, Aunty Carly?'

'I know, I know. I'm sorry. But you know how it is, I've been busy, these past few weeks.'

Gemma catching the look Carly flashed to Steve, and suddenly understanding what her friend's *busy* really meant, she had to smile to herself. Carly never changed, she thought.

'Are you joining us for dinner, Jess?' Carly asked innocently.

'Er, no, she isn't,' Dave hastily interjected. 'She and Henry, have already eaten.'

'What he really means, Aunt Carly,' emphasised Jessica, drawing herself up to her full height of five-seven as she placed her hands on her all too voluptuous hips, 'is now we're all one big *happy family*, I'm no longer invited to have dinner with the adults, like I used to be.'

Jessica presenting her father with a disparaging look as she childishly stuck out her bottom lip, along with her ample bosom, Gemma winced for him. His daughter looking far older than her fifteen years, a child in a woman's body, she briefly speculated on how Dave might react when the boys came knocking? She did not envy him, or them.

'Jessica,' Dave admonished, his colourless face turning a deep beetroot red as his daughter rudely challenged his authority.

'What?' Jessica rudely retaliated.

Inwardly cringing at the girl's tiresome and unwanted behaviour, Gemma shook her head. *Damn the girl,* she thought as she bit down on her irritation. *It's one thing her being mean to me, but when she's rude to her father…*

Looking visibly uncomfortable, concerned, Carly gently took hold of Jessica's arm. She gave it a small squeeze. 'Hey, come on beautiful, please don't talk to your father like that. We'll get together soon, I promise.'

Jessica threw her aunt a pleading, almost desperate look. 'Really? You mean it?'

Gemma watched as Carly flashed her brother a questioning look. Dave acquiescing with a pained nod, she thought sourly, how Jessica's poor conduct really did not deserve the amount of attention it was receiving.

'Of course I do. Let me have a word with your dad and Gem first and between us, we'll sort out a date and time for you to come over to mine.'

'Can I stay over?'

'Well, I don't exactly have a lot of room, so you'll have to sleep on the floor.'

'That's OK, I don't mind, really I don't,' insisted Jessica, suddenly all sweetness and light as she beamed from ear to ear.

'Hmm, but only so long as my housemates don't mind sharing a bathroom with you?' teased Carly.

'I won't hog the bathroom, I promise.'

Carly grinned at her earnest young niece. 'OK, leave it with me then and I'll see what I can do.'

'You promise?'

'Yes.'

'Soon?'

'*Yes!*'

'Jessica, it's getting late. I think it is time you finished your homework,' Dave prompted his daughter. 'Lights out no later than nine, remember. Oh, and I'll take your phone off you now, please.'

'But dad, it's still early, can't I give it to you later?' Jessica whined.

'Jessica, I'm not doing this with you now. You know the rules.'

'But dad...'

'If you want the phone back tomorrow?' said Dave, cutting his daughter off as he stood his ground. He held out his hand.

21

Reluctantly slapping her phone into Dave's waiting hand, Jessica's coal black appraising eyes, gave her father a long and disdainful look.

'Yeah, and I love you too, dad,' she muttered scornfully under her breath. Then, with a rebellious toss of her thick black hair — another legacy from the Italian side of her family — she turned smartly on her heel as she headed at breakneck speed, for the yawning door.

'Slam the door, if you dare,' Dave called after his defiant daughter.

Jessica pretending not to hear, she flounced angrily out of the room. She left the kitchen door, wide open.

All four adults looked self-consciously across the room at each other and for a couple of uneasy seconds, no one spoke.

Breaking the spell, Gemma walked over to the kitchen door and firmly closed it. Fifteen and already she's a handful, God help us, she thought painfully.

'Wow! Well, that was embarrassing,' said Dave with a somewhat false laugh as he referenced the awkward display of teenage indignation his daughter had delivered. 'Kids, eh? It's true what they say, you can't live without them and you certainly can't live with them.'

Steve, so far silent throughout all that had happened, suddenly agreed with obvious feeling, 'Yeah, you got that one right.'

'Said like a man who knows what he's talking about,' said Gemma, without thinking.   Her face coloured. 'Sorry Steve, I didn't mean to pry. Brain, mouth…'

'Hey, you have nothing to apologise for,' Steve said disarmingly. 'And in answer to your unasked question, no, I do not have a child of my own, but I do have a very close nephew.'

'Oh?' Gemma queried.

'Remind me, how old is Jessica?' Steve asked Gemma.

'Fifteen,' Gemma answered weakly, her legs reacting to the magnificent and engaging smile Steve had bestowed on her, she could do with sitting down.

Steve nodded, turned his blessed attention to Dave.

'The same age as my nephew, who at times, if you'll pardon my saying, is a right royal pain in the arse.'

'Typical teenager, then?' Dave queried, sounding desperately optimistic.

The amount of hope in Dave's voice, on his face, clearly visible for all three of them to see, Gemma felt awful for him.

'Oh yes,' Steve emphasised. 'Rebellious, and angry, he despises authority. It's a difficult age, I know.'

'Yeah, Jessica seems to be getting more and difficult, almost by the day.'

'Yeah, everyone goes on about your school days being the best time of your life, but it is hard being a teenager,' Steve said tactfully.

Registering Steve's diplomacy toward Dave's discernible discomfort, Gemma gratefully flashed him a warm and appreciative smile. She received one in return. He really was quite likeable, charming, she mused thoughtfully, well done Carly.

Carly threw her brother a questioning look, then hesitantly asked, 'Dave, is everything OK between you and Jess, only you seem really worried?'

For a second or two, Dave looked like a rabbit in the headlights.

'I've never seen her behave quite like that before. And she used to be such a sweet kid,' Carly pressed home.

'She's fine, Carly,' Gemma interrupted before Dave could give a more direct and honest answer. The last thing she wanted was a discussion on Jessica, taking over the evening. 'As Steve said, she's turning into your typical tortured adolescent.'

Dave looking distinctly uncomfortable again, even humiliated. Knowing that Carly was just itching to ask more questions, Gemma threw her friend a surreptitious look of warning. One that said, *later...* *I'll explain it all to you, later.*

CHAPTER FOUR

Thirty minutes later, Henry fast asleep, and with no further noise coming from Jessica's room — having been told to turn her music down at least three times before it finally fell silent — the four adults were greedily studying Gemma's hastily concocted supper of Spaghetti Bolognese with Parmesan cheese and garlic bread.

'Hmm, this looks delicious, Gemma,' said Carly.

Carly's eyes devilish, she flashed Gemma a blatant, knowing smile.

'Thanks,' Gemma responded, feeling her face flush pink with guilt. 'All my own hard work,' she confirmed with a light and almost embarrassed chuckle. 'But I didn't have enough time to make a dessert, so make the most of it.'

'Really, no pudding? Thank God for small mercies,' Carly replied.

Carly unashamedly giggling her head off between a couple of mouthfuls, Gemma's cheeks reddened even more.

'Yep, Gemma has slaved like a Trojan since coming home from work,' added Dave, for good measure, his face also creasing up with mirth.

'Oh, you are such a wicked, wicked, pair,' said Carly, before she burst out laughing. 'Don't forget, I *know* you two…'

Gemma's eyes watering with merriment, though her face was still beetroot red, she realised the game was up.

'OK, I give in,' she said, no longer able to keep up the pretence. 'You're absolutely right, of course. As usual, your dinner *is* out of a jar.'

'Actually, it's out of *two* jars,' Dave chipped in, still grinning from ear to ear. 'Though I can honestly confirm, Gemma did cook the spaghetti all by herself.'

Steve frowning down at his dinner plate before flashing Carly an openly quizzical look with those penetrating eyes of his, Gemma took pity on him. She gently patted the top of his hand across the kitchen table.

'It's OK,' she reassured him. 'Carly knows me too well and although it pains me to say this, a magnificent cook, I most certainly am not. Consequently, this,' she gestured to the food on her plate, the spaghetti and Bolognese saucepans sitting in the middle of the table, 'I can assure you, is a real treat.'

Still looking confused, Steve shook his head at Gemma as he waited for further information.

Gemma coughed, cleared her throat as she prepared to be brutally honest.

'In other words, you don't want to have to eat *anything* I might have prepared from scratch and cooked, as it is usually a disaster.'

'Yeah, I can second that,' Carly quipped before sprinkling a load more Parmesan on her pasta. 'Gemma's home-cooked food not only tastes awful, but it also has the potential to leave you needing to quite frequently use the bathroom.'

Now looking shell-shocked by all that had been divulged, Steve pushed the food around his plate, without tasting it. He nodded to himself.

'I see.'

'Come on then, eat up,' said Carly as she mercilessly teased her reluctant looking beau. 'This meal is all out of a jar or packet so you can be rest assured, not only does it taste good, it won't poison you either.' Twirling her pasta around on her fork to eat, Carly smacked her lips with a hearty pleasure as though to demonstrate her point.

'Carly, really?' said Gemma, in defence of herself.

Steve took a tentative mouthful, swallowed it down, then took a sip of his wine.

Carly chuckled.

'See, I told you, it is good, isn't it?'

'That's enough, Carly,' Gemma admonished in warning tones. 'Although I readily admit to being a rotten cook, in fact we both are,' she gesticulated to Dave, 'never, have I ever poisoned anyone.'

Carly raised her eyebrows at Gemma.

'Oh, come on Carly, that one time you got sick after eating one of my more adventurous meals, you had a winter vomiting bug, you know you did.'

Gemma's question purely rhetorical, Carly dispatched her mildly disgruntled friend a cheeky wink in tacit agreement.

Steve forked a second mouthful of spaghetti dripping with Bolognese sauce into his mouth. He hoped, he was not going to regret it later.

Dave tactfully changed the subject.

'The last time we talked, you were still single as a Pringle, so how did you two meet?' he asked his sister.

Carly snorted with laughter.

'Ha, *single as a Pringle*, where the hell did that come from?'

Dave blushed, threw his sister a weak grin and shrugged his shoulders.

'Probably Jessica, but come on, answer the question, where did you two meet?' he asked again.

Now it was Carly's turn to pink up as she cast Steve a brazenly coy, if slightly perturbed look across the table.

'Do you want to tell them, or should I?'

Shifting in his seat as he visibly got more comfortable, Steve lifted up his wine glass, then toasted it in Carly's direction.

'Oh, I think,' he started to say, almost smirking, 'you should be the one to tell that story.' He took a slow, drawn out sip of red wine.

'OK,' Carly replied, taking up the challenge even though she sounded uncomfortable. 'We both met on the day I literally fell into Steve's arms.'

Carly's statement delivered quite matter of factly, as though he should know exactly what she meant but none the wiser, Dave's brows knitted with puzzlement.

'Excuse me?' he queried.

'Don't look so surprised,' Carly admonished lightly, without offering any further explanation.

Dave shook his head at Carly.

'Carly, what the hell are you talking about?'

The sister poked a tongue out at her brother.

Knowing her friend as well as she did, Gemma couldn't help but wonder at Carly's unexpected reticence, her need to procrastinate? Carly's eyes briefly darting to Steve's face, as though needing some encouragement or perhaps even some reassurance from him, Gemma felt a prick of alarm. Then she shook her misgivings away, silently told herself, she was being daft.

'I was on my way into the Underground as Steve was coming out and I literally fell into his waiting arms,' Carly continued, just as inexplicably.

At Carly's mention of the Underground, Gemma flinched. She hated the place, avoided it like the plague. So much so, she would rather spend precious hours walking, driving, or even using the capricious London buses.

Dave, still looking none the wiser and just as puzzled, asked, 'The Underground?'

'Yes, it happened on the same day as that awful accident. That one a couple of months back. Around the end of August, I think.'

Gemma remembered. How could she possibly forget?

Dave pulled a face, slowly shook his head.

'No, what accident?'

'Oh, come on, Dave... The one where that woman was killed when she slipped and fell on to the live rail at Piccadilly Circus, right in front of her child.'

Gemma flinched with horror at the thought of what the poor child must have witnessed, of what the poor woman had gone through.

His face inscrutable, Steve took another sip of wine.

Dave shook his head again.

'But you must remember? It was all *over* the news at the time.'

The incident happening during the school summer holidays, and the day before Dave and Jessica had moved in with Henry and herself, the event was forever etched on Gemma's mind. The poor woman unwittingly pushed on to the tracks by the crowd, it was Gemma's worst nightmare. That and the ever present threat of being blown up by a terrorist bomb.

'Nope, I'm telling you, I don't remember,' Dave insisted.

'Yes, you do. According to the news, instead of paying attention to what was happening around her, the stupid woman had been texting on her mobile and in the commuter crush, she lost her footing and fell,' said Carly.

Carly's tone oddly cold, Gemma thought of the number of times she had been distracted by her phone whilst waiting for a bus, or simply walking along the street. Wincing at her friend's apparent lack of sensitivity toward the *stupid woman,* the tragic senselessness of it all, she could not help but think, but for the grace of God…

Again, Dave shrugged his shoulders.

'But you were right there, that day.'

'What?'

Carly sighed.

'You met me in town and we had a drink in that coffee shop, the one near the statue of Eros in Piccadilly Circus.'

News to me, Gemma thought to herself as she wondered how Dave could forget such a horrific event so easily.

Carly exasperated, she sent Dave a questioning look.

'Look, it was a very busy time back then. Don't forget, I was just about to move in here,' Dave justified.

Carly shook her head as though in disbelief.

'Whatever… Anyway, around the same time as the accident happened, Steve was exiting the station just as I was entering it. Both of us suddenly caught up in all the commotion, you know, people stampeding everywhere, I tripped over my own feet, started to fall down the steps and Steve caught me. Helped to get me safely out of there, then took me across the road to the pub. Bought me a drink to steady my nerves.'

Dave snorted with derision.

'Seriously? You, of all people, had to be taken to a pub to steady your nerves?' he scoffed as he winked at Steve. 'I reckon she saw you coming, mate.'

'I have absolutely no idea what you could mean?' said Carly, with a feigned air of innocence. 'It was a terrible experience, horrible. Everyone was upset, including me,' she declared forcefully. But there was a mischievous twinkle in her eye.

'Yeah, I get the poor woman's accident was horrendous, but you, helpless, I don't buy it,' said Dave. Chuckling, he turned to Gemma as he cast her a knowing smile. 'Talk about getting away with murder, don't you think?'

Though smiling sweetly back at Dave, Gemma courteously held her own counsel as she neither agreed, nor disagreed, with his summation of his sister's personality. Knowing her friend had never been one to shy away from anything dark or difficult. That she was naturally audacious and typically one of those self-assured lucky people who possessed nerves of steel, privately, Gemma could not agree more with Dave. But tonight, Carly blatantly out to impress, Gemma was not about to burst her friend's carefully constructed bubble of feminine vulnerability.

'My turn for a similar question,' Steve piped up. 'I know you both met through Carly, but when was that, exactly?'

'If memory serves me right, it was last year, around early June, I think,' answered Dave.

He looked to Gemma for confirmation.

She nodded.

'And where did you meet?' asked Steve.

'Round Carly's. Gemma popped in to see Carly and the rest as they say, is history.'

'So even though these two have known each other for years,' said Steve, gesturing to Gemma and Carly, 'you two had never met before?'

'No, strangely enough, we hadn't,' said Dave, looking somewhat surprised at the truth of the matter.

'And how long have you been living together?'

'A couple of months, I think?'

Steve chuckled. 'You don't sound too certain.'

'I'm not, the whole thing has been a bit of a whirlwind,' said Dave.

'You and Jessica moved in the third week of August,' Gemma interjected.

Steve nodded. His wide and expressive mouth presented a beatific smile that did not quite reach, Gemma thought, his eyes.

'If you don't mind my saying, your daughter, she doesn't look a bit like you,' said Steve to Dave.

'No, she's had a lucky break there,' Dave agreed with a wistful smile.

'How come?' he asked.

Realising where the conversation was heading and starting to feel uncomfortable, Gemma wriggled in her seat. She swallowed down a sigh before it could escape.

'She's the spitting image of her mother, Sarah,' said Dave. His smile slowly fading, there was a sense of sadness and tragedy behind his eyes.

Feeling an unwanted sting at the mention of Sarah's name, Gemma hid her face in her wine glass. Even after all this time, she still hated it whenever Sarah's name came up in conversation. She hated herself even more, for being so petty about it.

Steve gave Dave a contemplative look.

'Carly told me what happened to your wife and I just want to say, I'm sorry for your loss. It must have been hard?'

Gemma spluttered on her wine. Carly gave her a sharp look. Dave looking pained, he dropped his gaze for a second as he concentrated hard on rubbing out a spot on the table.

'Thanks,' he mumbled.

'Sarah, would I be right in thinking she was of Italian descent?' Steve asked.

Reaching for his wine glass, Dave slugged back a large gulp as he gave himself a minute.

Feeling upset for Dave, and for herself, Gemma tried not to glare at Steve as she wished he would change he subject. Struggling to ignore the all too familiar stirrings of latent jealousy, her irrational envy, it was with some disgust that she firmly told herself not to be so pathetic. There was no way, she could compete with a woman who had been so stunningly beautiful and even more so, now she was *dead*.

'Yes, practically all of Sarah's family live in and around Rome. In fact, she was born in Rome. She and her parents moved to England, when she was still very young,' said Dave.

'Makes sense. Explains Jessica's obvious Latino looks, the feisty temperament,' Steve deliberated. He switched his ultra-cool gaze from Dave to Gemma. 'Why don't you tell me a bit more about your son, Gemma? How old is he?'

Still flustered by her uncharitable thoughts toward Sarah, toward Carly's clearly impertinent new boyfriend, Gemma cleared her throat. She hoped, her hot cheeks had not given away her discomfort.

'Not much to tell. He's just your average seven year old.'

'And the apple of his mother's eye,' Carly interposed from the sidelines.

'What about his father? Does he still see him?' Steve asked.

Taken aback by not only the boldness of Steve's question but the tactlessness of it, Gemma started. Perhaps he was not quite as charming as she had originally thought?

'Of course he does,' she shot back defensively.

Steve nodded.

'Good to hear. I'm a firm believer in boys needing their father to be around,' he stated.

Shocked at Steve's obliviousness to her sensitivities on the subject, Gemma felt a swell of anger almost lifting her from her seat. How dare he preach to her about something he knew nothing about?

'Really?' she challenged.

'Gem, he's only interested,' Carly tired to pacify.

'Sorry, have I upset you?' Steve asked Gemma, a look of surprise on his face.

Furious with the inconsiderateness of Steve's bald-faced questions and comments, no longer able to look at him — and she had been trying so hard to like him — Gemma briefly buried her face in her wine glass. She took a greedy, stalling, gulp.

Carly looking hotly embarrassed whilst Steve had a bemused look on his face. Dave somewhere else entirely as he continued to gaze off into the distance. Gemma still apoplectic with anger, the silence only lengthened.

Resolving she'd had enough, that it was time to change the subject, Gemma ruthlessly served the conversation to Carly, batted enough lobs her friend's way to keep her going for a while. Steve was her boyfriend after all, so who better than her to amuse him, she thought truculently.

CHAPTER FIVE

Wanting nothing more than for their guests to be gone so she could go to bed, curl up with a book and forget the day's tensions, Gemma suddenly realised, Steve was trying to catch her attention. Empty plates all round, he was volunteering to help clear away the dishes as he removed a sheet of kitchen towel tucked down the collar of his immaculate white shirt.

His copybook blotted from earlier on, throughout dinner, Gemma had been unable to warm to Steve and she had tried. She had really tried. In spite of the superficial charm, Steve saying nothing that was remarkable or particularly interesting, touching lightly on a variety of subjects, she judged him to have a calculated aloofness. So far unimpressed, she reasoned that perhaps, it was more a clash of personalities rather than a definite dislike. Either way, there was something about him that jarred. Yet if you were to ask her *why* she felt that way, she knew she would be unable to explain.

Steve waiting expectantly, Gemma galvanised herself into action before he could. She did not want his help.

Desperate to talk to Carly about her errant niece, Gemma politely thanked Steve for his kind gesture then requested of her friend, that she should stay behind instead. It would be good to have a girly catchup, she explained.

Packing a more than happy Dave but a visibly reluctant Steve off to the lounge with a full cheese board and a fresh bottle of wine, Gemma determinedly shooed both men out of her kitchen. She shut the door behind them. At last, she would have Carly to herself.

'So, what do you think?' Carly insisted on knowing as soon as the two men left the kitchen.

Her friend's emerald green eyes dancing with an undisguised merriment, a happy expectation, Gemma pushed Carly toward the kitchen sink. She passed over a stack of dirty plates for Carly to rinse off. She needed some time to reflect, to get her thoughts in order before she answered her impatient friend's, probing question.

'Gem, stop stalling, tell me what you think,' said Carly as she turned on the hot tap.

'About?' Gemma delayed as she began to load the dishwasher.

'Stop it, Gem.'

Briefly looking up from what she had been doing, Gemma forced out an impish grin.

'Stop what?'

'Gem,' Carly whined.

'Oh, I see,' Gemma teased, 'you want to know what I think of Steve.'

Carly vigorously nodded her head.

'Now you get it.'

'I think,' Gemma paused, reluctant to admit to how she really felt, 'it's still too early to tell. I've only just met him.'

Carly sighed, ran a hand through her already wild curls.

'But I really like this one, Gem. Every time I see him, he gives me a serious case of butterflies.'

'No, really?' Gemma said, with a spiky smile. 'I would never have guessed from the way you were eating his face off when I opened the front door to the two of you.'

Carly blushed.

'You saw?'

'Yep... Anyway, why are you asking *me* about Steve? I am not exactly the best judge of character, am I? Wouldn't you be better off asking your brother?'

'What are you talking about? You're a great judge of character, you know you are.'

'You think? What about Paul?'

'Paul's not that bad, you just got bored and outgrew the poor...'

Carly hesitating, leaving the sentence hanging, she threw Gemma a cautious look.

'Go on, you can't stop there,' Gemma prodded, prickling with unease as she began to feel her hackles rise. It wasn't Carly's fault she didn't know the truth about Paul, she reminded herself.

'Sorry Gem, but at the time, I felt quite sorry for Paul.'

Now it was Gemma's turn to blush.

'You felt sorry for Paul? Why?'

'Well, it's not like he cheated on you or anything, is it?'

Carly's candid observation sharply reminding Gemma just how badly everyone felt she had behaved toward her ex-husband, she experienced an uncomfortable pang of guilty conscience. In a way, she wished Paul had cheated on her. At least then, in the eyes of her family and friends, she would have been seen to have had a good reason to the end the marriage. As it was, most of her family and especially her mother, thought she had been mad to leave such a *perfect* husband.

'Anyway, regardless of what happened between you and Paul,' Carly continued, 'you *know* you're a much better judge of character than I am,' she emphasised, throwing Gemma an expectant look.

Shaking away her maudlin thoughts of Paul, Gemma examined her friend's animated and earnest face, her make-up free and unsullied porcelain skin. Not for the first time, she envied Carly her forest of curly red hair, her piercing green eyes, her willowy figure honed and toned from years of teaching yoga and Pilates. A gorgeous creature, who at thirty-six, still had the body and the enthusiasm for life of an eighteen-year-old, Carly was a real force of nature. His little *pocket-rocket,* her brother affectionately called her.

Gemma's constant fear of putting on weight defeated by her never-ending love of food, now they were living together, she briefly contemplated if Dave might babysit Henry for a couple hours a week, so she could join one of Carly's classes. Knowing she could do with getting to grips with her insidiously expanding body, but both time and money a serious issue, it was not that easy. With two extra bodies in the house to take care of and think about, she had been slowly disappearing up her own backside and with Dave's job on the line, though relatively immune to the lures of wealth, still, she could not escape the fact, they were as poor as church mice.

'Gem, where have you gone? You're miles away again.'

Dragging her mind back to the present, Gemma flashed her visibly irritated friend a weak smile.

'Sorry, where were we?'

'Steve, I *really* need to know what you think about Steve?'

Rapidly concluding that during dinner, she and Dave had only been allowed to *flirt* with the peripheries of Steve's life. That any gleaned information was purely basic — he worked in insurance, he had a fifteen year old nephew, he lived somewhere in London. That he had asked far more questions than he had answered, which in itself was strange as most people had an almost irresistible urge to talk about themselves, Gemma began to realise she was genuinely stumped on what to say. Also uncertain as to how well a noticeably besotted Carly might respond to a brutally honest observation of the new man in her life, she decided that for now at least, it would be best to err on the side of caution, and say little.

'First impressions, he's more mature than your usual sort.'

'Hey,' Carly objected with a light-hearted chuckle as she bumped up against Gemma.

'Stop it, or you'll have me sitting in the dishwasher,' Gemma lightly complained.

'Serves you right. Explain yourself,' Carly demanded in mock overtones. 'What do you mean, he's more mature?'

'You know exactly what I mean.'

'No, I don't.'

'Oh come on, Carly,' Gemma insisted seriously. 'The last couple of men you've dated have been younger than you, and irresponsible with it.'

Carly's earlier good humour sliding from her face as she obviously struggled with some unpalatable thoughts, she eventually nodded her head at Gemma.

'Yeah, I suppose you've got a point. But Steve *is* different, right?'

Gemma wracked her brains searching for some more positives on Steve.

'Sounds like he has decent job. So I doubt he'll try and steal from you.'

Looking distinctly uneasy, Carly avoided Gemma's keen gaze for a second or two.

'Yeah, the last one almost put me off dating, *for good*,' she emphasised bitterly.

Recalling how awful the last boyfriend had been, how he had stolen nearly a thousand pounds from Carly, and how nasty he had got when she had finally given him his marching orders, Gemma shivered. Trust Carly to hurtle full pelt into a relationship without properly getting to know the man's background, his story. Talk about walking on edge. Yet, Gemma reminded herself, she had spent a good deal of time getting to know Paul before she married him, or at least she thought she had, and what good had that done her?

'Yeah and with that in mind, don't you think you should take a bit more care this time.'

'Care?'

'Yes,' Gemma nodded. 'Keep Steve at arms length for now. Get to know him a *lot, lot* better before you give him full access to your life, or to that beautiful heart of yours,' Gemma counselled.

'You don't like him, do you?' Carly accused miserably.

Realising Carly knew her too well. That she had picked up on her antipathy toward Steve, Gemma could kick herself. She had never been able to lie that convincingly and certainly not to those with whom she was close. Also recognising just how much her opinion mattered to Carly, she resolved to try harder as the last thing she wanted, God forbid, was for their friendship to suffer as the result of a man.

'Carly, it's not that I don't like him… I just don't know him, yet,' she replied cautiously. 'And naturally, I'm worried for you. I don't want to see you getting hurt again.'

'But he talked masses and masses over dinner,' said Carly as she hotly defended her new boyfriend. 'He told you loads of stuff about himself, I heard him.'

Gemma hesitated. Carly's eyes glittering wetly, she felt an immediate stab of guilt, followed by a second stab of pity for her naive and impetuous friend.

'Did he? I remember him asking Dave and I a lot of questions about us and our lives, but I don't recall him saying a lot about himself.'

'He's just diplomatic. It's the first time he's met the both of you and he obviously wants to make a good first impression. He was trying not to be rude, not to monopolise the conversation,' Carly protested. 'He's a good listener, Gem. Really he is.'

Carly's voice rising with her emotion, hearing the passion behind her response, Gemma was taken aback slightly. Whatever she said now, she knew it was already too late. Carly was infatuated with the man, seeing everything he said or did through those great big rosy coloured spectacles of hers. Nonetheless, she had to try.

'Maybe so, but those kind of traits don't exactly make it easy for us to get to know him, do they?'

The dishwasher loaded, Carly removed herself from the sink and leaned up against the kitchen countertop.

The look of hurt and disappoint on Carly's beautiful face plucked at Gemma's conscience as she began to ruthlessly question herself. Why was she being so harsh about Steve? After Carly's previous disasters, why couldn't she just be happy for her friend? Why couldn't she see Steve, the same way Carly did? Was her own situation with Paul, with Dave, clouding her judgement? Was she jealous? No, it was more than that. She was sure it was.

Carly again running her fingers through her wild and untamed hair, she flicked away a stray tear. She sighed.

'I'm sorry Carly, I didn't mean to upset you, truly I didn't.'

'Yeah, I know. Look, in a minute, I'll fill you in on some of the gaps. But I know you. You analyse everything and everyone, so you can't just stand there and tell me, hand on heart, you haven't already formulated an opinion of sorts?' she robustly insisted.

Carly obviously determined to have her answer and right on the button, in a tight spot, Gemma suddenly needed a distraction. Turning away from Carly, filing the kettle, she flicked it on and set about the business of making herself a coffee. Holding her liquor weakly at the best of times, there was no way she could drink any more alcohol tonight.

Carly watching Gemma's every move, her eyes becoming more and more pained by the second, her mouth trembling with emotion, she poured herself another glass of red wine, slugged back a huge mouthful.

Knowing she could prevaricate no longer, that she had to give her anxious friend at least something more to go on and keen to loosen the tightening tension, Gemma forced out a grin. It was time to highlight some of Steve's more obvious and favourable characteristics.

'He's more mature, he's sophisticated, and he obviously takes a pride in his appearance. That suit he's wearing, is lovely, must have cost a fortune. Puts your brother's carefully chosen ensemble to shame,' she quipped, referencing Dave's clean but old jeans, his navy polo shirt.

A weak smile of pride twitched at the corners of Carly's mouth.

'Yeah, but he's not vain. He just likes to make a good, first impression,' she said.

Gemma nodded.

'He's also quite a few years older than you, isn't he?'

'Forty-two, same age gap as between you and Dave.'

Conceding the point, Gemma gave a slight nod of her head. She flashed Carly another reassuring smile.

'I also heard him tell Dave he has some sort of job in insurance. One that sounded important and responsible?'

'Yeah, he's a commercial fraud investigator. Not that I know what that means.'

Carly sounding proudly dismissive, Gemma heard the slight hint of desperation in her friend's voice and instantly sorry for her. Carly's previous boyfriends having been so awful, in that moment she genuinely hoped, Steve *would* prove the exception.

'You know me,' Carly added, 'I can't stand any of that *big business* crap any more, or the *corporate-vampires* who work for them,' she stated bitterly.

'Hey, you were like that once,' Gemma objected mildly.

'Yeah, but not anymore,' Carly emphasised with feeling.

Five years ago, with the tragic death of her sister-in-law, Sarah, acting as a catalyst, Carly had experienced an epiphany of sorts, Gemma remembered. Almost overnight, Carly had thrown up everything that had, up until that point, been a constant in her life. Stating life was too short to waste, she had quit her well paid job in advertising, dumped her partner of two years and had then — having sold her flat to raise the money she needed to kick-start a new direction in life — taken herself off to India. Returning home some weeks later, she had set herself up as a freelance yoga instructor and thriving on her chosen path, had slowly but surely expanded her repertoire to include Pilates, Reiki, and a host of other specialist skills and qualifications Gemma could no longer remember the names of.

'And yes, in case you're wondering,' said Carly, 'so far, he's paid for everything when we're out together. He's really generous, Gem, to a fault sometimes. But it makes for a pleasant change, don't you think?'

Gemma nodded her agreement.

'Shows he's a gentleman.'

'What about family? If he's got a nephew, he must have a brother or sister, somewhere?'

Carly looking suddenly uneasy, almost furtive, Gemma pursed her lips. She knew it, she just knew it. Nothing was ever that simple with Carly.

'What? What haven't you told me?' Gemma demanded.

Carly dropped her gaze.

'Carly, answer me, that look on your face, you're starting to make me nervous.'

Carly dropped her shifting gaze to the floor.

'Carly?'

'Uh, if I tell you something, do you promise not to tell Dave?'

'If it's too personal to talk about, we can skip it,' Gemma replied, but only out of courtesy. Her antenna now on high alert, there was no way she could really not know. She had to have the inside story.

'You have to promise not to tell Dave,' Carly insisted.

'OK, OK, I promise.'

'Uh, Steve doesn't have a nephew, or any siblings.'

Thrown momentarily, then puzzled, Gemma threw Carly a suspicious look.

'Go on.'

'What he does have…' Carly hesitated, 'is a fifteen year old son.'

'What?' Gemma squawked. 'But he said he had a nephew, I distinctly heard him? You heard him. How could you let him lie to us like that? Why didn't you say something?'

'I'm sorry. He… no, we, we told you a fib. But it was for a good reason,' Carly rushed out, looking at Gemma as though her last statement explained everything.

Shocked that Steve could so *easily* lie to them, that Carly could be so complicit in his deceit, Gemma was furious. She should have trusted her instincts. She should not have let Carly's desperation for her to like Steve, get in the way of her usual common-sense.

'Gem?'

Gemma shook her head. She needed to get her emotions under control. There was more to come, she could feel it and for that, she was certain she would need a clear head.

'Sorry, but you're going to have to give me a minute.'

Carly hastily moved away from Gemma. Again, she refilled her empty wine glass. Taking another large slurp, she smacked her lips as the fortifying alcohol obviously hit the desired spot.

Gemma thought. She gathered her wits. She was ready.

'OK, if Steve has a son, where's the wife, the boy's mother?'

A deathly silence.

Carly looking decidedly shifty as she visibly struggled to answer what was an obvious and straightforward question, her brilliant green eyes could not settle as they flickered all over Gemma's worried face.

Stiffening, Gemma braced herself for what she thought was to come. But Carly still saying nothing, in the end, she was forced to ask.

'You're having an affair with a married man, aren't you?'

Carly biting her lip, to Gemma, it seemed she was reluctant to confirm one way or the other.

'Carly?'

'No! No, of course I'm not. What do you take me for?'

More irritated than relieved. Angry with Carly's sudden inability to give a direct answer to a direct question, Gemma took a deep, long pause. If she was to get to the bottom of whatever Carly was hiding, she needed to compose herself.

'OK, so where is she? Where is Steve's wife?'

Again, Carly hesitated. She took another rejuvenating mouthful of wine.

'Carly, this is stupid. Just tell me.'

'There is no wife.' Carly shot out, in hushed tones.

Gemma reeled with confusion. What the hell was she talking about? Of course there had to be a wife.

'What do you mean there's no wife? There's a child, so there has to be a mother,' Gemma insisted.

This time Carly's reply was instantaneous.

'He's a widower, Gem. Steve's wife is dead.'

The dishwasher whooshed noisily into the sudden silence.

Trying not to show her incredulity, Gemma blinked rapidly as she fought to digest Carly's shocking announcement.

'You OK?'

Sensing from her stiffness of manner, Carly had yet even more to share and that the news was unlikely to be good and not quite ready to hear it, again, Gemma looked to buy herself some much needed time.

'No, not really, I need a minute.'

Turning her back on Carly, Gemma opened the kitchen cupboard door above her head, grabbed herself a mug and reboiling the kettle, she made herself another mug of instant coffee. Her hand lightly shaking as she poured the hot water on to the coffee, added milk, she lifted the mug with both hands, drank and took a reviving sip.

After a couple more minutes, her defiant thoughts now collected and back under control, Gemma avoided the inescapable next question. The answer to that one, was not one she could face, at least not just yet.

'So where is Steve's son in all of this? Where is he tonight whilst you're out with his father?'

Carly looked toward the kitchen door as though checking to see if it was properly closed. It was.

'He lives with his grandparents, with Steve's in-laws.'

'What?'

From what Steve had stated during dinner, about sons needing to spend time with their fathers, his own son not living with him was quite the surprise, and the last thing Gemma had expected to hear Carly say.

'It's not what you think, Steve sees Brian, his son, as often as he can,' Carly rushed out awkwardly, almost as though she had heard what Gemma had been thinking.

Gemma's brows knitted.

'OK, so how does that little arrangement work?' she asked, trying not to sound as caustic as she felt.

'They live in a place called Deal. It's a small sea-side town somewhere on the East Kent coastline, I think. And every Friday evening, Steve goes down to their place for the weekend, so he can spend some quality time with Brian.'

'So Monday to Friday, Steve lives in London on his own?'

'Yes.'

'And he goes down to Deal to see his son, *every* weekend?'

'More or less,' said Carly, an expression of guilt hovering at the corners of her mouth again.

'Ah…' Gemma nodded, left the sentence hanging.

'Look, I know what you're thinking but I promise you, it's not me who's been stopping Steve from going down there *every* weekend.' Carly said stiffly.

Could she hear herself Gemma thought, feeling sorry for the innocent teenager unwittingly caught up in the middle of his father's new relationship?

'So why does Brian live with his grandparents, instead of his father?'

'They live in the same town as Brian and his mother did, you know, before she died. And Steve didn't want to move his son away from everything he was used to. He wanted him to be able to go to the same school, to stay with friends and all that.'

Gemma nodded.

'Right.'

Though it all sounded like an eminently sensible and tidy arrangement, it still seemed odd to Gemma that Steve would leave his in-laws to bring up his *only* child. Was he really being incredibly unselfish or was he, she wondered, more than happy to offload the responsibility? Beginning to wonder what Dave would make of it all, the parallels to his own life and how hard he had fought to keep Jessica from living with her maternal grandparents, she guessed he was unlikely to be that impressed.

'Remind me, how long have you and Steve been seeing each other?'

'A couple of months, maybe? About the same length of time you and Dave have been living together?'

'And what about Steve's parents, where are they in all of this?'

'They're dead.'

'Dead?'

'Yes, they died years ago in a car crash, when Steve was still a teenager.'

Rough, Gemma thought.

'And no other family? Grandparents, aunts, uncles?'

'No, Steve became an orphan after the death of his parents.'

Really rough.

'Have you met his son?'

'No, Steve only lost his wife about four months ago. So as you can imagine, he's not too keen on Brian being introduced to anyone new. At least not just yet,' Carly rushed out.

'Four months?' Gemma squeaked as her jaw dropped open.

'Yes, and I can already guess what you're thinking but it's not like that, honestly it's not. The marriage was on the rocks long before I came on to the scene. In fact, I would go so far as to say, they were on the brink of separating,' Carly reassured rapidly.

Gemma shook her head. Once again, she was struggling to believe what she was hearing.

'Sorry?'

'Gemma, stop looking at me like that. I am not a bad person. In case you've forgotten, it's not like you and Dave gave it a lot of time from dating, to moving in together. And you had *two* children to think about,' said Carly hotly.

Was she for real, Gemma asked herself?

'Come on, Carly, I'd been separated from Paul for almost a year before I met your brother. And Dave had been on his own for a lot longer than that.'

On the receiving end of a mutinous look, Gemma decided she was ready to ask the question she had so far, been putting off.

'Tell me, how did Steve's wife die?'

Carly hesitated. Her cheeks suffusing to pink, she looked even more guilty, if that were at all possible.

Refusing to go where her instincts were taking her, had taken her all along, Gemma shook her head at herself, surely not?

'It was all a bit... unexpected.'

'Sorry?'

She couldn't be right, could she? Hoping she had to have misheard, not wanting to think the unthinkable, Gemma searched her friend's face for some much needed clues.

As though agreeing with Gemma's unspoken conjecture, Carly nodded.

'It's true, Gemma. She took her own life, just like...'

Gemma's thoughts immediately turning to Sarah, the long shadow her awful death had cast over Dave, over Jessica, she shuddered. For something to do, she drank some cold coffee, spluttered as it went down the wrong way.

Carly thumped Gemma on the back.

'You OK,' she asked?

'Suicide?' Gemma stammered out apprehensively, barely able to say the dreaded word. Poor Dave, how on earth was he going to feel when he found out about all of this?

'Yes.'

'But how? How did it happen?'

'She drowned herself. Walked out into the sea…'

'Dear God!'

Gemma's face under her make-up was grey, her lips bloodless. She felt as though, any minute, she could collapse.

'Gemma, you OK? Do you need to sit down?'

Gemma shook Carly's stabilising hand off her arm. The last thing she needed was to sit down. Suddenly unable to keep still, she began to pace.

'The sea? And it w-wasn't an accident?' she managed to stutter out as she walked.

'No, accident, she left a note. Brian found it.'

Imagining the horror of what it must have been like for the poor boy, of the nightmares he must have experienced since, must still be experiencing, Gemma was unable to help herself.

'Jesus, Carly,' she protested weakly.

On either side of Carly's face, there was a bright spot of pink rapidly appearing, darkening.

'I know, I know. But she was ill, Gem, mentally ill,' Carly explained, seemingly with no emotion wasted.

Struggling, her own emotions lurching all over the place, Gemma drank some more of the cold, now bitter tasting coffee. She shook her head.

'I'm sorry, Carly, but I don't know what to say to you.'

As she came abreast, Carly gave Gemma's forearm a quick, hard squeeze before letting her continue her pacing.

'Then don't, don't say anything. I'll do all the talking. You're worrying about Dave, aren't you? About how he's gonna react to all of this, when he finds out?'

'Of course I am, but that's not *all* I'm worried about. I'm also worrying about you, and that poor boy. How do you think he's going to feel when he finds out how quickly his father has moved on from his mother?'

The dark pink spots on Carly's cheeks reddened even further. Again, her eyes misted over.

'How should I know? But we certainly don't plan on telling him any time soon. We figured we'll work that one out when we need to.'

To Gemma's ears, Carly sounding more irritated than upset, angry even, she was sorry. She wanted to help Carly, not fight with her.

'The same goes for Dave,' Carly stated firmly. 'There is no point in discussing any of this with him, it's too soon.'

Gemma stopped her pacing.

'Look Carly, I know I initially agreed not to say anything to Dave, but he's your brother,' she reasoned. 'And he's also my partner, the man I'm meant to spending the rest of my life with. I shouldn't be keeping these sorts of secrets from him. And neither, in my humble opinion, should you.'

Carly shook her head.

'Please, Gem, I'm begging you. I've told you all of this in confidence. You're my best friend, so be my friend.'

Before she could stop herself, Gemma threw Carly a look of astonishment and disbelief.

'Don't, Carly. Don't try and manipulate me. I don't appreciate it. And as for Dave, don't you think he has a right to know what his sister is getting herself into?' Gemma pleaded.

'*No! No, I don't,*' Carly hissed out under her breath, her eyes glittering angrily all of a sudden. Then she sighed. 'Look Gem, we need to know we have a viable relationship before we start seriously rocking *anyone's* boat,' she insisted.

'So you and Steve are on the same page about this?'

'Yes, and he's really sensitive about it all, so you can't discuss it with him, either.'

How convenient, Gemma thought resentfully?

'You have to understand, Gem. He's had an awful time with his wife's family. Ridiculously, they blame him for her taking her own life,' Carly tried to explain.

Just like Sarah's family, Gemma thought sadly. Even though Sarah's parents had never said anything directly to Dave, there was still a subversive undercurrent of blame that was hard to ignore. But where Steve was concerned and for all Carly knew, Gemma thought worriedly, his wife's family might be on to something. He obviously had no trouble telling a bald-faced lie to his girlfriend's brother and close friend, not to mention manipulating Carly into doing the same. Gemma shivered.

She gave Carly a good hard, sceptical stare.

'Carly, you sure about this?'

'Sure about what? About not telling Dave? Or about going out with Steve?' Carly asked, sounding edgy and instantly on the defensive again.

'About *everything*,' Gemma stressed carefully, wisely choosing not to single out Steve. 'Your brother, Steve's son, his wife's recent death, her family, everything combined, it all seems so very complicated. Surely you can see that? You could get seriously hurt, Carly,' Gemma tried to persuade.

Carly gave Gemma's forearm another squeeze.

'Thanks, Gem. Thanks for caring. For interfering and poking your nose in. I love that you care about me, but I'm a big girl now, and I'll be fine,' she insisted, though there was a brittle edge to her voice, tears glistening at the corner of her eyes.

Gemma sighed, heavily.

'OK, I won't say anything for now but only provided, you understand, you can't keep this from your brother forever. At some point, you're going to have to tell him. And if you don't, I will.'

Carly delivered Gemma a weak smile of reassurance.

'Look, Gem, most of the men in my life don't last more than a couple of months, so there's no point in worrying and panicking about all the ifs and maybes, not at this stage. Let's just see what happens over the next few weeks, shall we?'

Carly's tone of voice expecting no answer, her question purely rhetorical, Gemma knew it was time to quit. She would get no further with Carly tonight. Realising in that moment, just how much she disliked Steve, how little she trusted him, Gemma could not help but hope, God help her, the relationship would fail.

'Carly, you do know, don't you, I'm always here for you?'

'Yeah, I know.' Carly smiled, tossed the tea towel at Gemma to catch. 'Now shut up and let's change the subject? Tell me what's been going on between you and my beautiful niece.'

CHAPTER SIX

Gemma sucked in a deep breath. Determinedly flicking her worries for her friend to one side, she blinked back the tears that were suddenly threatening to fall. She did not want to feel sorry for herself. She did not deserve to feel sorry for herself.

Carly looked into Gemma's eyes with a great deal of concern.

'Hey,' she said. 'Why the tears?'

'She hates me, Carly.'

'Oh, Gem, she doesn't hate you. Nobody could hate you,' Carly soothed.

'Yes, she does. And I know she's your niece and that rightly, you adore her but...' Gemma stalled, feeling like the traitor she was as she struggled to get out what she needed to say. 'She can be such a *bitch*,' Gemma rushed out before she could change her mind.

'Wow, that bad, huh?' said Carly, the ghost of a smile pulling at the corners of her mouth.

'Please, Carly, don't make fun of me. Every day, it's a challenge...' she hesitated, the words not coming easily. 'I'm seriously struggling here. I keep trying to talk to her, but she either ignores me, or gives me a tirade of abuse.'

Carly rubbed a hand up and down Gemma's arm in a calming motion.

'I'm not making fun of you, Gem? It's just that it sounds so unlike my pretty little niece, I'm finding it a bit hard to take it all in, that's all.'

'I know, I don't believe it myself sometimes. But I really need your help because I don't know what to do about it any more? No matter what I do, try, or say, I can't seem to get through to her. And now it's got to a point where I feel so totally out of my depth, I'm frightened.'

Carly's eyes widened in surprise.

'Frightened?'

Gemma hung her head in shame.

'Yeah, I'm scared I'm gonna do something, I'm bound to regret.'

'Like what for God's sake?'

There was a beat of silence as Gemma continued to grapple with the onslaught of her pent-up emotions.

'Gem, whatever it is, spit it out.'

Unable to look Carly in the eye, her cheeks awash with pink, Gemma falteringly divulged, 'There are t-times... I could quite easily... smack her one.'

Hating that she could admit to wanting to harm Dave's daughter, his one and only child who was the spitting image of her beautiful but dead mother, Gemma was wishing she could sink through the floor and disappear.

'Oh, Gem, I'm sure anyone trying to raise kids, never mind someone else's kid, feels that way at times. I know I would,' said Carly as she tried to dispel some of Gemma's angst.

'You think?'

'Of course, and you haven't hit her yet, have you?' Carly asked, her face wreathed with concern.

Gemma shook her head vehemently.

'No, and even though I have wanted to... I don't think I would,' she finished, struggling to believe herself.

'Well, there you go then.' Carly smiled, shaking her head at Gemma. 'Having never had or even wanted any children of my own, I can only imagine what you've been going through. And I can't say I'm an expert. But I'm pretty sure it's all quite normal to feel the way you've been feeling,' Carly sympathised kindly.

'Yeah, well, that might all change if you *do* get serious with Steve,' Gemma said almost nastily, in spite of herself.

'Hmm, well, as I've already said, let's just take it one step at a time, shall we?' Carly reflected with a low chuckle, not taking Gemma's barbed comment the least bit seriously. 'But getting back to Jessica, you two *had* been getting along fine, right?'

'Yes, that's what makes it even more worrying.'

'So apart from the obvious, you all moving in together, I mean, what else has changed?'

'I don't know?' Gemma replied with a heavy heart. 'Apart from moving in together, nothing else has changed, at least not that I am aware of.'

'Well, I can clearly remember you and Dave talking to Jessica about the move and she seemed fine with it all, even excited, so it can't be that. Are you sure there's nothing else?'

Gemma shook her head miserably.

Carly gave her a quick hug.

'No, she still goes to the same school, has the same set of friends.'

'Strange.'

'Yeah, it is like someone has flipped a switch somewhere and boom, Jessica's suddenly morphed into this hideous, uncontrollable monster. And I tell you, it's doing my head in.'

Looking contemplative for a second or two, Carly eventually shook her head as though stumped.

'What does Dave make of it all?'

Gemma shrugged.

'What does that mean?'

'I haven't told him yet.'

'What? But surely he's noticed?'

'Not really... He knows she can be a bit difficult, like tonight, but I haven't had the heart to tell him just how badly she's been behaving toward me. And she's not daft, she's at her worst, when he's not around.'

'How is she with Henry?'

'OK, I think, but there's such a big age gap, they don't really spend that much time together. It seems to be just lucky old me, she singles out.'

Carly nodded. She thought for a couple of seconds.

'Gem, I know she's my beautiful, adorable niece, but don't you think you owe it to yourself to be honest with Dave? After all, he is her father.'

Gemma shook her head dejectedly.

'Look,' Carly said, her voice soothingly calm yet firm, 'if you two are to stand any chance of working as a couple, I really don't think it's a good idea for you to keep this to yourself. He needs to know.'

So it was OK for Carly to keep secrets from Dave, to outright lie to him, and yet when the boot was on the other foot...Gemma thought belligerently, before reminding herself, Carly was only trying to help.

'Easier said than done,' she snapped out a little more tartly than she had intended.

Carly sighed, then smiled as she smoothed away her discernible irritation.

'I know, but you have to try, right?'

'It's difficult... I don't want to cause any trouble between the two of them. And I wanted to give her every chance I could, you know, to properly settle in before I tittle-tattled on her.'

'I'm sorry, Gem, but you *have* to tell him. Otherwise, in a roundabout way, you're not doing Jessica any favours. She needs to be told when she's behaving this badly,' Carly lectured.

What a hypocrite, shouted Gemma, but in her head! Not very happy with her friend in that moment yet unable to ignore her point, she sighed out bitterly.

'You think?' she asked, not quite managing to hide her sarcasm.

'Come on, Gem. How would you feel if it was Henry behaving like a little shit toward to Dave, and *you* didn't know about it?' Carly asked.

Carly was right, and Gemma knew it.

'I would hate it, you know I would.'

Looking pensive, Carly unexpectedly said, 'You know what, I've just realised, in the next couple of days, it's going to be the anniversary of Sarah's death.'

Gemma started, with the chaos of the last few weeks, she had totally forgotten. Jessica only ten when her mother had died perhaps, that was it? With the anniversary of her mother's death almost on her perhaps, she was struggling with painful memories that left her pining for her mum?

'So are you saying, all this acting out, it might have something to do with her mum?' Gemma asked hopefully.

'Dunno, but she's right on the brink of womanhood, Gem. And although I think Dave's done a fantastic job bringing her up almost single-handedly these last few years, it's still not the same as having your mum around,' said Carly, her tone matter-of-fact, not critical. 'And maybe, finding herself living in the same house as another woman who is still not her mum, the anniversary of her mother's death has become just a little more unbearable?'

Unable to imagine not having her own mother around and she was thirty-six not fifteen, suddenly, Gemma felt terribly sorry for Jessica.

'I wonder if that *is* it? I wonder if moving in with me, seeing me being a mother to Henry, has made this year especially poignant for her?'

Carly nodded.

'Makes perfect sense to me. Doesn't excuse the bad behaviour mind, but it might go some way to explaining where it's all coming from.'

'Carly, she trusts you, can't you talk to her for me?'

Another couple of tears escaping as she thought about what Jessica might have been going through, Gemma swiped them away. No more tears, it was time for action.

Carly shamelessly inspecting Gemma's damp face, she eyed her suspiciously as she gave her a shrewd once-over.

'You know what I think, I think this is just a bump on the rocky road to nirvana. Once Jessica gets over this milestone, and herself, she'll realise just how great you are. Then, like me, she'll love you to bits.'

'Oh God, I do hope so. But will you still talk to her for me please? Find out if we are right?'

Carly stared at Gemma as she deliberated. Then she smiled broadly, reassuringly.

'Yeah, OK,' she nodded. 'I'll talk to Dave about organising that weekend I promised her. Then we'll take it from there.'

Gemma's sigh of relief was heartfelt as she seriously hoped, they were on the right track.

Watching Dave pull his shirt up over his head, drop his trousers down to his ankles, then hop around the room as he struggled with his socks whilst trying not to fall over his underpants, Gemma was unsure whether to laugh or admonish him.

'Dave, you could at least put your clothes in washing bin,' she scolded as he left his discarded clothes in a tangled heap on the floor.

'Yes, miss,' Dave hiccuped as he swiped up the offending clothes.

Men they were all the bloody same, she thought tiredly.

Sat propped up with pillows against the headboard, Gemma twitched back Dave's side of the quilt as she made ready for him to get into the bed beside her. Though the state he was obviously in, she would much rather he slept on the couch.

Buck naked and grinning stupidly, more than slightly inebriated, his little buddha belly leading before him, Dave weaved his way toward Gemma and the bed. Chuckling foolishly as he stumbled over his own feet, he sat heavily down on the edge of it.

Not trusting the sudden gleam in Dave's eye, Gemma seriously hoped he was not going to come over all amorous with her. He in no fit state, she was definitely not in the mood. She shifted down in the bed, pulled the quilt up a little higher as she eyed him suspiciously.

It had been some time since Gemma had seen Dave this tipsy. The evening still early, only just ten o'clock, she had no idea how on he had managed to down quite so much booze in such a short amount of time? He would have a terrible hangover for work in the morning. Serve him right, she thought truculently.

'So what did you think of our Carly's new boy wonder?' Dave asked over his shoulder in exaggerated whisper as he drew out his words.

Dave always an easy talker, someone who liked to *chat* regardless of what his audience might be in the middle of doing or how they were feeling, and aware he was becoming even more expansive under the benign influence of the booze, Gemma braced herself. Exhausted, wanting only to go to sleep and put the exacting evening behind her, she hoped she could discourage him.

'I dunno,' she answered economically, chose her words carefully.

'You dunno?' Dave slurred, struggling to get the words out as his body swayed from side-to-side. 'That's not like you,' his lisped. 'You always have an opinion?'

'Dave, I'm tired.'

'Better than those idiots she's dated in the past,' he mused, not missing a beat. 'But I tell you, he's a watcher that one. He watches everything.'

He burped, giggled foolishly.

Not wanting to talk about Steve, Carly, or their rotten secrets, Gemma held her own counsel. Hopefully, soon, Dave would pass out and she could go to sleep.

'Kept his cards really close to his chest, didn't he?'

As usual, he hadn't missed much, Gemma thought worriedly. Dave's insights starting to make her nervous, she wriggled even further down in the bed.

'For all his fancy pants, his posh voice,' Dave mumbled as he gossiped on, 'I reckon that one's got a bucket load of secrets.' He widened his eyes at her, tapped his forefinger to the side of his temple. 'I'm a man, I know how other men think. I bet I'm right, you'll see.'

Dave gave Gemma a lopsided grin. Desperate to hide her guilt, Gemma barely managed to return a weak smile.

'You know what I think? I think, Carly should listen to me more. She should listen to her big bro, I'd put her straight.'

He nodded to himself sagely.

Glad Dave was too drunk to want an answer from her. Relieved he had not noticed her blush as she again flashed on everything Carly had revealed about Steve's messy personal life, his glib lies, she anxiously turned off her bedside light. She hoped he would get the hint.

'Didn't stay long, did they? He didn't drink much, either.' Dave hiccuped. Rubbing a hand backward and forward over his lightly stubbled head, he yawned widely. 'He's not normal, that one.'

Wisely keeping her mouth shut, Gemma said nothing.

'I reckon he didn't like us, found us common and boring. He's a snob.'

'No,' Gemma corrected impatiently. Not liking the direction in which the one-sided conversation was going, this time, she just had to say something. 'Don't you remember, he told us he needed to keep a clear head? He's got an early start tomorrow morning, he has a lot of driving to do.'

Dave shook his head, pulled a face, scratched the side of his jaw. 'Did he?'

Dave about to say something more, Gemma having had enough, she cut him off.

'Dave, I'm exhausted,' she snapped out. 'I've got work in the morning. I need to sleep.'

'OK,' he grinned good-naturedly, patted the top of her head, like she was his favourite dog.

Dave falling sideways, laying prone on the bed next to her, within seconds, he was snoring loudly, belching out wind from both ends.

Christ, Gemma thought with exasperation and distaste.

Leaning across Dave to switch off his bedside light, Gemma looked down at him as he lay there, irritatingly reposeful. All right for some, she thought.

Turning over to her side of the bed. Facing away from Dave and his alcohol tainted breath, Gemma settled down for a sleep that would not come. Her head busily chewing over everything she had learnt from Carly that evening, her worry that Steve was not quite all he seemed in spite of her best friend's protestations, her concerns about Jessica, not to mention the fact she was already lying to Dave, her brain refused to switch off.

She was kept restlessly tossing and turning, for most of the night.

CHAPTER SEVEN

Christ, I am bored.

A recurrent throbbing to the left-hand side of my head and face, a sharp pain directly over my eye and I know have the beginnings of a migraine. Experiencing a tinge of nausea and having no choice but to continue to lie on my bed, I briefly close my eyes against the incessant thump in my head, the unimportance of the outside world. Tuning inwards instead, I start to think. A rather dangerous preoccupation for me, as I have a tendency to obsess.

Why is it, nothing about my life feels real or authentic and yet here I am, tethered to its illusion? I do not live, I merely exist. Long periods of tediousness vying with despair, I am one of those people who has to have an outlet. I have to have a relief from the repetitive, mundane trivialities of life. And right now, it is time for a change, I know it is. I just need to work out how…

You see, I am not really so different, from the likes of you.

I typically try to forget most things as soon as they happen, but as my eyes squeeze tightly shut against the agony of migraine, I slowly begin to realise, the unfortunate event that recently took place down in the tube station, is one I have not been able to so easily dismiss. Even now, lying here, consumed with pain, my pulsating brain is determined I should revisit the incident. That I should relive everything that happened, in glorious detail. That I should gourmet on the juicy memory, feed off each off each and every juicy ingredient — the woman's bloodcurdling scream —the screeching train — the babbling mob scrabbling to find their mobiles — the smell of the fear — the terrified faces of those reeling away from the horrific scene — the ghoulish media reports hypothesising over what had happened, and why.

The accident-suicide — as it was eventually headlined by the mainstream media — particularly easy to execute, to get away with. It is as I think about that one, random act of violence, my malaise, like a beautiful moth unfurling from the claustrophobic confines of its chrysalis, suddenly pings free.

Weary of avoiding life, of not truly living. Recalling how present I felt in the flux of that moment, how the inherent danger of being seen, of getting caught, added a beauty, a depth and a challenge to the perceived security of my boring, bogus life, I have a sudden realisation, an epiphany of sorts...

Living dangerously, suits me.

Some people, I suppose, get scared when they kill, but not me. The idea of killing does not shock or upset me. So there is no reason, I can think of, for me to stop there. Why should I not continue to use London's man-made labyrinth, to pump some much needed respite into my colourless life? It would be so easy, so very, very, easy. The London Underground, an environment for disappearing into, for blending... Used daily, a necessity for those living, working, and surviving in the great metropolis, the unwitting victims supplied by the city's subterranean network of tunnels, would be limitless,

'Forgive me, but I can't help but exult!'

My thoughts potent, electrifying, the pressure that has been insidiously building inside my head, alleviates. Visceral pain replaced with an intoxicating anticipation, a bubble of satisfaction bursts deep and carnal somewhere inside of me, and I sigh out with relief.

Even though I have to admit to one critical moment of hesitation — due to an unexpected blip of moral conscience as I question the sanctity of life — my momentary misgiving is soon abandoned.

'If life is meant to be so precious, then why is it so tenuous?'

All uncertainty gone, the clearance replaced with a heady feeling of euphoria, a thrill of omnipotence, I leap out of bed and like an excited child, jump around the room. Punching at the air with an undignified glee, I cannot wait to execute my next event.

'At last, I have fixed on something that excites me, that makes me want to dive into the depths of life. You should try it.'

London, such a big and overpopulated city, with so many unhappy humans switched off from their surroundings, from each other as they mindlessly plug into their faceless devices, they will be such easy pickings. Thinking ahead, I realise my plans do not have to be difficult or complicated. By rejecting method and conscious decision, in favour of opportunity and chance, of going with the flow, I soon ascertain that I already have my template. That small, random acts of violence, are the obvious way forward.

Mind the Gap!

CHAPTER EIGHT

Staring at the innocuous white envelope clutched between her fingers as though it was about to bite, Gemma could resist no longer. Suspiciously holding the missive up to the light coming off the standard lamp, she flipped the item over from front to back a couple of times, but could see nothing through its opacity. The recipient's name and address neatly typed out. The envelope bearing a local postmark and looking exactly like one they had received only a couple of weeks ago, she was certain the letter would be from Jessica's school. Though still curious as to its contents, she was quite relieved it was addressed not to herself, but to Dave.

Disgusted at the depths of her cowardice, her ability to so easily detach herself from the letter's news, Gemma grimaced. Then suddenly hearing someone running down the stairs, she hastily moved herself away from the lamp and guiltily propped the envelope on top of the pine mantlepiece. Left it clearly visible for Dave to find.

'Hi mum, can I watch some telly, please?' Henry asked.

Affectionately running her hands through the top of her son's hair, enjoying the feel of it slipping through her fingers, Gemma leant down and kissed the side of his peach soft cheek.

'OK, but keep the sound down. Jessica's upstairs trying to do her homework.'

'Uh, no, she's not,' said Henry, singsonging his disagreement.

'Sorry?'

Throwing himself down on the sofa, Henry grabbed up the remote and clicked on the TV.

'Henry?'

'She went out.'

'What? When?'

'Dunno…' he answered, shrugging his shoulders.

Grabbing a hold of one of the cushions, Henry pulled it comfortingly into his stomach. Then tucking his feet up under his legs, laid his head down on to the arm of the sofa and without a care in the world, fixed his gaze firmly on the telly.

Gemma exited the living-room and wearily climbed the stairs.

The door to Jessica's bedroom ajar, loud music trickling through the crack, she knocked and waited.

There was no response.

Tentatively pushing open the door, expecting to yelled at any minute, Gemma quickly saw the room was empty.

Flicking her eyes to the open blinds at the window, six-twenty in the evening, and already the day had died. Outside dark and cold, with Jessica technically missing again, it was not a comforting thought.

Looking for clues, Gemma agitatedly scanned the low lit, unkempt room. The plump new quilt trailing off the end of the bed, used items of crockery poking out from beneath the newly bought divan, unwashed clothes exploding out across the floor, a ton of dust, empty crisp packets and chocolate wrappers littering the top of the bedside table, the dressing table covered in toiletries and make-up, the grubby disarray was a depressing sight. And yet, she had offered to help Jessica clean her room, numerous times.

Averting her offended eyes, Gemma alighted on a small brand new desk positioned just under the window. Her worried gaze instantly snared by a photo of Jessica with her mother, she crossed the room and gingerly picked up the white wooden frame, so she could examine the picture more closely. Mother and daughter standing under the dappled sunlight of a massive oak tree, Sarah looking young, happy and stunningly beautiful, Gemma felt an unwelcome but familiar stirring of jealousy. Sarah's long black hair lightly lifted by the wind, her tanned face laughing into the camera, the unseen photographer, her slim hand was clasped protectively over that of her daughter's. A much younger Jessica staring adoringly up at her mother, the family resemblance was so strong. The hope and contentment in the photo palpable, it was hard to believe that within a year of being diagnosed a manic depressive, and probably not long after the photo had been taken, Sarah had tragically ended her own life.

Carefully returning the photo, flipping up the lid of Jessica's laptop, seeing it was still switched on and that the child's mobile phone was laying face down next to it, Gemma sighed out her irritation along with her relief. The girl would not leave either device unattended for very long. She would not be far.

Just as she was concluding there was no need to panic, Gemma suddenly heard the front door being slammed off its hinges. The infuriating girl not even trying to sneak back into the house, as she had snuck out, Gemma was sure she had inherited the child from hell. She clenched her fists down by her sides.

'Damn you,' she whispered quietly to Sarah's photo, 'for taking your own life.'

Heavy footfalls hurrying up the stairs, Gemma swiftly removed herself from Jessica's desk. Reassured she had left everything exactly as she had found it, with a heavy sigh, she turned to face her pseudo-stepdaughter.

Jessica marched into the room with a proprietorial air.

'What are you doing in here,' she demanded to know?

Feeling guilty, in spite of herself, Gemma shifted uneasily as she instinctively steeled herself for battle.

Her room, her sanctum, Jessica's eyes danced possessively from one part of the room to the other as she looked to see if anything had been touched or disturbed. Crossing the room, she appraised her desk for a couple of seconds and grabbing up her phone, scanned the brightly lit screen. She threw Gemma a suspicious and accusatory look.

Gemma's cheeks reddening maddeningly, instantly on the defence, she went on the attack.

'Where have you been?'

Jessica glared at Gemma.

'I asked you question, young lady. Where have you been? And why did you go out without telling me, *again*?'

Jessica still refusing to reply, finding herself on the end of yet another mutinous look, one that pointedly said, *What's it to do with you?* Gemma could feel her anger rising.

'Jessica, I'm waiting. I need an explanation,' she insisted.

Her voice now rising along with her anger, Gemma could almost feel the steam coming out of her ears. She needed to calm down, or she would get nowhere, she reminded herself.

Looking contemptuous and equally annoyed, Jessica briefly closed her eyes as though she wanted nothing more than for Gemma to disappear.

'For Christ's sake Gemma, I'm fifteen. I am not a baby!'

'And your point is?'

'My point *is*,' Jessica stressed sarcastically, 'I'm old enough to go down to the corner shop without having to ask *your* permission, first.'

For a moment, Gemma could only look at Jessica with astonishment and disbelief. *Blast the child.* How many times had they had the exact same conversation? Mentally counting to five, Gemma reminded herself that it was *she* who was the adult, and that no matter what Jessica thought, said, or did, at fifteen, she was still a child, a vulnerable child. She took a deep breath.

'Look Jessica, I know you think you're a grown-up but believe me, in the eyes of the law, you're not. And in the absence of your father, I *expect* you to let me know *when* and *where* you want to go, *before* you leave the house,' she stressed.

Met with another firm silence and on the receiving end of yet another rebellious look, Gemma was so frustrated. But it was so important that she somehow, got her point across. She had to make the girl think. She tried again.

'Jessica, how do you think your father would feel if you went out without telling me where you were going and then, for whatever reason, you didn't come home? Please, think about it. How would we even know where to start looking for you?'

'Like that's ever going to happen,' Jessica snorted arrogantly, disrespectfully.

'Jessica, we live in a city, in London. Anything could happen to you.'

'No, you're just trying to manipulate me, to control me,' said Jessica viciously.

Vying between wanting to throw the girl out of the widow, and hug her tight, yet again, Gemma was out of depth. She was desperate to get through to the girl, to help her understand how open to attack she was, how dangerous it was for such a beautiful young girl to be on her own, out there.

The muffled sound of the front door being closed again, Gemma realised Dave was home from work and she could not be more relieved. This time, she decided, Jessica could deal with her father. Resolved to going downstairs, to telling Dave what his daughter had been up to tonight, these past few weeks, she made to leave the room.

'Gemma, please,' Jessica whispered urgently, her face paling as she heard her father coming into the house, 'don't tell dad.'

Woman and woman-child eyed each other, suspiciously and warily.

Jessica's tone having switched from adversarial to almost conspiratorial, Gemma was taken aback. Why the sudden change of heart, and what hell did she do now, she thought with exasperation and worry? If she told Dave the idiotic child kept disappearing on her, she would only incur even more of Jessica's wrath. Then again, if she didn't tell Dave what his daughter had been up to, and she did it again but with more serious consequences, he would be furious with her and rightly so. *Damn the girl!*

Jessica's eyes anxiously darting toward the bedroom door and back again, Gemma had a sudden realisation... Jessica's unexpected change of heart possibly had more to do with the letter sat on the mantlepiece, rather than a genuine remorse. Either way, she was exhausted. She no longer had the energy battle it out with the girl, never mind furnishing Dave with an explanation as why she had not yet told him of his daughter's regular need to abscond. She sighed.

'OK, but I am *not* going to do this with you again. Next time you leave this house without telling me, for your own safety, I *will* tell your father,' Gemma emphasised.

It was as she was crossing the threshold of Jessica's bedroom that Gemma heard a surprising, if hushed, 'Thank you.'

Visibly fuming, Dave was pacing up and down the minimal floorspace of their bedroom, angrily muttering to himself.

Sat on the edge of their double bed, watching him wear a hole in the already threadbare carpet, Gemma looked on with irritation and concern. Her earlier squall with Jessica, if Dave's intermittent expletives were anything to go by, now shaping up into becoming a full blown storm, she sighed, figured all she could do was hang tight until the worst of the anticipated uproar had blown over. After all, she reminded herself, it was not as if Jessica was her child.

Though it did not make Gemma feel any better to know it, she had been a hundred percent right earlier. The letter propped up on the mantelpiece *was* from the school. The school writing to say they suspected Jessica of forging a sick note so she could truant for a *whole* day, they were insisting Dave ring and schedule an appointment to see the Principle. The school stating they would be following up with a phone call if they did not hear from him by the end of the week, Dave had been apoplectic.

Unable to stand the pacing any longer, his constant to and fro threatening to give her a headache, in spite of herself, Gemma tentatively asked, 'Dave, have you ever known Jessica to do something like this before?'

Stopping mid-stride, Dave rubbed a hand backward and forward over his stubbled head as he turned to face Gemma. He sighed heavily.

'No, she's always been spirited, but she's never truanted from school before.' He shook his head. 'I can't think what's got into her? But what's really got me worried, is where in the hell did she get to that day, and who the hell was she with?'

His eyes look haunted, Gemma thought, her heart going out to him. He began to stride up and down the room.

'What do you think the school will do,' she asked?

'No idea? But as she's never done anything like this before, I'm seriously hoping, they won't suspend her.'

'They wouldn't expel her, would they? The thought of having to find her another school, in this oversubscribed borough, doesn't bear thinking about,' said Gemma, with feeling.

Dave dispatching her a withering look, she could have bitten her tongue off.

'Sorry, that wasn't exactly helpful, was it?'

'No,' Dave answered curtly.

Feeling suitably chastised, Gemma lowered her eyes. Shrinking from what she saw was mainly Dave's dilemma, she retreated into protective thoughts. *When I find some time, if I find some time, I will get myself another job, one that pays me more money and where I don't have to work for a psycho. And why should I put myself between Dave and his daughter? I hardly know the girl, and if she has anything to do with it, I never will? I know, I'll join one of Carly's yoga classes, get myself fit and svelte again.* It was bad enough having to deal with Dave's memory of his beautiful but dead wife, never mind trying to be a replacement mother to his woman-child of a daughter, who outright rejected her at every turn, she excused herself.

Dave stopped his pacing. He threw Gemma a resolute look.

'Right, come on then, let's do this.'

'What? You want *me* to go with you?' Gemma squeaked, automatically baulking at the thought.

'Yes, Jessica lives with you as well as me now. And this is just the sort of thing we need to provide a united front on. You have to be there.'

Gemma shook her head vigorously. She had an innate aversion to outright confrontation.

'Oh, I'm not so sure, Dave.'

Gemma could not believe Dave wanted *her* there when he chastised *his* daughter. Even though he was so much better at the whole parenting malarkey than she was, still, she could not help thinking he was making a *big* mistake. What if her presence served to only inflame what was already, in her opinion, a supremely volatile situation? He must be mad.

'Why?'

'Don't you think you should handle this one on your own?' she asked indecisively, hopefully.

'No, I don't,' Dave disagreed strongly. 'This is important, you have to be there.'

'But what if my being there only makes things worse?'

Wavering with uncertainty, she really did not want to go, but he seemed so certain. He caught her troubled look.

'Gemma, it's about time Jessica accepted *your* authority as well as my own.'

Taken by surprise at Dave's perceptive comment, but still full of doubt, Gemma shook her head again.

'I'm not so sure.'

Dave gave her a reassuring smile.

'Look, Gem, I *know* she's been giving you a hard time of late but I promise you, it's going to be OK.'

Surprised and feeling sheepish, Gemma found it hard to maintain eye contact.

'How? How did you know,' she asked?

Dave lifted her chin with his finger.

'That she's been giving you a hard time?'

'Yes.'

'Carly told me.'

Gemma gulped. She hoped Carly had not said too much. Only this was not the way she had wanted Dave to find out just how bad, her relationship with his daughter was.

'You've spoken to Carly?'

'Yes, she rang earlier today, to sort out a weekend for Jessica to go over and stay with her. She and that Steve left so early after dinner the other night, we never got a chance to sort it out then.'

'What did she tell you?'

'Not a lot, just let slip that Jessica's been a little trying lately and that when I got a chance, I might want to talk to you about it.'

Gemma cringed with embarrassment. Feeling ashamed of her flagrant lack of guardianship skills, she readily apologised.

'I'm so sorry, Dave. I have been trying, really I have,' she explained weakly. 'But no matter what I try, I don't seem to be able to get through to her.'

'Hey, it's not *you* who should be sorry. I should have been helping you more, listening to you more. Taking on someone else's child, is tough.'

Dave's statement said with real feeling, Gemma started. She had to ask.

'Have you been having problems with Henry?'

'No, no, it is fine.'

'You don't sound too sure?'

'All we've had, is the odd little skirmish. But it's nothing really. And he's a lot younger than Jessica. A lot easier to handle.'

Having no idea Henry had been difficult for Dave, Gemma felt awful, tired and depressed by it all.

'I'm sorry.'

He shook his head.

'Doesn't matter. And anyway, right now, Henry's not the problem.

Look, we haven't got time to get into this now, but there is one thing I would like to say…'

'Go on.'

He took a deep breath.

'Don't take this the wrong way but I sometimes think, you can be a bit *too nice* for your own good.'

Too nice, if only he knew, Gemma thought her conscience badly pricking. The amount of times she could have killed the girl. Not wanting to incriminate herself, Gemma maintained a studied silence lest she say something stupid, or undesirable. Dealing with Jessica was like handling Dave's heart and at times, the responsibility felt overwhelming. She was a terrible person, a terrible step-mother.

'You know what, it was the anniversary of Sarah's death the other day and I think,' Dave said as he unexpectedly went off-piste, 'she's just missing her mum.'

'So you feel the same way as Carly?'

He shrugged his shoulders.

'I dunno? Is that how she thinks? I wouldn't know? We haven't discussed it in any great depth.'

So Carly hadn't said too much, Gemma thought with not a small modicum of relief.

'Look, don't worry, Gem,' Dave said. 'Between us all, you, me, and Carly, we'll sort her out. You wait, with a little time and a little patience, she'll soon settle down again. I'm certain of it.'

Nodding her head in agreement, inside, Gemma was not so sure.

The atmosphere in the kitchen was toxic.

Jessica called down from her bedroom by her father a couple of minutes ago, she was sat slumped on one of the wooden chairs at the dining table. The girl chewing at a fingernail, she looked, Gemma thought as she surreptitiously studied the teenager sullenly trying to ignore her father, more wary than worried.

Leaning up against the countertop, feeling awkward and out of place in her own kitchen. Henry safely ensconced in his own room, tucked up in bed and out of the way, Gemma was wishing she could disappear upstairs and crawl into bed with him.

Dave passed the letter from the school over to his reluctant daughter. Pressing it into her hands, he insisted, in a deceptively mild voice, she read it.

Pushing herself more upright in her seat, Jessica grudgingly read the letter.

Waiting a couple of minutes for her finish, his tone turning authoritative, Dave demanded, 'Well, what have you got to say for yourself?'

Jessica jumping angrily to her feet in reply, behaving as though she had every right to be outraged, she promptly crumpled the letter up into a ball and threw it back at her father.

The missile hitting Dave in the chest before falling to the floor, he dispatched his vexed daughter an immutable look.

No longer able to ignore her father's stern and unforgiving face, Jessica dropped back down on to her chair again. For a brief moment she looked as though she was about to cry, but then her face hardened.

It struck Gemma that Jessica did not seem overly upset at being found out, visibly furious, but distressed, no, not particularly. In fact, if there were any feelings of remorse they appeared well guarded. But the rubbish parent she was, what did she know? Perhaps, the girl was just putting up a good front? Whatever the truth of Jessica's emotional state, Dave was having none of it though.

'I'm still waiting, young lady?'

'I'm sorry,' Jessica bellowed, not sounding in the least bit apologetic, her eyes dry, if shining. 'But since when has it been a crime to put some flowers on my mother's grave,' she spat out.

Dave visibly staggered, rocking on the balls of his feet, his face paling at Jessica's spitefully delivered revelation, Gemma could see he was struggling to compose himself. Her heart went out to him.

'But your mother's grave is miles away. How on earth did you get there?'

Jessica looked defiantly up her father.

'Buses and the Underground. It wasn't hard.'

Thinking of Jessica using the Underground on her own, Gemma's legs weakened. So many suicides, so many unexplained accidents, it was murder down there.

'What? All on your own?'

'Yes.'

Watching Jessica's eyes shiftily avoid those of her father's, there was no way Gemma believed her. Jessica had had company, she was sure of it.

'I don't believe you,' Dave hissed.

Dave's eyes, all of sudden, glittering dangerously with a barely contained fury, both fists thumping the tops of his legs, it was a side of him, Gemma had not seen before. For an awful couple of seconds, actually wondering if he was about to strike his daughter, she inwardly panicked as she wondered what to do, how to stop him? But not so Jessica, she just scowled back at her father. Met anger with anger.

'Prove it.'

As quickly as his hand raised, it dropped again.

Gemma stifled a sigh of relief.

His face working with effort, he changed tack.

'So after everything I've said to you about not using the Underground on your own, you did it anyway?'

'Yes!'

His face turning beetroot red again, betraying his anger, Dave glared equally back at his daughter.

'I'm fifteen, I know how to use the Tube!'

'It's not safe, not at your age!'

Both of them now yelling at each other, Gemma shrank back against the countertop. Wanting to leave but desperate not to draw any attention to herself, she stayed put.

'You're being stupid. All my friends use it. This is all because *she's* too chicken to use it, isn't it?' Jessica accused, her eyes swivelling to Gemma, sending her daggers.

Squirming, unable to hold the girl's defiant gaze, Gemma concentrated her focus on Dave.

Dave cast his daughter a look of warning.

'Jessica, you are *never*,' he emphasised through gritted teeth, 'to talk about your step-mother in that way again. Do you hear me?'

She refused to answer.

'Jessica?'

'She's not my step-mother. You're not married,' she pointed out sullenly.

'No, not yet, we're not. But as soon as Gemma's divorce is through, we *will* be.'

Dave emphasising his point, Gemma wished she could feel as confident as he did about their future together.

'And you are *never* to use the Underground on your own, *ever* again,' he insisted.

'Not like I had a lot of choice,' she objected angrily.

Sighing out his frustration and anger, Dave rubbed a hand over the top of his head. For a second or two, he looked totally distraught and his wits end. He took a couple of deep breaths.

'Jessica, you should have talked to me. If I had known just how strongly you felt about seeing your mother's grave, I would have taken you there myself, just not on a school day.'

'Mum's been dead five years and I've only seen her grave, twice,' Jessica accused furiously, her usually pale face now a ghoulish white. 'And you never talk to me about her, *ever!*' she yelled.

In spite of herself, Gemma experienced a wave of pity for Jessica's plight. Commiserating with the child who had lost her mother in such tragic circumstances, for the daughter struggling to communicate with her father, her eyes misted over. For even though she had known Dave found it difficult to visit his wife's grave, what she had not realised, was that he had altogether been avoiding going there. Nor had she appreciated quite how much Dave was neglecting to talk to his daughter, about her mother. The poor kid getting older, on the cusp of becoming an adult, a young woman herself, even without the added complexity of having to deal with her mother's suicide, it was such a confusing time. No wonder she was so bitter and angry all the time. Dave's own needs getting in the way of his child's, not such a great parent after all, she observed ironically, sadly. Beginning to understand just how it important it was for Dave to spend some quality time with his daughter, for him to help her to gain some perspective and closure before she went completely off the rails, Gemma resolved she would discuss her concerns with him, and soon.

Dave knelt down beside his daughter, went to put his arms around her shoulders but Jessica shrinking back from him, she remained stiff and stubbornly unapproachable.

Standing up again, his cheeks flaming, his fists bunched up down by his sides again, visibly stung, Gemma's heart went out to Dave as she watched him fight his emotions.

'I'm so sorry, Jess. I had no idea how much you needed to see your mother's grave. I wish you had told me,' he said quietly.

Jessica refusing to meet her father's concerned gaze, to say anything, tears dripping off her chin, Dave tried again.

'Jessica, please, I am trying to help you. Don't push me away. Your mother,' he mumbled awkwardly, 'she wanted you so much.'

'Well, she can't have wanted me that much, or she would never have killed herself,' Jessica moaned, the words spilling painfully out of her in a sudden gush.

The heightened emotion of the occasion seriously getting to her, Gemma stealthily put a finger up to her own face, swiped away a couple of tears that hovered for second before dropping economically on to her cheeks. This was not about her, she ruthlessly reminded herself.

Dave cleared his throat.

'Jessica, your mother was ill. Her mind wasn't right. But she would have been so proud of you, of how clever you've become and how beautiful you are.'

'I don't believe you.'

He shook his head.

'Please, Jessica. Don't make her death an albatross around *your* neck.'

Jessica visibly upset as the unchecked tears slid slowly down her bloodless face, Gemma could see just how desperate Dave was to comfort his stricken daughter, but he wisely kept his distance.

'That said,' Dave added quietly, 'it does not excuse your behaviour. You should have told me how you were feeling, not taken it on yourself to play hooky from school. And for that reason, you're grounded.'

Feeling very much an outsider as she watched Dave's firm but tender approach toward his troubled daughter, in that moment, Gemma felt so terribly sorry for them all — for Jessica, for Dave, for Henry and herself, even for Sarah.

CHAPTER NINE

Wednesday, the middle of the working day and the working week, Gemma had stepped out to get herself some lunch from the local eatery around the corner from where she worked. In a queue as she waited to place her order, for the first time since leaving the house that morning she took the opportunity to hastily check her mobile for text messages. Then immediately, wished she hadn't.

What the…?

Fumbling with the device, almost dropping it as she tried to get a closer look at what she was reading, Gemma stared down at the message on her screen with astonishment and disbelief. Searching for an accompanying name and telephone number but the information withheld, the text sent anonymously, a dark cloud passed over Gemma's palpitating heart.

Determined not to panic, to keep a rational mind, she urgently began to question herself.

Had it been sent to her number by mistake?

The queue shuffled.

'Miss, your order please?'

What if it wasn't a mistake?

What if it wasn't a wrong number?

'Miss, you order?'

'Miss!'

The sales assistant raising his voice to catch her attention. The man behind tapping her on the shoulder, Gemma shook her head at herself as she endeavoured to focus.

'Sorry, what did you say?'

'I need your order?' was the curt and impatient reply.

'Of course, I'm sorry,' Gemma apologised to the tetchy sales assistant. 'A strong latte with full fat milk, and a chicken salad baguette, please.'

'Eat in, or take out?'

Gemma thought fast. Too unsettled to go straight back to the office, to eat a brown-bag lunch at her desk as she usually did, she made her decision.

'Eat in, please.'

She handed over a ten pound note.

The meagre change thrust into her hand. The sales assistant already in spirit with the man behind, Gemma looked suspiciously around her. No one was looking at her, *watching* her.

Joining a small jumble of people all waiting for their orders to be fulfilled, Gemma's anxious eyes kept being drawn down to her phone. Firmly telling herself it was not going to bite, with an anticipatory dread, she reread the anonymous text message.

You can't trust him! He is NOT, what he seems.

Shaking her head at the device, still finding the message incredulous, the questions began all over again.

What did it mean? Don't trust who, she demanded of herself, Dave?

The message almost shouting at her, it felt too personal for it not to mean Dave. If indeed, she reminded herself, it was meant for her.

Her order arriving, Gemma gingerly put the phone back in her pocket, like it was a bottle of poison. Then scanning the heaving room, spotting a vacant table, she hurriedly made her way over to it before it was nabbed by someone else. Seconds later, having wedged herself behind a corner table by a window that was wet with condensation, not having long to spare, she attempted to concentrate on her lunch. Chewing the end off her baguette, sipping her latte but her head all over the place, the food was tasteless and the coffee uncommonly bitter.

Liberating her phone from the depths of her coat pocket, rereading the same text message for a third time, obsessing on it, Gemma glanced at her watch and decided there was still time.

'Carly, it's me,' Gemma said as soon as her call was intercepted.

'Hey, how's it going?' Carly responded.

Carly sounding puffed out, as though she was going somewhere in a hurry, Gemma hoped she could talk.

'Bad time?'

'No, not really, but I have just arrived at work and I have to teach in ten minutes.'

'Look, do you have the time, or don't you?' Gemma snapped out, cutting Carly off as she suddenly needed to get to the point.

Her tone sounding so much shorter than she would have liked, rude even, Gemma could have bitten off her own tongue. It was hardly Carly's fault she was feeling so stressed. She immediately apologised.

'Sorry, Carly, I didn't mean to snap at you.'

'So what's the problem?' said Carly as unflappable as ever, albeit between harried breaths. 'Is it Jessica?'

Gemma heaved a sigh.

'No, it's not Jessica. She's grounded, but she's fine.'

'Grounded? What on earth for?'

'Truanting.'

'Christ, really?'

'Yes, but that's not why I called.'

'Shoot.'

I will if you just shut up for a minute, Gemma thought belligerently, in spite of herself.

'I've received a really strange text message,' she rushed out, determined to get out what she needed to say.

'Sorry? A text message?'

By way of an explanation, Gemma expeditiously relayed the content of the message out to Carly.

'Can't you see who it's from?'

'No, the number is withheld.'

'And it's the only one you've received?' Carly asked crisply.

'Yes.'

'Then it's probably a prank.'

Gemma tried not to raise her voice.

'A prank? You think? But who would do something as nasty as that?'

'Perhaps it's a wrong number?' Carly mumbled down the phone between the heavy breaths, and not answering the question.

'But don't you think it's weird?'

'No, not if the message was sent to you by mistake.'

'But what if it wasn't?'

'Don't you think you might be overreacting a little? You've only had one message. And that's probably been sent by mistake.'

'But what if it hasn't?'

'Gemma, really?'

'I'm serious, Carly. It's really spooked me.'

Carly sighed down the phone.

'OK, look, I feel really guilty even thinking like this, but going back to the prank thing, what about...' Carly paused for a second, 'my troublesome, truanting niece. You don't think this could be anything to do with her being grounded, do you?'

Could Jessica really be that spiteful, Gemma asked herself.

'Seriously, you really think a fifteen year old girl could be that underhand, that devious?'

'When you say it like that, no, of course I don't. All do I know, is she's hot to handle at the moment.'

'If Jessica did send it, how come her number didn't show?'

In the brief silence, Gemma could almost hear Carly's brain ticking over down the phone.

'Perhaps she borrowed someone else's phone?'

'You think?' Gemma asked hesitantly.

'You know what, Gem, I'm sure it's been sent to you by mistake. And if I were in your shoes, I'd just forget about it.'

Carly's tone sounding dismissive and feeling suddenly foolish, Gemma began to think her friend was right. She was overreacting.

'Yeah, you're right.'

'Hey, look, I'm really sorry but I have to get to class. We'll talk soon, yeah?'

'Yeah, sure, thanks Carly.'

Within seconds of her phone going dead, it sprung into life again. Chimed like a bell.

He's CHEATING on you!

CHAPTER TEN

Sunday morning and past ten already, having had a restless nights sleep Gemma was still tired. Stretched out on the sofa mindlessly watching the TV, the house still smelling of sausage sandwiches and toasty warm, even if far from relaxed, at least she was comfortable and had a full belly.

Jessica still grounded as punishment for her truancy and moodily sulking in her bedroom. Dave begrudgingly out, picking up a couple of newspapers and some extra milk. Henry, after throwing a massive strop at having to do so, staying at his father's for his customary fortnightly weekend visit, though quiet, the atmosphere in the house was undeniably tense, icy conditions inside and out. Life apparently not getting any easier for any of them, yet somehow, Gemma mused ruefully, they were all staggering through the weekend.

Gemma's geriatric black and white cat, Poppy, sauntering into the living-room without a care in the world, she promptly lay on her back in front of the gas fire and exposed her soft white underbelly to the radiating warmth. Her hind legs akimbo but her furry lady parts modestly covered by a strategically placed coal black tail, white socked front paws dangling across her chest, she closed her eyes and within a couple of seconds, was lightly snoring.

Not in any hurry to get up and get on with the housework, or prepare vegetables for the Sunday roast Dave was so craving, envious of cat's ability to so easily unwind, Gemma mutinously closed her eyes. A five minute catnap, that was all she needed.

Within seconds of dozing off, Gemma was rudely awakened.

DING!

Her mobile shivering and chiming on the coffee table, signalling a text, she huffed out her irritation. The cat also disturbed, Poppy sneezed, yawned, then continued snoozing. Gemma determined to follow suit, she kept her curiosity firmly suppressed, and once again closed her eyes.

DING!

The phone again vibrating as it chimed urgently, Poppy threw her mistress a baleful look, chewed on her extended claws for a moment, then closed her eyes and slept again.

DING!

The cat's peace shattered, Poppy roused herself from the floor, stretched out to her full length, then her tail twitching angrily, she left the room.

Three messages received in the space of few minutes, the potential urgency of them getting to Gemma, knowing they could be from Dave, Henry, or even her mobile shy mother, feeling guilty, she reluctantly swung her outstretched legs off the sofa and down to the floor.

Leaning forward, reaching out for the offending item, Gemma looked down at the screen and sat bolt upright on her seat, with a start.

'No! Not again!' she exclaimed to the empty room as she scrolled through the messages.

Why is HE still there?

He is NOT who he seems!

Get rid of him!

DING!

He's LYING to you, CHEATING on you!

Gemma could hardly suppress her shock. What the hell was going on?

DING!

He's a STRANGER, and YOU'VE let him in!

The device falling ominously silent, shaken up, Gemma fumbled the phone and dropped it face up on the carpet, with a soft thud.

She looked wildly around her.

Frantically scanning the room as though she expected the perpetrator to suddenly jump out in front of her, Gemma sprang up from the sofa and hurried over to the living-room window.

Was he out there now?

Was he hiding down between the parked cars, watching her?

He?

Who said it was a he? It could be a she?

Stood in the recess of the bay, a cold, hard stone lodged in her midriff, straining to listen, all Gemma could hear was the muffled rumble of traffic on the main road at the end of the street. Craning her neck first to the left and then to the right, she searched up and down a quiet and frosty street that was full of parked cars, but discernibly empty of people.

A freezing breeze unexpectedly rattling the glass, with a squeal of surprise, Gemma jumped. Trembling, throwing her arms tight across her chest as she held her shivering body together, she scrutinised the shadowed windows of the houses opposite. Yet no matter how hard she peered into them, she saw not a single soul.

Positioned in full view of the street and suddenly realising just how exposed she was, for the first time ever, Gemma wished she had strung up a pair of the dreaded net curtains. Wanting to hide, humiliated by her visible distress, to anyone who might well be spying on her, Gemma pulled herself back from the naked window with a fearful start.

Her eyeballs prickling with unshed tears, her overactive brain feeling as though it was filled with a swarm of wasps, she rushed from the living-room. Even though the concept stung her conscience, there was no longer any choice. Tortured by the text messages, she had to know.

Taking the stairs two at a time, not stopping to hesitate, Gemma seized open the door to Jessica's room and burst in.

Jessica lying prone on the bed, her thumbs hovering mid-flight above her phone as it shone an uplight on her fine young cheekbones, she started with shock as her head flung around to face her unwanted intruder.

Jessica struggling to absorb what was happening, Gemma took the advantage. Launching herself into the room, she snatched Jessica's mobile from out of her hands.

'What the fu...'

Hastily stepping back from the bed and out of Jessica's reach, Gemma held the phone aloft as she peered up at the brightly lit screen. Flicking her eyes over the text message Jessica had been in the middle of writing, she immediately saw it was to some boy... a Dean someone?

'What the hell are you doing!' Jessica roared angrily.

Vexation mixed with fright flickering across Jessica's colourless face, she flung a hand up into the air and swiped for her phone.

Not answering her, holding the device even higher, Gemma began to rapidly scroll through the numerous text messages Jessica had recently sent and received.

In an instant, Jessica was up and off the bed. Her mouth set in a determined, hard line, she lunged for Gemma.

'Give it back to me!'

But Gemma was too quick for her. Already part way out of the room, she grabbed for the door handle and pulled it firmly shut behind her. Two minutes, that was all she needed.   Holding on tight to the door handle with her free hand, Gemma continued to interrogate Jessica's phone. So many text messages, a fair few of which had been received from *Dean* — an important piece of information she instinctively filed away for later — but not a single one had been sent from Jessica's phone to hers; not just now, and not any time over the last three days.

Jessica's temper blatantly well out of control, she was yelling at the top of her voice as she mercilessly kicked and pulled at the other side of her bedroom door.

All of a sudden spent, her courage evaporating under the obvious lack of evidence as well as the knotty situation she had so thoughtlessly created, Gemma experienced a pang of ruthless shame. Beginning to worry over what was going to happen when the bedroom door was inevitably opened, she could not throw off a feeling of wickedness.

Her hand aching, cramping with tension, Gemma finally let go of the handle. What else could she do?

Jessica propelled backward with force, from the sudden release of her bedroom door, she ended up on her backside on the floor. A tangle of teenage arms and legs, she howled out her rage and indignation. Within seconds, she was up on her feet, flew like a bat out of hell, toward her tormentor.

Finding Jessica suddenly looming over her petite, five foot two frame and unable to   stop herself from doing so, Gemma cringed with intimidation. Saying nothing in defence of herself or her inexcusable actions, she pushed the stolen phone out in front her, like a peace offering. Anything to get the furious girl away from her.

'You're mad! A mad, mad woman!' Jessica yelled, her lips quivering with anger as she seized on to her phone and quickly hid it behind her back.

In that moment, they both heard the front door snap close. Dave's feet travelling up the stairs at lightening speed, a look of horror crossed both their faces.

Gemma realising she had a serious predicament on her hands, and that she had a mere few seconds to come up with a plausible excuse for why she had done what she had done, she tried not to panic, to think. In times of stress, her father had always maintained there were at least a dozen solutions for every problem. Yet right now, her mind circling the problem as though it were a hologram, she could only come up with two; say the truth, or lie.

Could she even begin to tell Dave about the messages?

Weren't they about him?

What if they were true?

Could she hear herself?

She did not recognise herself.

Suddenly, Dave was there, on the landing, unavoidably coming toward them.

'What on *earth* is going on?' he demanded, of the both of them. 'I could hear Jessica's yells, out on the street.'

Dave's face alternating between confusion, concern and anger as his head turned from one to the other of them, he stopped about a foot away, then waited for an explanation.

'She's crazy. She stole my bloody phone,' Jessica growled.

Jessica's black eyes aflame with fury, she hastily shoved the said item into the back pocket of her jeans before it could be taken way from her again, Gemma assumed.

'Jessica, whatever has happened, there's no need to swear.'

Dave turned his gaze to Gemma.

'Are you going to tell me what's been going on?' He asked quietly.

Incredibly nervous, but trying to sound normal as she strived to keep the anxiety, the all pervading fear and guilt from out of her voice, Gemma stuttered out. 'I c-can explain, but not here.'

'Don't listen to her! I tell you, she's mad! She attacked me!'

Dave held up his hand to silence his yelling daughter.

'Let Gemma speak, I'll get to you in a minute.'

Not wanting to explain herself in front of Jessica. Becoming worried Dave had not heard her whispered plea, Gemma tried not to cry as she asked, 'Can we discuss this downstairs, please?'

Dave perused Gemma's bright red face as he thought for a second or two.

'OK,' he agreed tightly. 'You go on down. I'll join you in a couple of minutes.'

Hot faced with shame, and more than happy to leave Dave to pacify his enraged daughter, Gemma took her opportunity and scurried away like the rat she was.

Finding it impossible to identify a plausible reason to explain away her appalling behaviour toward his daughter, and not wanting to further compound her situation by lying, Gemma haltingly told Dave the truth. Then when she was done, she handed him her phone to backup her incredulous story.

Watching Dave scroll through her phone messages, avidly searching his face for a reaction, she hoped with all her heart that his look of stunned disbelief, was genuine.

'I don't know whose's been sending these,' he waggled her phone at her, 'but they're ridiculous.'

Dave sounding as incredulous as he looked, Gemma so wanted to believe in him, to trust him. But could she, could she really? She thought she knew him, but what if she didn't? Struggling to look him in the eye, panic and doubt constricting her throat, she held his self-imposed silence as he continued to scroll up and down her messages.

'What I don't understand,' he continued sadly, 'is how on earth you could think my daughter, your step-daughter, for Christ's sake, would be capable of sending these?' He shook his head at her. 'They're so vicious.'

Whilst she silently conceded, suspecting Jessica of sending the messages was not only ludicrous but cruel, her mixed feelings of suspicion and anger superimposing themselves over those of foolishness and shame, she was unable to answer.

'Gemma?' he demanded.

Confused, Gemma shook her head. Trying hard not to cry, her gaze fell to the floor.

Dave reached out as if to take her arm, then he dropped his hand.

She forced herself to look up at him, to speak.

'I'm sorry, Dave. I was just so upset, I wasn't thinking straight. Of course I know she wouldn't send me something so nasty.'

Dave looking doubtful, as though he did not quite believe her, Gemma added to her explanation.

'After all the trouble we've had with her lately, the way she seems to feel about me, I thought she might be trying to get back at me. But I was being stupid, I know that now. And I'm sorry, really I am,' she offered miserably.

Looking a little more convinced, Dave dug his hands deep into the pockets of his trousers as he rocked backwards and forwards on his heels. There was sympathy in his eyes.

'You don't believe the text messages, do you?'

Gemma hesitated, and Dave saw it.

'Of course I don't believe them,' she insisted as she worked on keeping the uncertainty from out of her voice.

Dave hearing the lie, his expression dissolving even further into sadness, Gemma's heart almost broke. He exhaled heavily.

'I get that you must have been worried sick about these,' he said looking down at her phone, then up at her, 'but it would have been better if you had shared them with me first. Then we could have decided what to do about them, together.'

She could not agree more.

'I know. I'm sorry.'

He thought for a couple of seconds. He brandished her phone at her again.

'Are these why you've been acting so weird, lately?'

Gemma started with surprise. She had no notion of behaving oddly.

'Sorry?'

'Well, you haven't exactly been yourself these couple of weeks, not since the night of the dinner with Carly and her new prat of a boyfriend.'

Gemma shook her head at him.

'I've been fine. I've just had a lot to think about lately, what with Jessica playing truant, her behaviour toward me, that first text message, Henry's outburst yesterday morning. I've never known him not to want to go to Paul's.'

He nodded.

She was relieved.

'That reminds me, why didn't you tell me about that first message? You got it on Wednesday,' he asked.

'I wanted to, but up until this morning, I was hoping it wasn't meant for me, that it had been sent to me by mistake. And I didn't see the point of us both being upset by it.'

'But you *don't* believe them, right?' he again asked.

Gemma stiffened with a pervading guilt. His pain unacceptable to her, she yearned to reassure him. Yet still confused, her feelings in sharp contrast with her thoughts, she found it impossible to be honest.

'I've already said,' she procrastinated.

Dave giving her a sharp, skeptical look, Gemma had a hard time not to be bitterly disappointed in herself.

'Dave, I really am sorry about this morning,' she gabbled on. 'I'll go up and apologise to her.'

'I suggest *we* tell her the truth about these, first.' He flourished her phone at her again. 'At least they'll go some way to helping understand, why you did, what you did.'

'You mean show her them?'

'No, of course not, we'll just talk to her about them. Do you agree?'

In truth, Gemma was so unnerved by everything that had happened since Dave and Jessica had moved in — his assumption they were on the path to marriage, his precarious job situation and their general lack of money, Jessica's tantrums, Carly's secrets, Henry's sudden and unexplained reticence to visit with his father, the anonymous text messages and the awful suspicions they had sparked — she was no longer sure of anything. But desperate to claw back at least some semblance of normality, she readily agreed with him.

Gemma vigorously nodding her head Dave's way as the tears began to flow, he gently put his arms around her. For a while, they stood in an awkward embrace, until the tension between them eased.

Feeling Dave release her, Gemma took back her phone.

'What do you want to do about the messages,' he asked?

'Sorry?'

'Do you want to go to the police, make a complaint?'

'The police?'

Dave offering up the police, Gemma noted with a measure of much needed reassurance, was hardly the act of a guilty man.

'Yes, they might be able to trace where the messages are coming from.'

Uncomfortable at involving the police, a case of a little too much too soon, Gemma shook her head at him.

'No, I don't. I'm certain it's all a horrible mistake. Someone, somewhere, has to have got the wrong number.'

'And what if the messages keep on coming? Look, Gemma, I would *rather* you went to the police,' he emphasised.

'Well, I don't,' she stated just as firmly, a tight, dry lump in her throat.

Dave throwing her a doubtful look, it appeared as though he was about to argue the point.

'I think we have more than enough our plates right now, without involving the police in our lives,' she hastily ejected before he could say anything.

Seeing her determined expression, Dave held up in hands in capitulation.

'All right, I won't insist, but if you receive just one more…'

Dave leaving the sentence hanging, his meaning all too clear, Gemma hastily shoved her phone into the back pocket of her jeans, and surreptitiously flicked it on to mute, just like Jessica had, only half an hour ago.

Later on that same afternoon, the ancient heater working hard to warm up the frozen car, Gemma was lost in contemplation as she drove over to Paul's place, to collect Henry. Revisiting Jessica's reaction — the look of total surprise followed by one of honest confusion — to Dave's *chat* on the anonymous text messages, Gemma knew there was no way the girl could be responsible for sending them.

So who then? But there was no answer, only the question. With only one best friend in the world, Carly, and lots of lovely trusted family, Gemma could think of no one, she knew, who would be so callous toward her, or Dave, for that matter.

Arriving at her destination, Gemma stopped the car, got out and checked her watch. She was late, and Henry had school tomorrow. Having struggled to find the place, then somewhere to park, dusk was already curling up the edges of the sky. It served her right for snubbing Paul, yesterday. She should have gratefully accepted the directions he had tried to press on her, when stopping by the house to collect Henry for the weekend. By cutting her nose off to spite her face, all she had done was give Paul a reason to crow.

Burying herself comfortingly into the depths of her coat, Gemma hastily walked to the end of the street and approached a large block of flats set back from the main road. A startlingly white, concrete monstrosity with a flat roof, hard edges, and apartments that still had their original metal window frames, the building was obviously a relic from the Art Deco period. Knowing these types of buildings could often be cold and damp, especially at this time of the year, and finding the idea of her son having to stay in one of them marginally disquieting, Gemma shivered. Then she reminded herself, Paul was not exactly floating in cash and this flat, unlike his previous one, had two bedrooms at least.

Reaching up, Gemma depressed the external buzzer to Paul's flat. Waiting some time in the bitter cold for a response, she shuffled her feet up and down on the icy flight of steps, figured they would benefit from having some salt or grit spread over them. Paul taking his time, she buried her frozen hands in the side pockets of her coat.

She buzzed again and this time, there was an almost immediate answer.

'Hello, who is it?'

'It's me.'

They spoke in unison.

'Fourth floor,' Paul instructed.

The sound of another buzzer, the huge plate glass door in front of Gemma automatically springing open, she hurried forward before it could close.

It might not be the prettiest of buildings but at least it was secure, she reassured herself.

Entering into a wide but shadowy concourse, glass doors ahead leading to some sort of atrium, an elevator to her right, a dimly lit concrete staircase to her left, Gemma chose the lift over the stairs. She crossed her fingers it would be working. It was.

The elevator creakily arriving at the fourth floor, in search of Paul's flat, Gemma stepped out and slowly made her way round a soulless and sunless concrete corridor.

Six concrete floors in total, all of them were painted a subdued leaf green. Every apartment's front door facing inwards and painted a glossy black, each flat was connected to its neighbour by a shared concrete balcony-cum-corridor that wrapped around an internal quadrangle — the atrium she had spotted through the glass doors down in the building's entrance foyer. The way the building had been designed, privacy for anyone entering or exiting one of the flats, Gemma surmised, was hardly guaranteed.

Carefully checking each door for its chrome flat number as she made her way round the poorly lit balcony-cum-corridor, Gemma noticed shoddy and peeling paint, rusted metal window frames, the odd whiff of food and foreign spices, and the sound of voices drifting out from behind some of the walls. Navigating between black bin bags, kicked off shoes, door mats, children's toys and even the occasional bike littering the walkway, she had to watch her step.

Stopping momentarily, Gemma briefly leant over the side of the concrete balcony. Looking up at a slowly darkening sky, then down on to a children's play area that was empty of its charges but full of dark green triffid like vegetation, in spite of its openness to the elements, the communal courtyard-cum-atrium, lacked natural light. Finding the building oppressive, Gemma had the distinct feeling no matter what the season, the structure's interior would always be dim and gloomy. Again, she shivered.

Walking on, Gemma reflected on how much one of the apartments might well sell for? The London property market always buoyant, she deduced they were likely to be pricey. Expensive to buy and probably out of the reach of most of the people living in them, she guessed, like Paul's, a lot of the flats were likely to be rented out and hence their dilapidated state. Feeling suddenly grateful for the cramped confines of own little home with its dated decor and messy back garden, Gemma hurried on.

No bell, Gemma rapped smartly on the front door of Paul's new flat. Slowly letting out a breath she never even knew she had been holding, she hoped Paul was in a reasonable mood and that Henry had had a good time. Although Gemma always made a concerted effort not to feel bitter about Paul spoiling their seven year old son in ways she could no longer afford, still, it rankled. Henry coming home from his father's full of his latest exploits, even after all this time, she would be eaten up with envy. One day, when she was earning more money, she promised herself.

Figuring Paul might not have heard her the first time, Gemma rapped again on the door.

As she waited, buried fragments from the past came hauntingly back. Winter, two years ago, Paul not prepared to wait until Henry was in bed, he had walked out of the front door and away from them both. Five year old Henry, bawling his eyes out as he clung to her leg, he had watched the father he adored, leave him without a backward glance. The stinging memories calling to mind that it was she, not Paul, who had been the driving force behind their separation and that it was she, after nine years of marriage, who had taken everything he cherished away from him, Gemma tried not to hate herself. Then wretchedly wondering if she had ever loved Paul, the way a wife should, she felt unsure? Their separation and the reasons for it weighing heavily on her mind, suddenly and unfairly, she wished she had never met Paul. Yet without Paul, she reasoned, there would be no Henry.

She shook her head at herself, banged even harder on the front door.

Where the hell was he?

Muffled footsteps, the front door at last opening, with gritted teeth and a grateful sigh, Gemma slammed down the lid on her troubling thoughts.

Henry scampering down Paul's corridor excited to see her, Gemma seeing only him, her heart swelled with all the love and pride she held for her only child. Acknowledging there was *nothing* she would not do to keep her son safe and happy. Sharply reminded of Dave and Jessica's splintered relationship, of how her actions that morning had unwittingly exacerbated an already tenuous situation, in that moment, she resolved to do all she could to help them glue their precious father-daughter bond back together again. As a minimum, she owed them that.

Leaning down, Gemma hugged her son tight.

'Mum,' Henry squealed.

'Hello, you,' Gemma replied as she cupped Henry's face in her hands, then smothered it in a quick succession of kisses.

'Stop, mum, I'm not a baby,' Henry keenly objected before skittering away from her again.

'Hi,' said Paul, his smile welcoming, if tight. 'You found us then?'

He checked his watch.

Gemma inwardly winced.

'Yes, sorry, I know I'm late.'

Paul did not apologise for keeping Gemma waiting.

'Got a bit lost trying to find the place, did you? I'm not surprised.'

Uncertain as to his tone, as to whether Paul was being merely chatty or condescending, Gemma returned a weak smile.

'You should use the Tube. It would be a lot easier and quicker,' he added, smiling engagingly.

Paul knowing full well why she didn't use the tube, Gemma said nothing. She did not want to get into an old argument.

'No worries, though, you're here now. Come on, come on in,' he invited.

Paul stepping back, he politely ushered her into his flat. She hesitating, but Paul already turning his back as he began to walk away, if she did not want to appear churlish, Gemma felt she had little choice but to follow him. Obediently trailing her estranged husband down a short hallway with rooms off both sides, in spite of herself, Gemma had to admit to being curious.

'You've had a long drive, why don't you take off your coat and stay for a few minutes?' Paul suggested as Gemma dutifully trailed him into the lounge-diner at end of the corridor.

'Thanks, I will, but just for a few minutes. Henry's got school in the morning,' she said unnecessarily.

Gemma removed her coat and Paul took it from her. Paul then telling his son to look after his mother for a minute, he promptly disappeared out of the room taking her coat with him.

As soon as Paul left, Henry grabbed a hold of Gemma's hand. Dragging her over to a dining table at the opposite end of the room, he began to enthusiastically show her an adult sized jigsaw puzzle of the cosmos he had been working on with his father. Henry excitably pointing out the names of the planets on the puzzle's box lid, Gemma listened politely to her son's childish babble, but it was with only half an ear as she took an opportunity to survey the room.

The space not overly large but big enough, a hissing gas fire a metre or so to her right and with a safety guard in situ, she was pleased to note, the room held a brown leather sofa, a forties oak dining table with four mismatched chairs, and an eighties style chrome and a glass topped coffee table. Paul's vintage radiogram squeezed into an alcove to the righthand side of the fireplace, an open shelving unit filling the whole of the far end wall was jam packed with books and his collection of 78 rpm's. An eclectic but pleasing mix of furniture, it was all very Paul, Gemma reminisced. Bright and colourful movie poster prints on the oatmeal coloured walls. Beige flecked wall-to-wall carpet. Various framed photographs of Henry, a couple of them including the three of them as a family unit, positioned across one half of the radiogram, everything carefully thought out and in its place, fundamentally, the room felt comfortable and tranquil.

Leaving Henry to his puzzle, Gemma walked across to the enormous metal framed window taking up almost the full width of the only outside wall. Looking out on to the bare canopies of a line of dormant horse chestnut trees, although the flat was bang slap in urban London, Gemma thought she could be forgiven for thinking she was in the countryside. Appreciating the contrast between what was outside the huge picture window and what lay the other side of the front door, Gemma guessed that in spring and summer, the trees in full foliage, the view from the Paul's lounge would be spectacular.

'Nice, isn't it?' Paul asked suddenly from behind her.

Startled by his silent return, Gemma jumped.

'Jeez, Paul, you gave me a fright.'

'Did I, sorry but what do you think,' he asked, nodding his head toward the window?

'I feel like I'm in a treehouse.'

Paul's faced creased into a generous smile.

'Yeah, great, isn't it? I know the building's a bit crap, but at least the flat's light and airy. The kitchen's too small, of course, and I have an internal bathroom to contend with but overall, I think it's a reasonable size. This though,' he said, sweeping his hand out toward the impressive vista, 'this is what makes it. That view, it makes up for everything. You like it too, don't you Henry?'

Henry nodding his head in agreement, he looked uncertainly from one parent to the other as he noticeably came to a decision.

'Can I go play on the iPad, dad?'

Paul threw his son a stern, expectant look.

'Please.' Henry remembered to say.

Paul turned to Gemma.

'That OK with you? Do you have time for a coffee?'

Hesitating for a fraction of a second as she tossed a mental coin, Gemma nodded.

'I think so.'

Dave was unlikely to mind, and it would be good to have a mental and emotional break from her own contentious home, even if it was for just a little while.

'Good.'

Paul left the room again, this time to make the coffee.

Henry also disappearing out of the room to play on the iPad, Gemma instinctively followed Paul as she trailed his familiar back. Paul turning left right before the front door, Gemma soon found herself in the kitchen. Swivelling her head first left and then right whilst Paul watched for her reaction, Gemma openly took in her surroundings; modern white cabinets, a black tiled floor, all the required white goods, clutter free work surfaces, and another metal framed window slightly running with condensation, overlooking the outside corridor-cum-balcony.

'So, what do you think?' he asked.

'I think,' she nodded her head appreciatively, 'it's not too shabby.'

'I would have preferred the kitchen to be bigger, more like our old one, but at least it has everything I need.'

Gemma could read nothing in Paul's face as he referenced their old kitchen, but his comment instantly bringing to mind how excited he had been when viewing their end of terrace, and especially the large kitchen extension that traversed the whole back of the house, she experienced an immediate prick of conscience. Paul a fabulous cordon bleu cook, she could see how the smaller than average size of the flat's kitchen, the lack of available worktop space, would irritate the hell out of him.

Reaching up into one of the kitchen cabinets, Paul extracted two plain white mugs. He reached for the percolator.

'Fresh?'

She nodded.

'Please.'

'I don't have any cream, just plain milk,' Paul said as he lifted the percolator, filled the two mugs.

'Milk's fine.'

Keeping his own coffee black, grabbing the milk from the fridge and pouring a drop into hers, Paul handed Gemma, her mug.

'Let's go back into the living-room. It's warmer and cheerier in there.'

On their way back to the living-cum-dining room, all the other doors off the main hallway closed, Gemma was unable to peek into any of them. Naturally nosey, she considered asking Paul to give her a tour, but common sense got the better of her. Even though they had been married for a number of years and had Henry between them, they were hardly the best of friends.

Perching on the edge of the creaking leather sofa, sipping at the delicious coffee — Paul always made good coffee — Gemma flicked her eyes around the pristinely clean and meticulously tidy room.

'Considering you've only just moved in, you already seem very settled,' she observed conversationally.

Paul pulled out one of the dining chairs, to sit on. He nodded.

'Yeah, well, it's not as if I have a lot of stuff to unpack,' he stated flatly.

His tone sounding a tinge bitter. His statement alluding to the fact that it was she who had kept hold of most of their joint possessions following the breakdown of their marriage, not wanting to get into an argument, Gemma thought it prudent not to comment. It wasn't like she hadn't suggested he take more of their stuff. Yet apart from his radiogram and record collection, he had point-blank refused. She tried not to show her discomfort.

'So, how are you?' Paul asked, skimming over any awkwardness.

Gazing into the same blue-grey eyes as those of her son, Gemma thought how good Paul looked. A man of middling height, he was a little thinner maybe, his face a smidge gaunt perhaps, but always elegant, his fine blonde hair was neatly trimmed and his clothes — unlike her own — were classically smart and well coordinated. Every so often, she got a whiff of his cologne, lemon and exotic spices — an all too familiar scent.

'I'm good,' she replied, nodding her head.

Reaching into the open shelving unit behind him, Paul grabbed a half bottle of whisky, poured a tot into his coffee, drank a couple of measured gulps. The alcohol taking Gemma by surprise, she reminded herself, it was none of her business and forced out a smile.

'You?'

Paul's eyes locked on to hers as he openly scrutinised her face.

'You sure you're OK?' he asked doubtfully. 'You don't look your normal self?'

Aware it had been a while — months rather than weeks — since they had spent any real time in each others company, and realising she had forgotten just how perceptive Paul could be, Gemma smoothed any worry from her face. Paul's face seemingly wreathed in concern as he waited for an answer, if only for a moment, Gemma was suddenly tempted to blurt out all her problems. Then she caught herself.

'I'm fine,' she said with a complete lack of truth, delivering him a determined smile.

Paul blatantly suspicious as he cast her a knowing stare, his lips pursed and he slowly shook his head.

'No, I don't think so. But have it your own way.'

After twelve years, Paul knew her too well, Gemma thought. She switched subject.

'Henry, has he settled in OK?' she asked tentatively.

Gemma thinking of Henry's reluctance to spend the weekend with his father, she wondered how Paul would respond to her carefully considered question.

'Yes, why? Is there a problem?'

Paul sounding stiff, even a little defensive, with no understanding of why, Gemma guessed she had hit a nerve. Something to follow up on with Henry directly, should his lack of enthusiasm to visit with his father, continue into the future?

'No, no, I was just asking.'

'Well, he's already got his room set up exactly how he likes it.'

Knowing how OCD her son could be, how like his father he was, Gemma was not surprised to hear Henry had his bedroom already sorted and organised. If she were honest, Henry's mildly escalating OCD, at such a tender age, actually gave her cause for concern. But not wanting to exacerbate the tension between Paul and herself, she forced out a light chuckle.

'God, he's so like you, isn't he?' she sweet-talked.

Gemma flatteringly pointing out the similarities between father and son, the cloud lifted from Paul's face and his features instantly softened.

'Oh yeah, he's definitely my son all right. A right chip off the old block,' said Paul, smiling smugly.

'Yes,' Gemma agreed readily.

In the past, she had been so mean to Paul about his OCD and his need to control everything, now she no longer had to put up with it anymore, it wasn't like it cost her anything to be kind.

'Do you think you'll stay in this flat?'

'I've certainly no intention of moving any time soon. Three moves in two years is more than enough for me,' he pointed out dryly.

Paul looking as though he was about to say something further, then thinking better of it, Gemma was left wondering.

'I hope you'll be really happy here,' she said with meaning.

'Why the hell shouldn't I be?' Paul demanded.

Paul's tone expressing traces of discontent and moody resentment, Gemma tried not to wince. Her desire to linger any longer, instantly quashed, she gulped down the last of her coffee, then asked Paul to fetch her coat. It was already dark outside and Henry had school in the morning, she excused herself.

In truth, it was time to leave before she outstayed her welcome and things between them, got *really* difficult.

CHAPTER ELEVEN

Thirsty, Carly took a long pull on the dregs of a bottle of coconut water she had bought from the vending machine, a couple of minutes ago. Sighing out with gratification, she swiped a hand across her damp mouth and smacked her lips together with a greedy pleasure. Taking a short ten minute break after instructing four classes almost back-to-back, and before delivering her fifth and final lesson of the day, only Tuesday, and already she was pooped.

Although Carly loved doing what she did for a living, being self-employed and frequently having to put in a six day week to make ends meet, there were times when she desperately wished she had the money to open up her own studio. The thought of having clients coming to her rather than the other way round was heady stuff, the stuff that dreams were made of. Still, one day, she promised herself, she would make it happen.

Returning to the studio she had been teaching in, Carly pushed open the door and stopped dead in her tracks. The canary yellow yoga mats no longer in uniformed rows but strewn all over the place, her coat splayed out across the middle of the floor like a dead crow, the contents of her backpack flung to the far corners of the room by some unseen hand, she was struggling to believe her eyes.

Her jaw dropping, for a split second, Carly could not quite work out how it could have happened and then the answer hit her, smack in the face. Being so tired, she had forgotten to lock the classroom door; an oversight, the studio could sack her for.

Short on time, expecting pupils to be arriving within a few minutes and not wanting to be fired, Carly sprinted across the sprung wooden floor and rapidly collected up her stuff. Next straightening up all the scattered yoga mats, she puffed with the effort. Appalled at the amount of chaos caused, the delinquency of the act committed, Carly was beyond contempt for her unseen perpetrator.

Five frantic minutes later, the first of Carly's clients swung through the heavy door.

Carly's face almost as red as her hair, taking a couple of deep breaths to compose herself as she pasted on her usual smile of welcome, the delinquent room once again tamed, she hoped her clients, and the studio, would be none the wiser.

Later that same evening, her last class finished and her long troubling day finally at an end, Carly was stood in front of the ticket barriers inside the nearest Underground station, to where she had worked. Hastily rooting through her backpack for the third time, no matter how hard she scrabbled around in its cavernous mouth, she kept coming up empty. Her travel card wallet, her coin purse, her house keys, all three items were missing, likely stolen.

Patting herself down, people tut-tutting with impatience, some even swearing at her as they swerved with agitation around her firmly rooted form, as a last resort, Carly shoved her hands deep into the pockets of her coat. Her fingers unexpectedly plunging straight through, she was staggered to discover the lining had been slashed, to shreds.

'What the…' she ejected out loud to a confused passer-by. 'Sorry, sorry…'

No travel card, no money and no house keys, how in the hell was she going to get to Steve's now, or even home, for that matter? Relieved she had forgotten to bring her iPad with her that morning, and even though she could really do with them right now, thank God she had also left her credit and bank cards at home, she thought bitterly.

Angry and frustrated, Carly told herself she needed to calm down and think, or she would get nowhere.

Unzipping the side of her yoga pants, anxiously diving her hand down into the hidden pocket, she was relieved to find her mobile; *of course*. Her phone her lifeline to work, her ability to earn money depending on it, she never went anywhere without it. Consequently, the device rarely left her person and it was just what she needed to use, right now.

Slinging her backpack over her shoulder again, pushing her way through the crowd as she exited the station concourse, Carly speculated on whether she could ring Steve for help? Thinking she could ask him to come and find her, to meet her a little earlier than they had arranged, she slowly began to realise that contacting Steve, was not necessarily the best idea? Steve being a nerdy insurance man, he had the potential to insist she report the theft to the studio and that, she could not do. Nor did she want to row with him about it.

Perhaps, it would just be easier, to call someone else. Not Gemma and Dave as they would be busy at home with the kids and really, they were too far away. Deciding to ring one of her more reliable housemates, Carly begged Susie to come and meet her with the spare set of house keys, and some money she could borrow. That way, at least, she could get a new travel card, then get herself over to Steve's flat more-or-less at the allotted time, leaving him none the wiser.

Whilst waiting for Susie to arrive, Carly replayed over and over in her head, what had happened to her at the studio. For five years, she had taught out of a number of different studios, without a single problem. And despite a whole lifetime living in the big, bad, city of London, not once had she experienced something quite so vindictive. The theft was one thing but savaging her coat pockets the way they had, that was just spiteful. What's more, she suddenly realised with a shiver that had nothing to do with the cold, whoever it was, they had carried a knife…

Grabbed and swept up into an embrace as soon as the front door was flung open, Carly relaxed into Steve's broad and familiar chest.

'Get in here, you whore, I've missed you,' he teased. 'And you're late.'

Luxuriating in the feel of Steve's solid frame pushing up against her own, his strong and familiar hands sliding up and down her tensed back, for the first time since her run in with the thief and the uncertainty she subsequently felt, Carly felt safe.

'Hey, let me get in the door first,' she whispered into his ear, before flicking her tongue sensuously around its soft pink shell.

Groaning, Steve grabbed Carly by the hand and dragged her into his flat. Using his foot to slam the front door shut behind them, he unceremoniously stripped off her backpack and flung it against the wall.

Steve propelling her toward the couch, without being asked, Carly found herself pounced on. Steve frantically undressing her of every item of her clothing, unabashed, she stretched out nude on the couch in front of him.

The sexual tension in the room was suddenly electric.

Later, Steve lying under her, his arms enfolding her as he lightly scratched her back, she started to get chilly. Lifting herself off him, Carly jumped off the sofa and grabbing for her scattered clothes, began to slowly put them on.

'What are you doing?' Steve asked, his hand lunging for her.

The stirrings of his desire again obvious, Gemma skittered out of his reach. Hungry, she needed sustenance.

'What does it look like I'm doing? I'm getting dressed.'

She gave him a wicked smile.

He raised an eyebrow at her. Openly voyeuristic and perfectly relaxed about it, Steve watched her every move as she finished dressing. Then he got up and pulled on his own clothes.

'Well, now we're both boringly dressed, I suppose I had better feed you?'

Carly laughed. Running her fingers through the tousled mane of curly red hair cascading down her back like a flaming lava flow, she pulled it up into a rough topknot and secured it with a clear plastic scrunchy.

'If you don't want me to faint with hunger, yes, please? Do you need any help?'

'No, just take a seat,' Steve instructed, sauntering out of the room, like the cat who had got the cream.

Collecting up the cushions scattered across the floor, Carly tidied the couch. Then crossing the open plan living-cum-dining-room, she headed for the rectangular glass dining table already laid out for dinner. Delicious odours permeating through from the kitchen and now ravenous, she took up her usual seat and looked forward to the meal Steve had spent precious time, cooking for her.

Looking round the room, not for the first time, Carly admired the striking modern furniture, the expensive looking soft furnishings, the original pieces of modern art peppering the surfaces and walls. Steve's flat located in one of London's more prestigious streets, she idly wondered, again not for the first time, where his wealth had come from? One day, perhaps, she would ask him? Her travelling gaze alighting on a number of glass votives placed strategically around the room, with lit tea lights in them, she thought on how fortunate she was to have such a romantic and thoughtful man in her life.

Returning from the kitchen, Steve carefully positioned a plate of slow cooked beef stroganoff with wild rice in front of Carly.

'Tuck in,' he instructed.

Sniffing appreciatively at the steam curling up off her plate, Carly's mouth began to salivate.

'Mmm, yummy,' she said.

Setting about the serious business of demolishing her meal in record time, Carly barely stopped to breath.

'Wow, someone's hungry,' Steve commented wryly.

'Delicious,' Carly mumbled, between the last few mouthfuls.

Steve waggled a bottle of Burgundy in front of her.

'Wine?'

Knowing she had an early start in the morning, Carly deliberated. Though trying to be good, the wine an exceptionally nice one, she was unable to resist.

'OK, but just a small one, I have to be up at the crack of dawn.'

Steve raised an eyebrow as he poured out two small glasses of red wine.

'You could always stay here, tonight?'

Taken aback, Carly pondered for a moment. Steve protective over his personal space, she was rarely encouraged to stay over, nor was she allowed to leave anything of hers, behind.

'You know I've come straight from work, right?'

'Yes.'

'So, I need to go home and change my clothes, and I don't have any toiletries here, not even a toothbrush,' she pointed out, unable to withstand the opportunity to have a small dig.

He gave her an amused look.

'It was just a suggestion.'

Steve accepting defeat far too easily for Carly's liking, she tried not to show how miffed she was. She forced out a smile.

'Yeah, well, it's easier if I just go home. Anyway, I thought you didn't like me staying over?' she challenged lightly, trying to keep the mildly hurt belligerence from out of her voice.

Steve contemplated.

'True, but she's been dead for four months now. So I reckon, a few more weeks, and we should be able to relax the rules.'

Steve blatantly impervious to how his statement might sound to someone less calculating, Carly's smile faded as she winced at his indifference.

'What's the matter?' Steve said, not taking his dark eyes off her. 'You look upset?'

'I'm not upset,' she denied.

'Oh, I think you are,' he pressed, almost mockingly.

'It's just sometimes…' she paused, searching for the words, 'you sound so cold when you talk about Helen. You know, you don't even say her name.'

'Really?' he said coolly.

Registering Steve's tone had an air of finality about it, that he was not really asking a question and that he most definitely did not want to talk about his dead wife, Carly changed the subject.

'Aren't you nervous about what your family and friends are going to say, when they finally find out about us? I know I am.'

'Hell, no!' he laughed derisively. 'Aside from my son, I don't give a crap what anyone else thinks about me, or our relationship.'

'Seriously?'

'Of course. I don't need anyone else's approval on how to run my life.'

'You think?' Carly questioned, trying not to look as doubtful as she felt.

A cynical smile creased Steve's lips.

'I keep telling you, all family and friends ever do is interfere,' he said disparagingly. 'They give you opinions you don't want, and advice you didn't ask for.'

'Well, I don't agree with you,' Carly ejected robustly. 'There's no way I would be where I am today, without the advice and support of my family and friends. I keep telling you that.'

A silence.

Steve frowned and shook his head.

'I know you do. But then my experience of family, is not quite so benign as yours.'

'What's that supposed to mean?'

Becoming reflective, Steve sighed heavily.

'If Helen's family is anything to go by, they've always have had *far* too much of a say in how I run my life. And all I can say is, thank God, I'm an orphan. I couldn't imagine having two sets of parents, to deal with.'

Appalled, Carly sat up straighter on her chair.

'Steve, you can't say something like that about your poor old mum and dad, or yourself,' she catapulted out, finding herself unexpectedly occupying the moral high ground.

'I just did,' he shot back.

Steve sounding unattractively pugnacious, Carly was shocked. How could he possibly think it was OK to talk about his dead parents in such an offhand manner, his being an orphan? Both sets of Steve's grandparents already dead before he was born. His parents technically orphans themselves and both only children, when they had been tragically killed in a head-on collision with a drunk driver, they had left Steve all alone in the world when he was but still a young teenager. As a result, she expected him to be at least a bit more perturbed by what had happened to them all. After all, it couldn't have been much fun being brought up in a succession of foster homes? Then everyone dealt with their grief in vastly different ways, she reminded herself. Perhaps, she excused him guiltily, Steve's show of outward indifference was just his way of protecting himself from the internal pain of it all?

The silence lengthened.

Realising Steve had lapsed into what felt like, a sullen silence, his behaviour reminding Carly of a rebellious child, she wracked her brains for a change of subject. Deciding it was time to move the increasingly fractious conversation on to the one family member she knew he would not have a problem talking about, she asked him about Brian.

'You know, one day, I would love to meet your son.'

'You want to meet Brian?'

She nodded, smiled.

'Of course I do.'

Steve staring into the distance for a second or two as his eyes filmed over with thought, Carly allowed her own gaze to drift toward the sideboard positioned behind his chair. Surreptitiously, studying a silver framed photo — the only photo in the flat — of Steve with a young boy nestled in his lap, she thought how proud and happy they both looked. The boy appearing to be no more than three or four years of age, Steve looking quite a bit younger, his hair darker, his frame slimmer, it slowly began to dawn on Carly, she had never seen an up-to-date photo of the now fifteen year old Brian. Nor, she realised disquietingly, had she seen a single picture of the boy's mother. An oversight she would have address, at some point.

Nodding, Steve eventually said, 'Maybe soon, we'll see.'

He seemed happier now they were on less tetchy ground.

'That would be nice,' she smiled.

'At least you got to introduce me to Dave and Gemma, the other week.'

'Yeah, Gem's like a sister to me, and I don't know what I would do without Dave? He's the best brother, ever.'

Steve sent her a searching look, one she did not quite understand.

'I liked your story.'

'Story?'

'Yeah, the one you spun them on how we met. It was inspired,' he said, grinning wickedly.

Finding Steve's amusement inappropriate and not nearly as comfortable as he obviously was with her duplicity, Carly dropped her gaze for a second as she cajoled her thoughts. He doesn't mean it, she persuaded herself. His sense of humour is just naturally dark, black.

'I should have realised they were bound to ask us how we met. And you certainly put me on the spot, didn't you?'

Steve lifted an eyebrow.

'Did I? But most of what you said was true. We were both there that day. You did stumble into me on your way down into the Tube. And I did save you from falling and breaking your neck.'

'Yes, but I used that poor woman's awful accident, as if it was our first meeting… And it wasn't, was it?'

'No, but it was a clever and creative use of the facts, well done you.'

Flashing Steve a sharp look, Carly briefly closed her eyes. Knowing she was as much disappointed in herself as she was with him, she had the sudden wish she were somewhere else entirely. Remembering her after dinner conversation with Gemma, in the kitchen that night, the lies she had told through the facts she had omitted, she felt so vile and underhand.

'Steve, please, you *have* to understand. I hate that I have lied to them both. If Dave knew I'd been having an affair with a married man for almost a year, and that you don't have a nephew but a son, he would be so hurt, and angry... And not only with me.' She sent him a pointed look.

'But the truth is always subjective, my darling. And anyway, you're a grown-up, an adult. Surely you realise you don't need your brother's permission to be in a relationship, regardless of whether the man involved, is single or married?'

Her head in a whirl, hearing the logic in Steve's statement but instinctively disagreeing with it, upset and disconsolate with herself, with Steve, Carly shook her head doubtfully.

'Don't be so discouraged,' Steve continued on. 'It's our prerogative to protect the privacy of our relationship and if that results in us having to tell a few little white lies for while, then so be it.'

Carly's brain ached. It had been a long and testing day. Feeling drained and exhausted, Steve's arguments sounding more and more unscrupulous by the minute to her ears and unable to work out if he was being deliberately obtuse or not, she was also becoming increasingly exasperated. Struggling to find the right words to get her point of view across, she was close to giving up, and going home.

'Don't you agree?' he demanded to know.

She tried again.

'Steve, can't you understand, I feel guilty and disloyal toward my family. And if there is one person I would never normally lie to, even over Gemma, it's my brother. You know, he would *never* lie about anything, not to anyone. Nor would he mess around with a married woman.'

'Really? Sounds like you have your brother on a bit of pedestal. Everyone lies, my darling. Surely you're not so naive as to believe otherwise?'

'Stop it, Steve,' she entreated. 'You're making my head spin.'

But Steve on a roll, it seemed he was not going to be stopped from forcing home *his* point.

'Taking the lovely Gemma as an example, isn't she still married?' he pressed on.

'But that's different,' Carly shot back, her head somersaulting all over the place as she tried to get a fix on Steve's twisted logic. 'You're not comparing apples with apples.'

'Aren't I? You can't deny she's still married?'

Carly thought, tried to get her ducks in a row before she set about presenting the defence case, for her brother and best friend.

'No, but she and Paul had been separated for over a year before she started dating Dave. *And* she's in the process of getting a divorce. Our situation is totally different to theirs.'

'Her husband might not agree with you. But whatever?'

Shrugging his shoulders, Steve calmly took a sip of wine.

'Steve, you were still living with your wife when we got together. You know it's different,' Carly insisted as she tried to stand firm.

He smirked infuriatingly.

'Do I? Helen and I had emotionally separated long before I met you. It was just out of convenience, financial and for Brian, we were still living together.'

'Yes, but that's my point, Gemma and Paul were no longer living together when she met Dave. But you and Helen, you *were* still living together when we first met. For anyone on the outside looking in, they would assume we were having an affair.'

'Well, you know what assumptions make,' he chortled, his smile not quite reaching his eyes, 'an *ass* of you and *me.*'

Suddenly, she had to ask.

'Steve, I know you told me she didn't, but what if Helen *did* commit suicide because of us? Are you sure she didn't find out about us, about me?'

'*No*, she did not find out about us and *no*, she did *not* commit suicide because of you,' Steve emphasised firmly.

Unable to stop herself, Carly's mind grimly zeroed in on Sarah, Dave's first wife. Sharply recalling how wretchedly unhappy Sarah had been during the last year of her life. Hating how she had so easily allowed her superficial lifestyle to get in the way of her ability to help her fragile sister-in-law, at time when she had so desperately needed her support, Carly was suddenly full of remorse and self-reproach. Back then, she had been a selfish and terrible sister-in-law to Sarah, not to mention an awful sister to her brother, and she would never forgive herself.

Becoming aware of Steve's dark and inscrutable eyes watching her, a strange and almost twisted little smile playing at the corners of his mouth, Carly snapped her thoughts back to the present.

'But still...'

'*No*,' he emphasised, cutting her off. 'I know what you're thinking and I won't have you assuming you're to blame for Helen's suicide. Just like your brother's wife, she was mentally unstable, had been for years. And long before I met her.'

'But if she was already so ill when you first met her, why on earth would you marry her?' Carly asked, her curiosity getting the better of her.

This being the first time Steve had ever truly opened up about his wife, the woman who up until her death had always been a shadowy figure hovering somewhere in the background, she was desperate for more information.

'Because *I* didn't know,' he emphasised bitterly. 'When I first met Helen, she was funny, alluring, and extremely cute at hiding her instability. But that family of hers, they all knew. Couldn't wait to palm her off on a naive young man who knew no better, and had no family of his own to look out for him.'

Hearing the resentment, the bitterness flooding through Steve's voice, in spite of her earlier exasperation, her anger, it caused Carly to pause for thought. From her experience with Sarah, she knew only too well what it was like to live in the sphere of someone who was emotionally and mentally challenged, how destabilising their illness could be, for all concerned. Still, there was a principle at stake here, and she could not leave it there.

'Even so, Dave's going to hate it once he realises you and I have been together for nearly a year without him knowing. And that we were already together when your wife took her own life. He would presume we didn't care about Helen, or her state of mind.'

'Then that would be an incorrect assumption on his part, wouldn't it?' Steve replied coolly, his eyes calculating as he studied her face.

'But how can you say that? If we cared about her, then why have we been screwing around with each other, all this time? That's the question Dave will ask.'

Carly hated that she sounded so needy all of a sudden, but Steve talking so openly about Helen had stirred up a whole host of mixed emotions she had not been expecting and right now, she was desperate for some reassurance. She had to know she was not just Steve's bit on the side, the wanton and immoral tart responsible for the break-up of his marriage, for potentially driving his wife into suicide.

Somewhat incongruously, Steve laughed.

'Then I would have to put him straight, wouldn't I? I would have to make sure he understood, just how little my wife cared for me. How as soon as we were married, she made my life a living hell even though I did everything I could to help her, and her illness. I would also have to ensure he understands, just how much I love you.'

Tears not far off, Carly dispatched him a watery smile.

'You know what,' Steve continued, 'I think you've been approaching all of this, from entirely the wrong angle. You seem to think everyone has a right to know how long we've actually been together, but they don't, do they? Who's going to tell them? I'm certainly not. So why you would put yourself, through the agony?'

Confused, Carly shook her head at him.

'Sorry?'

Steve smiled at Carly's obvious uncertainty, her visible doubt.

'Put simply, we could adopt the little while lie you told the other night. Leave everyone, including your brother, Gemma, and Brian, all in ignorant bliss.'

He nodded to himself, to her.

'Trust me, it would be better for all concerned.'

126

Carly started, then wavered. Never, had she considered not telling their families the absolute truth of how they had met, of how long they had actually been together. And there was still the little matter of explaining to Dave, why they had lied to him about Steve having a nephew, instead of a son. But right at this moment, unable to think straight, Steve's proposal was becoming more and more tempting by the second.

'And of course, your brother would have to be told,' Steve continued with a wolfish grin, 'that from the first time I met you, I found you completely irresistible.'

Blushing, her vanity satiated whilst her conscience was still stricken, and not wanting to argue any longer, when Steve, the desire and lust flaming in his eyes, got up, took her hand and pulled her away from the dining table toward the bedroom, she did not put up a fight.

A little before midnight, back in the house she had to share, even though she was exhausted and wanted only to crawl into her bed, Carly tipped the contents of her backpack out on to the floor. She had to take one last look, just in case she had missed something.

Pulling apart her tangled gym clothes, carefully patting down each item in turn and discovering nothing hidden in their folds, she gathered them together and dropped them into the laundry bin in the corner of the room. Then rifling through what little remained — notebook, diary, phone charger, scraps of paper, make-up bag, hairbrush, and a spare pair of trainers — it was soon obvious all three items — the coin purse, travel card and door keys — were still missing, presumed stolen.

A sheet of stark white paper snagging at Carly's attention, not recognising it, she flipped open the folded piece of A5 paper, then swore to herself.

Reading what was written, then reading it again, and again. Scrutinising the message upside down and sideways as she fingered the dreadful letters, the awful words, Carly collapsed down on to her bed in a state of shock.

Staring vacuously at the wall ahead of her, a snake of fear uncoiling in the pit of her roiling stomach, was she, Carly asked herself, in serious trouble?

CHAPTER TWELVE

Hey YOU...

Yes, YOU, I am talking to you, reader.

Come on, keep up.

I bet after all this time, you had forgotten about me, hadn't you?

Well, try not to be puzzled or confused as all it does, is show your unattractive lack of intelligence.

Yes, I am still here, hiding in the shadows of these pages, the confines of this story.

But I should also be lurking around the periphery of your thoughts, or at least the fringes of your vision as you navigate the London Underground, busily perusing your smartphone, waiting for the train...

Tell me, and be honest now, how often have you looked over your shoulder lately... checked to see who is standing, right behind you?

Boo!

Cautiously keeping my distance, watching the comings and goings of the station through the reflection of a darkened bookshop window, I occasionally catch the eye of a sales assistant weighted down with boredom. Though blatantly curious, the nosy cow rudely ignores me when I send her a flirty wink.

The pavement teeming with people, from my vantage point across the road, the entrance to the Underground looks murderously busy and precisely how I need it to be.

Then, almost as if by pure chance, I suddenly see her. Catching sight of that unmissable red hair, loosely pinned on top of her head, I find it impossible not to turn round. I have to get a better look, to truly see her.

She is smiling, and beautiful, sickeningly beautiful.

Exiting the station, ignoring the crossing at the intersection a few yards away, barely looking to her left or right, her red hair bobbing precariously each time she sharply turns her head, she sprints across the road. Seemingly impassive to the flowing traffic, the tooting cars, the motorcycles and bikes having to weave round her, unerringly, she heads straight toward me, looks right at me.

Suddenly, it's as if all the air has been sucked out of me.

In the void, I gasp for breath and feel a chill.

Then aware she is not seeing me but through me, I breath again.

Still, I cannot afford to be careless.

Bracing my back against the glass window behind me, I shrink even further into the gloomy recess of shop's overhang. Finding the shadows, I fade away.

Stepping on to the pavement a mere two to three paces from where I stand, not noticing me, she veers right and begins to move past me.

So close, right within my reach, I could do anything to her... anything...

For a couple of precious seconds, a slight eddy of cool air plays across my naked face as I quickly reach out, let my fingers flutter imperceptibly across the top of her right arm, inhale the faintest trace of a lingering perfume, before she passes me by.

Then as quickly as she has appeared, she is gone. Spirited away by the crowd, she leaves me bereft. Hating the feeling, needing to relieve the loneliness, I begin to move. There will be another time, another day.

Slipping out of the shadows, I meld in with the passing crowd and cross the busy road.

Entering the Underground, I approach the down escalator.

Watching, noticing everyone, the feeling of desertion already gone, there is a familiar stirring deep within my gut, and I smack my lips with an anticipatory pleasure. Truly, I have developed a taste for what is to come.

My eyes peeled, scanning as I walk, suddenly, I see him, my next unhappy human.

Old and ancient, looking as though he has lived his life at least twice over, he is out of place amongst all the young and smartly dressed commuters racing to get home before they have to turn around, and do it all over again. Grey-faced, stubbled cheeks, sparse white hair snaking down on to his collar, scuffed black shoes too big for his shrunken feet, a tweed coat that is patchily stained, his right hand — conveniently — clutches the top of a wooden cane. Nicotine stained fingers, grime sitting under the bed of his nails — closer now — his fusty smelling clothes hang loose about his tall and skinny frame. Decrepit and wearing an air of sadness, sweat forming a sheen on his corpse-like face, too dead for this world, I have to briefly wonder, will he be missed?

For a moment, the old man catches my speculative gaze. His hostile eyes becoming watchful and alert — something abut me bothers him — he feebly tries to get a spurt on.

The old man shambling toward the top of the escalator, I watch his right foot hover unsteadily above the moving treads. Wobbling precariously, struggling to keep his balance, I can't help but think, he is an accident waiting to happen.

'Dead man walking,' I whisper under my breath as I step on to the escalator.

Taking the fast lane, I walk down the metal treads at a steady pace.

Close now... my breathing speeds up, shallows.

My ears humming, I enjoy the rush of adrenaline, the surge of optimism.

Right behind him now, without faltering, my foot catches his cane, kicks it out from under his grasp.

Whoops...

There he goes.

Hearing an almost inhuman howl of fright, I resist the desire to turn round, to watch.

A terrified, blood-curdling, scream.

My heart flips in my chest. I feel so... alive.

A cacophony of horror-stricken shrieks and yells, and there it is again, that feeling of intoxication, of rapture.

Within seconds I am off the escalator, long before he hits — and those poor unfortunates he has taken down with him — the bottom.

So random...

So thrilling...

CHAPTER THIRTEEN

Friday the twentieth, well into the middle of October, and Gemma was on her way to have lunch with Carly. Hopping off the bus as it roared to an impatient stop, a biting wind swirling around her lightly clad legs, she fenced her way down the street, at a fast pace. Entering the coffee shop they had agreed to meet in, stepping past crowded tables, she scanned faces eagerly looking for her friend.

Bouncing up to the table that Carly was sat at, puffing and panting between breaths, Gemma would be glad to sit down.

'Sorry, sorry, I know I'm late, but I got here as quickly as I could. For some unknown reason the bus was delayed and then it was so packed, I almost couldn't get on it,' Gemma explained.

'No worries. Sit down before you fall down,' Carly commanded warmly, though her face was far from serene.

Noticing Carly's worried face as she plated an air kiss to the side of her cheek, Gemma shrugged off her coat and scarf, shoved them on to the back of the empty seat opposite, then plonked herself down with a grateful sigh. She flashed Carly a smile.

'So, what's up? What's so important, you couldn't talk to me about it on the phone,' she asked, getting straight to the point?

'Do you know, the Central line's completely closed again? An accident on the escalator or something,' said Carly, rather obscurely.

Gemma shivered, the Underground again. She shoved her horror away. Mystified by her friend's obtuse response, not for the first time since she had received Carly's cryptic phone call, she wondered what the hell was going on? Time to try again.

'Explains why the bus was so full, but not why you asked me here?'

'How long have you got?'

'Forty-five minutes or so, Katie's out of the office for the next couple of hours and I've managed to get one of the girls to cover for me.'

'Great, I took the liberty of ordering for us,' said Carly, pointing to two steaming mugs and a couple of cellophane wrapped baguettes. 'I trust that's OK?'

The aroma of roasted coffee and pastries hitting the back of Gemma's nose, suddenly, her stomach growled.

'Are you kidding,' she gushed. 'I'm starving.'

Carly seemingly determined to procrastinate, Gemma took the opportunity to take a greedy drag of coffee before unwrapping the hugely calorific baguette brazenly taunting her. God help her waistline, she thought ruefully as she took a big bite.

A couple of minutes later, Gemma clocked her watch. Time was ticking.

'Right, Carly Rogers, enough of the dithering. You've obviously got me here for a reason, so spill?'

Carly gave Gemma a considered look. She bent forward conspiratorially.

'OK, well there's no other way to say this, so I'm just gonna spit it out.'

Gemma wished she would.

'I think, I'm being *stalked.*'

Gemma's eyes widened in shock. Almost choking on a mouthful of roll, she took a large gulp of her drink to help clear the food seemingly stuck in her throat.

'Stalked?' she spluttered with astonishment.

Carly nodded before looking furtively around the room.

'Go on, say it, you think I'm crazy, don't you?'

Gemma felt an unexpected chill shiver up her spine. Did Carly really say *stalked?*

'I think, I need some context.'

Though she nodded, Carly said nothing, at least not immediately.

'Sorry, my head's all over the place and I can't think straight,' she said eventually.

Carly looking off into the distance as though she was somewhere else entirely, and obviously not quite ready to continue talking, Gemma realised she had no choice but to bridle her impatience. Giving Carly some extra time to compose herself, to gather her thoughts, she focused on her lunch and ate in silence for a couple of minutes.

'OK, I'm ready,' Carly said.

'Go on,' Gemma encouraged.

'A couple of really odd things have happened to me over the last few days and it's seriously starting to freak me out...'

Carly stalling, closing up like a clam as her bright red hair bobbed wildly up and down, like a bright orange buoy on a tempestuous sea, Gemma could see how her usually unflappable friend was badly shaken.

'What things?' she prompted, even more keen to get to the bottom of the matter.

Carly stopped looking out of the window at the passing traffic. She returned her disturbed gaze back to Gemma.

'You know when you get that prickling sensation at the back of your neck, the one that says you're being watched but then when you look around, there's no one there?'

Carly intently staring at her for several seconds, putting her quite on edge, Gemma slowly nodded her head up and down.

'Yes.'

'Well, lately, I've been getting that feeling... *a lot,*' Carly emphasised sinisterly.

Carly visibly gearing herself up to say more, Gemma held on to the silence as she did her own thinking. Spooked by Carly's weird and out of character behaviour, her friend's situation uncomfortably reminding her of the anonymous text messages she was still tortuously receiving, and hiding, she worriedly swept her eyes up and down the packed out room. She saw nothing overtly suspicious. No one appeared to be watching Carly, or her, come to that.

'Right, sorry about that,' said Carly, clearing her throat. 'A few days ago, I was the victim of a theft and since then, things only seem to have gotten worse.'

Hearing the loaded tension in Carly's voice, the implication that there was more than one bad thing going on in her life, Gemma glanced at her friend, from beneath her lashes. Wondering if Carly was being, perhaps, a little over anxious, Gemma had to admit, her friend did not look too good. Carly looking pale and tired, like she was not sleeping well, Gemma guessed there had to be some substance to what she was saying.

'OK, well why don't you start with the theft?'

'Tuesday evening, I had my coin purse, travel card and front door keys stolen. Oh, and whoever it was, they also trashed my coat.'

Gemma started with confusion.

'Trashed your coat?'

'Yeah, they slashed the pockets with a knife.'

'Christ.'

'You can say that again.'

'And where did this all happen?'

'At the studio, I came back from a short break to find they'd thrown all the stuff in my backpack across the floor, destroyed my coat, and for good measure, scattered all the yoga mats I'd spent ages laying out, all over the place.'

'God, that's awful,' seethed Gemma, her anger readily flaring on behalf of her friend. 'What else?'

Carly sighed.

'Since the theft, I've found a couple of really odd… no, really nasty notes, shoved into my backpack.'

Carly's extra news, a little too close to home for comfort, feeling a little sick, Gemma flicked her an alarmed look.

'Really nasty notes?'

'Yep.'

Gemma's attention momentarily distracted by the hiss of coffee machines punctuating a background cacophony of adult chatter and a surfeit of babies and children too young to be in school, she suddenly found it difficult to concentrate. Breathing hard, she took another slurp of coffee, then biting down hard on what little was left of her baguette, looked to give herself a much needed minute.

But Carly was too impatient to wait.

'Gem, for Christ's sake, stop eating and tell me what you think?'

Spluttering, Gemma swallowed down the last of her food.

'Sorry, so this all happened at one of the yoga studios you work out of?'

'The theft, yes, the notes,' Carly shook her head, 'I don't know?'

'Sorry?'

'I found the first note on the same night as the theft, but I didn't find the second one until yesterday afternoon.'

Gemma sought clarification.

'Yesterday, this Thursday?'

'Yes.'

'And the theft happened this Tuesday, three evenings ago?'

'Yes.'

'And you think the notes were put into your backpack, on two separate occasions?'

'Yes.'

'You're sure of it?'

'Yes, since Tuesday night, I've been thoroughly checking my backpack, *every* day.'

'And you couldn't have missed the second note?'

Carly shook her head.

'No, but what's worse, is that all week, I've had the most awful feeling I'm being followed. And for someone to have shoved a note into my backpack without me noticing, well…'

What Carly was implying, did not bear thinking about, Gemma thought as she shook her head at her visibly anxious friend.

'Sorry, you're going to have to give me a minute.'

Shell-shocked by what Carly had divulged, Gemma had to think for a moment. A definite theft along with nasty notes, a potential stalker, everything that was happening to Carly, it was almost unbelievable.

'Have you upset anyone, lately?'

'No, at least not that I'm aware of.'

'One of your students, perhaps?'

'No one has complained, they all say they love me. Some of them even follow me around from studio to studio.'

Gemma ghosted a smile.

'Like that's not creepy?' she pointed out.

'It's not like that, they just enjoy the way I teach. Most of my students have been with me for years, although there are a couple of newish ones.'

'How new?'

'One joined about a month ago and the other,' she thought, 'about six weeks ago.'

'Perhaps you should check them out?'

'And how on earth do you expect me to do that?'

Gemma shrugged.

'I've no idea. Have you reported the theft to the studio? Can't they help you?'

Carly shook her heard vigorously.

'No way, I can't.'

The vehemence in Carly's tone, Gemma's brow creased into a puzzled frown.

'Why not?'

'Look, the studios provide my bread and butter work, and they all talk to each other. The last thing I need is for them to think I'm trouble.'

Gemma was none the wiser.

'But it wasn't your fault.'

Carly's cheeks reddened. She cleared her throat.

'Er… I'm rather afraid, it sort of was.'

'What was?'

'When I took my break, I forgot to lock the classroom door behind me. A big, big, fat no, no, I'm so stupid. What can I say? I was tired. And I probably should have put my stuff in a locker.'

'Mistakes happen.'

'Not those kind of mistakes.'

'But what if you weren't the only instructor targeted that night?'

'I've casually asked around, re the theft, not the notes, but no one else seems to have had any problems.'

'But if you won't say anything, what makes you think any of the others would?'

'Although none of us are likely to say anything to the studio, that doesn't mean we don't talk to each other. You know, off the record, so to speak.'

'Out of everything you've told me so far, it's the theft of your keys and the nasty notes, I find the most disconcerting,' said Gemma. 'Have you brought them with you? The notes, I mean. Can I take a look at them?'

Again, Carly's cheeks suffused to pink. She shifted around in her seat.

'Er... no... unfortunately, I haven't got them any more.'

'I don't understand, where are they?'

Carly sighed.

'Er... I burnt them.'

Gemma delivered Carly a pained look of disbelief.

'Yeah, I know, not helpful, right? But I was so angry at the time.'

Sighing with disappointment, Gemma shook her head at Carly.

'Not OK, but I'm assuming you can remember what they said?'

Carly smiled her apology.

'The first one said, *I know who you are, bitch.*'

'And the second one?'

'*I'm watching you, bitch.*'

The tone of the notes uncomfortably reminding Gemma of her own situation, of how tense and intimated the anonymous text messages she was still receiving, and hiding, had left her feeling, her temper flared. Suddenly furious with the sick individuals who had so maliciously erupted into her life, and that of her friend's, in that moment, she wanted to kill them; *how dare they*? Her heart beating a little too fast, Gemma reminded herself she needed to remain calm and relaxed. Otherwise, she would be of no use to Carly. But it was not easy.

'Shit!'

Carly nodded.

'Yeah.'

There was a minute of silence.

'And what about your house keys?' Gemma asked.

'My keys?'

'Yeah, if you *are* being stalked, aren't you worried whoever it is might follow you home one day, then use them to get into your house?'

An immediate look of shock passing across Carly's face, Gemma almost felt guilty, but how could she not have asked?

'Christ, I hadn't thought of that.'

Unable to shake off a strong feeling of horror as she thought through the ramifications of someone, a stranger, having unfettered access to Carly's home, Gemma shivered.

Carly sighed with resignation.

'I need to get the locks changed, don't I?'

Gemma nodded.

'Yeah, I would say that's a good idea.'

'Hmm, expensive, and I can't afford it at the moment.'

At times like these, Gemma wished she had more money.

'What about your housemates, can't they help out?'

'No, they're all just as broke as I am.'

'The landlord, would he help?'

'He would, but he's a nightmare to get hold of. And he would only pass the costs straight back on to me, I know he would.'

'Carly…' Gemma appealed.

'I know,' Carly interjected. 'It's OK, Gem, I hear what you're saying… I'll get a hold of the landlord. He should probably do it, anyway. With any luck, he'll get done by the end of the month. Gives me some time to scrape up some extra money.'

Though the end of the month was still a whole, eleven days away, somewhat mollified, Gemma nodded.

'Good, going back to the stalking, have you actually *seen* anyone following you?'

Carly shook her head, flicked her eyes anxiously round the coffee shop again, the disinterested customers minding their own business.

'No, but I can't stop looking over my shoulder, cos all my instincts are screaming at me.'

'But you're not sure? You could just be spooked by what's happened.'

Carly delivered Gemma an uncertain look.

'No, I'm not sure, but…'

Carly leaving the sentence hanging, looking particularly nervous, Gemma had to suggest it.

'Carly, perhaps you should go to the police?'

'I can't, not without proof. They'll think I'm a nut-job.'

Gemma nodded.

'Yeah, possibly, but if you get any more nasty notes, can I recommend you keep a hold of them this time?'

Carly dispatched Gemma a rueful smile.

'I will, I promise.'

'Good.'

Carly threw Gemma an enquiring look.

'Sorry Gem, but I have to ask, have you received any more of those anonymous text messages?'

Gemma hesitated, and Carly saw it.

'You have, haven't you? Why haven't you rung and told me, already?'

Gemma shrugged.

'I don't know, really. I think, I haven't quite been able to believe, what I've been receiving.'

'Have you told Dave about them?'

'Yes.'

Gemma blinked rapidly. Omitting to tell Carly the full facts of the situation, that although Dave did know about those first few messages, he had no idea about the ones she had received since, she tried not to show how guilty she felt. She hated lying to Dave, to her best friend.

'And what did he say?'

'What can he say? Like me, he has no idea who they might be from and obviously, he strenuously denies what they accuse him of.'

'Look, I know he's my brother and that I'm biased, but Dave hates telling lies and he's *not* a cheat,' Carly reassured.

'Yeah, I know, but it feels good to hear you say that. Thanks, Carly. He also suggested, I should go to the police, which in itself is reassuring, I suppose.'

'But you haven't?'

'No, I can't face going to the police. We've got enough on our plates at the moment, without involving them in our lives.'

'You mean with Jessica?'

Gemma nodded.

'Yeah, but to be fair, it's not just her, Henry's also been acting up a bit.' She sighed. 'And there's Dave's job.'

'Sounds like you have got your hands full?' Carly commiserated.

Gemma sent Carly a weak smile.

'Yeah, but we'll muddle through.'

Feeling decidedly uncomfortable, not wanting Carly to know how strained her relationship with Dave had become these last few weeks, Gemma chose not to elaborate. Although Carly was her best friend, first and foremost, she was Dave's sister.

'Gem…' Carly hesitated, 'your anonymous text messages and what's been happening to me, you don't think they could all be connected, do you?'

Gemma thought. Could there seriously be a link between what was happening to Carly, and herself? She doubted it, could see no motive for it. She shook her head at Carly.

'I'd be very surprised. It's more likely to be some weird coincidence, don't you think?' She shook her head at herself. 'That said, how the hell should I know? Perhaps, we should both go to the police?'

'No way,' Carly ejected vehemently. 'There's no way I can go to the police, not yet. As I said earlier, I don't have any evidence, and it would be tantamount to professional suicide if any of the studios got wind of what's been happening to me.'

'You sure about that?'

All of sudden, Carly's manner turned brittle.

'Trust me,' she nodded, 'if the studios think something funny's going on, they'll forget to book me and before I know it, I won't have any classes. Worse, once the word gets around, and it always does, my private clients will suddenly disappear. And then before *you* know it, I'll be sleeping on your couch.'

As much as she loved Carly, not at all keen on the idea of having to squash her friend into their already overflowing house, Gemma hastily nodded her head.

'Yeah, I get it,' she empathised.

Both thinking, the friends lapsed briefly into silence.

Having quickly evaluated everything they had discussed, Gemma unexpectedly found herself beginning to formulate a plan of sorts, and though it seemed totally crazy, she decided to put to Carly.

'Look, other than me having to go through the pain of changing my mobile number, I don't know what, if anything, I can do about my anonymous text messages. But that doesn't mean, I can't help you.'

Carly sat bolt upright in her chair as she looked expectantly across the table.

'You help me? How?'

Gemma took a deep breath.

'Look, this is going to sound really wacky, but bear with me. If Dave's up for a bit of babysitting, I could sign myself up for your Tuesday yoga class, come along and see if I can winkle out if any of your students have it in for you, especially those two new ones. I could even follow you to the pub, after class. See if anyone is really stalking you.'

'You would do that, for me?'

Her idea taking hold the more she talked about it, Gemma was actually becoming excited by it.

'Course I would. It'll be an adventure,' she said enthusiastically.

'Christ, Gem, you're mad. But OK, why not?'

Carly's face became serious again.

'But we're not private detectives, Gem. What if my thief and the stalker, turn out to be one and the same person? Remember my coat? He had a knife…'

At the mention of the knife, all Gemma's instincts suddenly reared up and said, *Run!* But her sense of adventure, along with an almost desperate need to distract herself from her own problems for a while, conspiring against her, she was still persuaded to give it a shot.

She shrugged.

'What can I say? I'll be super careful and anyway, we'll have the upper hand. Whoever they are, they won't be expecting me to be in the picture.'

Carly grinned. Her eyes, for the first time since Gemma had arrived, twinkling brightly, she too looked excited.

'OK, let's do it.'

Gemma pulled a wry face.

'Just one thing, I can't afford to pay an annual studio fee.'

'Don't worry about it, I can handle that one.' Carly winked.

'Great, then we have a plan. I'll talk to Dave about babysitting Henry for me. You sign me up for your Tuesday class, and don't forget to text me the details; location and time.'

A conspiratorial smile passed between the two women. They'd got this.

'OK, done, one thing though, please tell me you're not intending to tell Dave about any of this?'

'Of course not, he'd be furious. That reminds me, is Steve still around?'

'Yes, he's still around. And no, I haven't said anything to him about what's been happening.'

'How come?'

'He's in insurance, so he's bound to want me to go to the police. And anyway, we've not exactly been seeing eye-to-eye over a few things, lately.'

Gemma nodded. Still not a fan of Steve's, she was glad Carly had kept him in the dark. She was also secretly pleased to hear that Carly and he were not, perhaps, getting on quite as well as they might have hoped. There were better men out there for Carly, she was sure of it.

Ten minutes later, their business concluded and their lunch finished, the two friends left the coffee shop together. Gemma's fingers tucked into the crook of Carly's arm, both of them giggling at something silly as they looked to relieve some of the angst created from their edgy discussion of earlier, neither woman noticed a dark clothed individual slither out from the shadows of a building opposite, and follow them.

CHAPTER FOURTEEN

Gemma screwed the dripping sink tap, even tighter. Looking out of the kitchen window at the anonymous backs of houses in the next street up, she saw snatches of other people's lives, and a new moon hanging low in an ink black sky. Remembering her father telling her it was bad luck to catch the first glimpse of a new moon through glass, she hastily averted her gaze. Already nervous enough about the evening ahead, she hoped, it was not a bad omen.

Dave strode into the kitchen.

'Time you left, isn't it?' he asked cheerfully. 'What time does your yoga class start?'

Still miles away, deep in the mineshaft of her own thoughts, Gemma dried her hands on a tea towel, distractedly left it scrunched up on the countertop, then turned to face Dave.

'Sorry, what?'

'I said, what time is your class due to start?'

She sighed, as though she had the weight of the world on her shoulders.

'I have to be there for seven-thirty.'

Dave flicked his eyes down at his watch. 'Did you know it's six already? Shouldn't you get going?' he encouraged.

She nodded.

'Yes, I suppose so.'

Yet Gemma made no immediate effort to move. Now she was minutes away from having to leave the house, she no longer wanted to go. Brainlessly omitting to factor into her excitable plans that Carly's yoga studio was based in west London and that to get to it, she had no choice but to use the Underground, she could kick herself. Feeling sick to her stomach, she shrank from what lay ahead. Her worst nightmare, ever!

Dave smiled encouragingly into Gemma's pale face.

'OK, well don't you think you should go and get your stuff?'

Shivering with an unwanted spasm of fear, Gemma tried not to give into it. She had promised Carly she would be there. She had to go.

'It's just the Tube, Gemma,' Dave said. 'And these days, it's so secure, you'll be fine, you know you will. And you won't be on your own, there'll be hundreds of others travelling with you.'

Yes, thought Gemma miserably, and that was one of the problems. Her claustrophobic fear of being hemmed in, of being suffocated by numbers if she needed to get out, suddenly threatening to overwhelm her, she struggled not to cry.

Dave grinning cheerily at her, Gemma tried not to be irritated. He was only trying to help.

'Come on, Gemma, you must have realised you were going to have to use the Tube when you booked the class with Carly?'

Gemma gulped down her fear, her unshed tears. She could not afford for Dave to become suspicious, to ask difficult questions.

'Of course, I did,' she said with a complete lack of truth. 'I just thought I'd be more ready, than this.'

'It's OK. You'll be OK,' he coaxed.

He obviously doesn't watch the news, Gemma thought bitterly as Dave pulled her in close. The latest report telling of an elderly man missing his footing on the down escalator, causing the death of himself and at least one other, not to mention the numbers injured, it was horrifying.

'Gemma, come on, buck up,' Dave chided gently over the top of her head. 'What happened to you, happened over twelve years ago. And it's not like you haven't used the Underground, since.'

Dave was right, she *had* ridden the Tube a handful of times since that dreadful day, but this would be the first time she had used it on her own, in twelve years! Tension raking at her skin, a rising panic, Gemma fought with her fear, her natural inclination to run upstairs, bury her head under the pillows and never go out again. Dave still holding her, saying everything he could to reassure her, Gemma listened to his heart beating under her head. She took comfort from its rhythmic thump.

'Gemma, what do you want to do?' Dave asked, tilting her head up so he could look down into her face, her glistening eyes. 'If you really don't want to do this, then don't. Carly will understand.'

What Dave did not know or understand, Gemma thought as she battled with her nerves, was that Carly was depending on her. She needed her. Pulling herself away from him, Gemma stood tall again. This was not a question of *if* she could go, she *had* to go.

'It's OK, I'll be fine,' she reassured him.

Dave searched her face.

'You sure?'

'Yes, I just needed a minute, that's all,' she explained.

'You know if I didn't have to babysit, I'd come with you?' Dave said, his face serious, his eyes earnest.

She squeezed his hand.

'I know. But it is time I got over this.'

Dave smiled. He looked relieved.

'What time does the class finish?'

Gemma thought.

'It's an hour long, so around half eight, I think. But if it's OK with you, I'll probably join Carly for a quick drink afterwards? Think I might need it.'

'Of course it's OK, take all the time you need. Just text me when you leave the pub, so I know when to expect you in.'

Gemma rewarded Dave with a watery smile.

'Sure, thanks, Dave.'

'How long did you say this course goes on for? Perhaps I should start organising a regular boys night out with Steve.'

In her present mood, her current turmoil, not picking up on Dave's teasing tone, his comment worrying her, pricking at her guilty conscience, Gemma threw him an anxious look.

'You *don't* mind, do you? Looking after Henry, I mean?'

'Of course I don't mind. I'm teasing, silly. Go on,' he urged.

Dave pushing her gently away from him, he playfully swatted her ample backside.

'Go on, go and enjoy yourself. And don't worry, I'll take care of everything here. Henry's in safe hands with me.'

Not according to her new text pal, Gemma thought savagely, but did not say.

Dave's mention of Henry reminding Gemma that he was still occasionally playing him up, she truly hoped her son would behave himself tonight. In the meantime, the hostilities between Jessica and herself dramatically calming down over the course of the last few days, she allowed herself a small tight smile. Even though they were still not talking, at least not in any true sense of the word, Jessica making a determined effort as was she, for first time in a long time, she was hopeful. Her emotions heightened by what lay in the past, the future, and more specifically, the present, Gemma felt a couple of tears spring unbidden to her eyes. Not wanting Dave to see, she sniffed them hastily away before they could fall.

'Oh, and don't forget to say hello to my errant sister for me,' Dave called out to Gemma's stiffened back as she strode determinedly out of the house, without a backward glance.

The gaping mouth of the station silently yelling at her, tormenting her, Gemma stood as though transfixed. Commuters unconcernedly hurrying in and out around her, a lonely figure, she could not move. Standing in the cold, her breath clouding around her face, her feet seemingly stuck to the pavement, dread knotted Gemma's stomach as she faced the one thing she feared most in the world, the Underground.

I am not afraid, she tried to convince herself.

Terrorist attacks were everywhere these days, not just on the London Underground, she firmly reasoned with herself. Unfortunate enough to have been around that catastrophic day, to have witnessed first-hand the traumatic aftermath of London's 7/7 bombings in 2005, unlike the scores killed, the hundreds left horrendously injured, *she* had been one of the lucky ones. Left miraculously unscathed by the bomb that went off down in the station from which she had just exited, *she* had survived. So what right, she angrily chastised herself, had she got to whinge, to be so afraid?

I am not afraid.

I am NOT afraid.

On their way past, somebody nudged Gemma's arm. She squealed with fright.

'Sorry, love,' said a startled commuter, his puzzled eyes only briefly locking on to hers before he hastily passed her by.

The commuter looking at her as though she was mad, Gemma was humiliated.

I am NOT afraid!

Knocked into again, this time, somehow, the curse was broken. Stiffening with a new resolve, Gemma doused her paranoia and took charge of herself. Unerringly placing one foot in front of the of the other, without hesitation, she made her way into the brightly lit station as though she was taking a stroll in the park.

Tapping her Oyster card on the station barrier, Gemma automatically hurried her stride as she joined the crowd and drifted away with it. Following directional signs hanging from the ceiling, those stamped in big bold letters along the white tiled walls, not once faltering, she made her way toward the platform for the Central line; the busiest line on the Tube and the same one she had used on seven July 2005.

Now standing on the open platform but well away from those crowding toward the dizzying edge — the *live* rail — her back almost touching the station wall, Gemma was extra vigilant. She noticed every single person stood within a few feet of her, and what they were carrying. She caught no ones eyes. Her well reasoned fear still percolating somewhere in the deeper recesses of her mind and threatening to bubble to the surface at any minute, she urged for the train to arrive.

Waiting, her palms beginning to sweat, waiting, her breath becoming ragged, Gemma willed away the panic.

She had been doing well.

She was doing well.

Taking long, deep breaths, she worked on calming her nerves.

She was fine.

She could do this.

Focusing on what she was seeing to still her overanxious mind, Gemma watched an occasional puff of wind sweeping up the tracks, stirring bits of paper, billowing out people's hair. Then she heard the tapping of shoes, the sound amplified by the sheer numbers now thronging on to the platform, that and the change in air pressure, she knew the train was coming.

So many people.

Too many people.

Keep away from me, she suddenly wanted to yell!

Another whoosh of air and the monstrous train swung into view. Fighting a feeling of asphyxiation as everyone seemed to press and heave against her, Gemma allowed herself to be silently pushed forward as they took her with them.

Someone was behind her!

Hot breath trickling down the back of her neck, the experience alien and disturbing, it was all the extra encouragement Gemma needed, to throw herself on to the train.

The door alarm ceasing right before the train lurched forward and away from the station, bodies hemming her in on all sides, Gemma clutched for a space on the stanchion in front of her. Grasping on to the cool, metal surface of the stabilising pole, preparing to do battle with the swaying rhythm of the train, she tensed her non-existent core muscles and held on tight as she blinked back tears of fright, tinged with pride.

One change and twenty Tube stops later, followed by a five minute walk through a cold and intermittent rain, Gemma arrived safe and sound at her destination with only minutes to spare. Feeling ridiculously pleased with herself, with the headway she had made in managing her not inconsiderable paranoia, she could so easily have jumped in the air and whooped out her triumph.

She had done it!

Walking into the studio building, a broad, self-satisfied smile playing on her face, Gemma gave her name to the bubbly front receptionist, signed in and got the directions she needed to find Carly's yoga class.

Hurrying her stride, passing a lot of closed doors on the way — some reverberating the rhythmic thump of energetic music, others deathly silent — with a front receptionist to get through, it would be less than easy for just any old passer-by to sneak into the building, Gemma deduced. Made her theory for Carly's thief being one of her students, far more likely, she concluded.

Reaching the classroom, Gemma hung back in the open doorway and waited for Carly to join her.

'You made it then,' Carly called out, in her brightest teacher voice as she walked toward her newest student.

For effect, Gemma nodded and gave a small wave.

'You look a bit pale, you all right?' Carly whispered, carefully keeping her back to the students milling around their yoga mats as she came alongside.

Taking her cue from Carly, Gemma also kept her voice low.

'Just about, can you believe it, I totally forgot I'd have to use the damn Tube to get here?'

Carly's face creased with concern.

'Oh my God, Gem, I'm so sorry. I didn't give it a second thought. You're OK though, right?'

Gemma nodded. Still buoyed up with her success, she flashed Carly a broad smile.

'Surprisingly enough, yes, I am.'

'Good for you,' Carly enthused.

'Yeah, in a weird sort of way, having to use the Central Line again, has sort of done me a big favour.'

Carly grinned.

'I'm so pleased for you, Gem. You can't let the past pull you under.'

Gemma shot Carly an old fashioned look.

'Blimey, where did that bit of philosophy come from?'

Carly shook her head.

'No idea, but I need to get this class started. You ready?'

'Hang on a minute, has anything else happened since I last saw you?'

Carly's instant change of expression, told it all. She nodded.

'Yeah, another note appeared in my backpack. God knows how it got there? And I'm still certain, I'm being watched.'

Her lips compressing as a chill snaked its way up her spine, Gemma shivered it off.

'OK, well I'll focus on getting to know those two new students, tonight. See if I can find out what they think of you.'

'Are you still following me to the pub tonight?'

'Yep, after what I've been through to get here tonight, I bloody need one.'

Gemma gave Carly a cheeky wink.

'Come on then teacher, your class is getting fidgety.'

CHAPTER FIFTEEN

The morning after her yoga class, Gemma returned straight home after dropping the kids off at school, then called in sick for work. She had slept for less than three hours the night before and now, she was bone-tired. Shattered from travelling on the Tube twice in quick succession, even more from the shock of witnessing some nutter stalking her best friend, for once, she needed not to have to work and to allow her day to drift. Today, she thought, the irony not lost on her, it was her turn to play truant.

Still in her work clothes, Gemma lay as flat as she could on a rickety two-seater sofa that over the years had had most of the stuffing knocked out of it. Using a faded cushion to prop her head up on the arm whilst her feet hung off the other end, still uncomfortable, she sighed out with tiredness and tension.

Grinding the heels of her hands into her eyes, trying to relieve the pressure beating away behind them, Gemma was desperate to unwind. If only she could relax for a while, even have a doze, then perhaps, she would think more clearly?

Gemma used to like living, but wracked with worry and indecision of late, of feeling acutely miserable with how life was generally treating her, she wondered briefly, if it would be easier to just slit her throat and be done with it. Not normally the suicidal type, but this the day after she had witnessed something that had filled her with an abject-terror, she was seriously struggling. She shook her head at herself. What was she thinking? She had to be tired!

Five minutes later, the events of the last few weeks, days and hours, all still busily dominating Gemma's mind and overriding her ability to settle, she gave up and got up.

Needing something to do, something to occupy the monkey chattering away inside her overactive brain, Gemma stripped off her work clothes, donned her dressing gown and started to clean. Starting with the kitchen and keeping well clear of Jessica's room, Gemma cleaned the living-room, Henry's room, the bathroom and finally, their bedroom. Then closing all the windows she had earlier opened to air the house, the last of her reserves spent, she headed back to the bathroom and turned on the bath.

Whilst the tub filled, Gemma undressed. Dropping a generous gush of scented oil into the bath water, she stepped in shakily exhausted, lay back and closed her eyes. Her muscles aching from the yoga postures so ruthlessly inflicted on her poor and out of condition body, a rock of tension in the pit of her stomach, she dipped her head under the bath water and put off all pending decisions. Cocooned in the warm, deliciously fragrant water, she let her mind drift and for a snippet of time, was utterly at peace with the world. Then, the present intruded.

Her purposeful mind refusing to be quiet as it ruthlessly dragged her back to the events of the previous evening, Gemma was disappointed all over again. What on earth had made her think an hour would be enough? Even though Carly had reserved a mat for her right between the two newbies — a nubile young woman in her early twenties, and a geeky middle-aged man with a relaxed sphincter — sixty minutes was no near enough time to get to know two perfect strangers. Aside from trading the odd pleasantry or embarrassed laugh between the body contorting moves, she had had next to no conversation with either of her neighbours. The recollection leaving her feeling both despondent and a failure, she thought how childish her original plan had been, it would take a lot more than just one session for her to get to know *any* of Carly's students. The trouble being, she deliberated worriedly as she dried her body and pressed a towel into her wet hair, after what she had witnessed on the way to the pub, she could not afford to wait.

Half an hour later, Gemma was dressed in jeans and a comfortable jumper. Her hair curling damply around her face, her cheeks still rouged from the heat of her bath, she gazed distractedly out of the kitchen window whilst waiting for the kettle to boil. The slanting rain pummelling the sodden back garden into submission, she watched a lone robin actively plucking at the overgrown lawn. The bird lifting its head then arching its neck to gobble down a worm, Gemma recoiled from the window as she recalled afresh, a feeling of menace leftover from the night before. The worm's demise uncomfortably reminding Gemma of what could be at stake for Carly if she did not act quickly enough, she shivered. She hoped, it was not an ominous omen.

Sipping her coffee, feeling as though she was about to jump into the abyss without a parachute, Gemma was uneasily aware of the enormity of the responsibility she had unthinkingly taken on, of the decisions she had yet to make. At this moment, Carly's safety, her life, literally in Gemma's hands, she wished it was otherwise.

She shook her head at herself.

'Could I be more stupid?' she whispered out loud.

Always an emotional eater, Gemma's stomach growled. Suddenly ravenous, needing something to soothe her unwanted fears, she set about raiding the fridge. Making herself a fried egg and bacon sandwich spread with lashings of butter and HP sauce, she poured herself another coffee then sat down at the kitchen table to eat and cogitate. Torn with indecision and a not insignificant amount of dread, she began a robust debate with herself.

She could call Carly, tell her what she had seen, then walk away. It was not as if it was her problem, she reasoned, with a pang of instant self-condemnation. In fact, she was still struggling to understand why, when in the pub and Carly had asked if she had seen anyone following her, she had not just told her the truth? Angry with herself, with her shilly-shallying and her cowardice, taunting herself that she was the one who had been yearning for an adventure, Gemma smacked her coffee cup down on the table, watched the bitter liquid jump and spill. Like hell, she could walk away!

Perhaps a better approach, would be to tell Dave, a problem shared and all that? But what with Jessica misbehaving, the threat of redundancy, his worries over her and the God awful text messages, how would that possibly be fair? Didn't Dave have more than enough to worry about at the moment? Anyway, Carly would never forgive her. Taking it upon herself to share everything that had been happening to Carly, with her brother, and without her permission, she would go nuts. No, talking to Dave, she deliberated, was a non-starter. Also, Dave would go straight to the police, she simply knew he would and that was the one thing, Carly was determined should not happen. At least not until she had some real proof, some tangible evidence that would not ruin her career.

Taking another greedy bite of sandwich, brown sauce dribbling down her finger, Gemma licked it off with a greedy pleasure, then washed down the remainder with the dregs of her coffee.

Refreshing herself of the facts, Gemma inevitably began to realise that she still had no idea if Carly's thief, the *nasty* author, and stalker, were three separate individuals or one and same? If she could hold her nerve, give herself a proper chance to expose Carly's stalker, then perhaps, it was a question she could get an answer to?

Feeling hugely daunted as she blinked away a couple of self-defeating tears, without giving herself time to reflect any further, Gemma finally settled on a decision. The only decision, in her opinion, she could take.

CHAPTER SIXTEEN

Shadows consume the city, giving it a feel of early winter. The end of October, the sky is sombre and loaded with low sullen clouds that block out most of the sun. Everything around me grey, dreary and uninteresting, I don't let it put me off as I continue to watch from my vantage point at the end of the street.

Mid-morning on a Wednesday, aside from an intermittent car traversing the concrete speed bumps in the road as they drive past, the boringly suburban street appears free from disturbance. Children in school, their parents working paltry jobs to pay off rents or mortgages they can ill-afford, how dully conventional their awful little lives must be.

No one arriving or leaving for the last hour, the bog-standard Victorian terrace I have been attentively watching is, I am now certain of it, empty of all human life.

A searingly cold wind blowing in from the North, feeling restless, I decide it is time to make my move.

Hooded and gloved, suitably dressed for a cold day and looking like any other person minding their own business as they walk down the street, I keep my eyes carefully peeled for any unseen curtain twitchers. Nothing moves.

Casually approaching the drab little mid-terrace, a house that is devoid of any kind of beauty or interest, almost there, I behave as though I have every right to be here.

Using the Yale key on the ring I procured from the redhead's backpack, I open the front door and deftly let myself in.

Inside the door, I listen.

The house is deathly quiet.

Standing in the dark hallway, looking to orientate myself, I quickly scan up and down its tatty and narrow confines. Guessing the property is a shared house, two closed doors — one to my right, the other at the end of the hallway — I go with the stairs directly in front of me. Treading lightly, at the top, I arrive at a small landing that splits both ways. Dog-legging left, using the only other key on the fob, I insert it into the lock of the door at the far end of the corridor; nothing doing. Walking slightly back on myself, I push the same key into a door to the left of me; still nothing doing. Moving forward, ignoring the bathroom and passing the head of the stairs, I make my way to the last room up here, the one that must straddle the whole front of the house.

This time, the key inserting effortlessly into the lock, it turns easily.

'Gotcha,' I whisper.

Letting myself in, standing on the threshold of the redhead's private bolt-hole, her safe refuge, I hold my breath for a couple of seconds, then sigh out with an anticipatory relish. This should be fun!

The room a reasonable size for such a pokey mid-terrace and benefiting from a large window opposite, it is definitely the master. Inside it, there is a double-bed, a bedside table, fitted wardrobes, a low coffee table, and a line of straggly plants. Cold, musty and slightly smelling of mould, the room in a general state of chaos, my nose wrinkles with distaste.

Flicking my gaze back to the double-bed, the pillows heaped against the centre of the headboard, the duvet pulled askew, it is as though she has just stepped out of the room and will be back any minute... At the thought, my heart skips a beat.

Again, I listen. It would not do to caught now. The house set well back from the main high street, there is minimal traffic noise. The only other disturbance, the billing and cooing of a randy pigeon strutting backwards and forwards on a concrete sill outside the window, there is silence, but not quite.

Stepping across the threshold, my mouth dry, my pulse rampant, I flick away my initial disgust for her aversion to cleaning, and allow the excitement to rise. I have been looking forward to this day.

Behaving like a private detective beginning a thorough investigation, keen to not miss a thing, I am determined to take my time, to pay attention as I conduct a slow and methodic prowl backwards and forwards across her room.

Winding my way through piles of books abandoned haphazardly to the floor, my eyes skim their spines. Curious as to what she reads — reference books on the human body, the brain, the mind, and even philosophy — I have to admit to feeling an element of surprise. I had not pegged her to be particularly academic or intelligent.

Fingering through numerous items trailing from hooks on the back of the door — scarves, coats, hats — the discarded items of clothing cluttering up precious floor space, I have to confess to being appalled at her relaxed attitude. Noticing her most intimate belongings are strewn across the top of the unmade bed, I decide not to go there yet.

Passing the struggling row of pot plants lined up on the floor against the end wall. Observing their brown tipped leaves straining to catch what little they can succour from the available daylight, their earth bone dry, she was no horticulturist, I realised.

Looking for photos, my gaze travelling over the minimal surfaces, around the white painted walls with their garish hippie-dippy posters, I soon realise there is dearth of visible information on friends and family. With nothing to go by, to compare her resemblance to, nothing even of that fat little friend of hers, I have to confess to being disappointed.

Walking over to the wooden coffee table positioned directly under the window, my eyes slowly glide over a wasteland of paperwork. Seeing the lid of a laptop poking out from under the mess, I pull it out, but it is powered down.

Wardrobe doors left wide open, I run my hands along slithery items of clothing, then purposely slide them shut.

Having no affinity with the way she lives, the room more typical of that of a teenager or a student, for a woman who is meant to be in her thirties, I can't quite believe how immature and unsophisticated she is. Not the turn-on, I had expected.

Returning to the coffee table, looking through a stack of discarded mail — letters, bank statements, bills, receipts, handwritten notes and reminders — I wish I have more time. On fire to know what the documents contain but restraining myself, proud of my self-control, I focus on the task in hand. Picking out crumpled sheets of paper from the wastepaper bin, I line each and every one them neatly across the top of her laptop lid, followed by a mug of cold coffee artistically placed bang in the centre. Standing back to admire my handiwork, I straighten up the piles of paperwork, the scattered books, leave everything on the coffee table looking neat and orderly, if a little bizarre. Happy with the results, I turn smartly away.

Returning to the bed, handling curled fragments of underwear — lacy black underpants, a black satin bra that smells strongly of her perfume — I feel a tightening tingle in my belly, a pulse in my temples.

Fascination vying with revulsion, breathing too fast and trying to modulate it, I drop the garments into the laundry bin as though scalded.

Is it still too soon to contemplate?

Am I even ready?

Soon, I tell myself, soon.

One last look. Secure in the knowledge I have tidied up enough to cast doubt, to confirm my visit, I am satisfied.

You see, it is important she knows I have been here. She has to know that she is not safe. Otherwise, where is the fun in it?

After a last squirt of her perfume which I leave lingering in the air, I let myself out and head for the Underground.

CHAPTER SEVENTEEN

It was 4 a.m., and she could no longer sleep.

Full of doubt, her mind was racing with what-if propositions. What if he doesn't show up? What if Dave gets suspicious and finds out she's been lying? What if work finds out she's been lying about being sick, and she loses her job? What if he does show up, and he attacks Carly? What if he shows up, spots her, then attacks her?

Staring grimly at the ceiling, the tears welled.

Worried about disturbing Dave, she turned over and watched the alarm clock. Finally, it was time to get up.

Careful to keep all three of them in blissful ignorance of her duplicity, Gemma kissed Dave goodbye as he left the house for work, then she dropped off the kids of at their respective schools as it though it were any other day.

Home thirty minutes later, she immediately called work and deliberately avoiding Katie, passed on her message through one of her peers. Extending her sick leave, self-certifying herself as having *picked up an awful sickness and diarrhoea bug*, and it being Thursday already, she confirmed she would not be back at work until after the weekend.

Still needing to collect the children from school later today and tomorrow, Gemma had worked out she had roughly five to six hours a day to work with. Not a huge amount of time, but it would have to do. She just had to get through each of the next two days, in one piece.

Committed to her decision to unmask Carly's stalker, Gemma had done her homework. Spending a significant portion of yesterday afternoon interrogating the internet, she had researched anything and everything she could find on stalkers. She had also spent some of her time, drilling out all the tips and tricks on how to successfully tail someone. Finally, she had made herself fully conversant — Carly publishing her daily itinerary on her website — with her friend's teaching schedule for the rest of the week; venues and times.

Now though, a quick change of clothes and she would be ready to leave.

The rain coming down in sheets, the pavement and buildings the same colour as the leaden sky, it was a miserable day to be out, thought Gemma sourly as she hurried her stride with difficulty. Tense, her whole body was feeling like a clenched fist as she willed herself not to vomit.

Continuing to weave in and out of the umbrella-shuffling pedestrians, unwittingly pushed into one gutter puddle after the other, Gemma's feet were soaked. Yet rapidly approaching the first of her destinations, for the first time since she had started out, Gemma was grateful to feel a quick rush of adrenaline override her cold, cold fear. Soon, she reassured herself, the almost paralysing fear would be replaced with considered action.

Arriving early, Carly's first class not due to end for another twenty minutes, Gemma stopped and took stock of her surroundings. Wondering where she could wait, she noticed there was a coffee shop right across the road from Carly's studio. The cold and damp really starting to bite, she headed straight toward it. Not only would the coffee shop provide her with the requisite cover she needed, it would also enable her to acquire a fortifying shot of caffeine.

Sat on a bar stool sipping at her drink, trying to appear casual as her right let jiggled up and down and her fingers shook, Gemma keenly watched all the comings and goings of Carly's building through the coffee shop window. Waiting for her friend to appear, time in hand, she begun to fret about the stalker, all over again. Her overactive brain hypothesising on all the *what ifs* and *maybes*, she could feel herself becoming more and more nervous by the minute. What if he doesn't turn up today or even tomorrow, for that matter? *Google* implying it was more a question of *when*, rather than *if* a stalker would show, but what if, at this moment in time, he was working or otherwise engaged? Maybe, she thought with a rising panic, he was only able to stalk Carly at night? What if putting her job at risk, lying to Dave and the kids, to Carly, had all been a complete waste of time?

The self-doubts mercilessly crowding in, challenging her sanity as they further frayed her already shredded nerves, all of a sudden, Gemma spotted Carly exiting through the main door of the studio. Knowing it was now or never, she fiercely pushed away her immobilising thoughts and her head instantly cleared. Whatever the outcome, she was here now, so she might as well get on with it.

Jumping off her bar stool in a rush, not noticing the coffee she sloshed all over the countertop, Gemma chucked her unfinished drink in the bin. Hastily leaving the seductive warmth — *the safety* — of the coffee shop, the rain still slashing down, she pulled the dark grey hood of her raincoat up and over her head. Then she got a wriggle on. Game on!

Carly wearing a scarlet rain mac and carrying an equally bright red umbrella with big white polka dots, amongst the sea of black and grey, she was definitely easy to see and follow,   thought Gemma

169

gratefully. Crossing the road so she was on the same side of the street as Carly, cautiously keeping her distance, Gemma constantly scanned the moving crowd for a likely suspect. On her guard, she watched for anyone and everyone who came within feet of her heedless friend.

Ten minutes later, still trudging down the rain soaked street and as of yet, the stalker nowhere to be seen, Gemma was left with nothing but a mounting frustration. Revisiting her earlier concerns about him being a possible no-show, again worrying about all the lies she had told, she felt a rotten stab of guilt as she mightily prayed, her deception would not all be for nothing.

Another five minutes, Carly ducking into the Underground station, Gemma followed her down with not an ounce of hesitation. She now managing her phobia instead of it managing her, she barely gave a second thought to the miles of subterranean tunnels she would have to journey in order to complete her mission.

Time passed. Two studios down and three, one hour classes later, Gemma was impatiently waiting for Carly's last class of the day to finish. Cold all over, her feet and calves throbbing, she was beginning to wonder if she had the stamina for much more. Also bored and measurably disappointed, she was finding it harder and harder to retain the concentration needed to remain vigilant. Checking the time, realising it had somehow become early afternoon already, she thought seriously about calling it a day. Pretty soon, she would need to go and pick the kids up from school. Then, out of the corner of her eye, she saw something.

Gemma's languor overwhelmed by a sudden sense of urgency flooding in. Her heart skipping a beat as her mouth dried, she tried to remain calm, but it was difficult. Her attention snagged by an individual skulking around in the semi-darkness of a derelict shop doorway right across the road from herself and from Carly's studio, every so often, he would dive shiftily in and out of the shadowy recess.

Trying not to gaze directly into the shop doorway, to look like any other innocent bystander waiting for someone to arrive, Gemma made a show of checking her watch a couple of times. She looked innocently up and down the street a couple of times, only once across the road. Could it really be him, she asked herself? A whole morning of following Carly without incident, her last shift of the day, it sort of made sense. After all, why would he turn up any sooner, put himself through the boredom of having to hang around class after class waiting for Carly, when there was really no need?

There he was again… out, in, out, in.

The person across the road seemingly watching Carly's studio building, his behaviour odd at best, suspicious at worst, Gemma's spirits rose. Becoming less and less uncertain, even a tad excited, she discreetly scrutinised his every move until she was convinced, she *had* her man.

The suspense building, the whole mad escapade becoming suddenly a lot more real, a sudden prickle of fear snaked its way down Gemma's spine. Fighting off an unwelcome desire to run, to get the hell out of there and away from him as fast as her legs could carry her, she had to force herself to stay put. This was it, wasn't it? This was what she had lied her arse off for. Having got what she had been hoping and praying for, waiting practically all day for, there was no way Gemma could allow herself to quit now, regardless of her understandable trepidation.

Contemplating her next move and realising what a dangerous move it was, a chill wind blew right through Gemma. From this point forward, she would no longer be trailing a benign and harmless, Carly. Instead, she would be hunting down a stalker — an obsessive with an unknown agenda, and possibly — if *Google* were to be believed — a potential killer.

The fear again returning, this time in a sudden rush, Gemma's breath was taken away as her heart thundered in her chest. Becoming awkward and ungainly, stumbling mid-stride, she prayed the stranger across the road, had not noticed.

Hastily revisiting her earlier plans, Gemma reminded herself that whenever she got the chance, she had to remember to use her smartphone to take photos. Similarly, if the opportunity arose, she would follow the stalker home, find out where he lived. Although it remained to be seen how easy either course of action would be, no matter what happened, the whole point of today's exercise was for her to gather evidence. Something tangible she could later pass on to Carly. Then she would support her friend in whatever decisions she took, thereafter. It was, after all, Carly's life and there was nothing worse, Gemma knew from bitter experience, than being coerced into taking a life-changing decision before one was truly ready for it.

Conducting a quick and shifty physical inventory of her prey, it wasn't long before Gemma felt thwarted. Assessing him to be of medium height and build, her quarry wearing a small black backpack, a pair of black boots, baggy jeans, a loose dark grey waterproof with the hood up over his head and a black scarf covering the lower half of his face, his style androgynous, his look was no different to thousands of others walking the streets of London on a cold and wet day. Not giving up, taking a second sneaky peak, if she were pushed to hazard a guess at his age, again, the way he was bundled up, she found it impossible to tell. Not a good start.

Nervously licking her lips, doubting herself and her abilities all over again, Gemma suddenly found she had a significant question for herself. What if she slipped up and it encouraged him to do more to Carly than simply stalk her? Then, she thought, as she queasily answered her own question, she would feel pretty sick for a very long time.

Seconds later, Carly leaving the studio, Gemma stilled her abhorrent thoughts along with every muscle in her body, and hung back. Waiting to see what her *mark* would do, she saw him lift himself out of the concealed doorway, cross the road and slide himself into the flow of pedestrians, a few paces behind Carly.

It was him! It was really him, thought Gemma as she spun hastily around. Following the stalker, following Carly, sweat breaking out along her hairline, all of a sudden, it was hard to breath again. Feeling light-headed, her stomach twisting, making her feel sick, terrified yet weirdly excited, Gemma forced herself to keep pace.

She *had* her man! It was time, she instructed herself, to beat the devil at his own game!

The chase on, no longer noticing the cold rain soaking through her shoes and clothes, hordes of pedestrians surging around her, like a predator focused solely on its prey, Gemma studied the stalker's every move. His step jaunty, at times daringly close to her unsuspecting friend, he displayed a calm but disrespectful nonchalance. Finding herself simultaneously fascinated and repulsed by him, awed by his gall, yet loathing the way he toyed with her friend in his twisted little game of cat and mouse, Gemma shivered with revulsion.

Carly striding out, the stalker following suit, Gemma puffed to keep pace as she worked hard to keep the pair of them in her sights. Speculating on how he had known what studio Carly was working out of? Then puzzling on whether Carly was his one and only victim? The second question impossible to answer, she concentrated only on the first and eventually, the penny dropped. Like herself, the stalker had to have interrogated Carly's website, found her rather too helpful timetable.

When all this was over and done with, Gemma promised herself as she panted up the street, she would warn Carly, strongly suggest she modify her website to take down the amount of dangerous detail being published for all and sundry — the weirdos out there — to see.

Hastily glancing down at her wrist-watch, with a nervous apprehension Gemma realised, it was getting late. In the not too distant future, the kids would need to be picked up from school. Worrying about the rapid passage of time and her responsibility toward the kids, her attention momentarily distracted from her task, Gemma collided with a person leaving a building and had no choice but to stop dead in her tracks, for a moment.

'Sorry, sorry,' she apologised to the startled young man.

Disentangling herself from her unwitting dance partner, peering down the street only to see Carly's brolly moving further and further away, Gemma lengthened her stride in a mounting panic. Where was he?

Flustered and disorientated, fearing she had lost sight of the stalker, Gemma picked up even more speed. Then finding herself to within a couple of feet of the stalker's back, breathing hard and almost down his neck, she instantly pulled back.

Alarmed and unnerved by what had almost happened, by just how close she had got, Gemma encouraged the distance between the two of them to steadily increase until she felt safe and back in control again.

Her thoughts turning to harvesting evidence, Carly walking purposely this whole time and without stopping, it had been a real challenge to get *any* photos of the stalker, never mind a decent one. His hood continuously up, his scarf permanently wrapped around the bottom half of his face, the entire time, all Gemma had really seen was the bridge of a nose, a pair of dark eyes, maybe? Concerned to realise that not once, had she managed to catch full sight of the whole of the stalker's face, Gemma hastily fumbled for her phone. Retrieving the device from her coat pocket, without looking, she flicked up the screen and put it on to camera mode. Shakily taking yet another snap of his back, his bobbing head, feeling amateur and stupid as she got funny looks from a couple of passers-by, she smartly returned the phone to her pocket. Fearful she would never get her moment, her chance to obtain some *real* photographic proof to put before her friend, Gemma experienced an almost overwhelming urge to tap him on the shoulder, tell him to drop his scarf, so she could stick her phone in his face.

'Christ!' Gemma ejected in shock and alarm before clapping a hand over her errant mouth.

Her earplugs urgently buzzing into her ears at the same time as her phone, on silent, began to oscillate in pocket, she had almost jumped out of her skin. The second time, in the last few minutes, since her phone had rung and again guessing it would only be work trying to track her down, she disregarded the call and let it go to voicemail. She dare not take her eyes off her target lest he elude her.

Five minutes later, all three of them down in the Underground, Gemma was obsessing. Fixated on the dwindling lack of time, on whether the stalker was going to follow Carly all the way home, on whether she would ever be able to get a decent photo of him or find out where he lived, distracted in spite of herself and the ticket barriers slowing her down even further, yet again, she almost had to run to catch up with the dissonant pair.

Breathless, her chest heaving, Gemma stopped short in surprise. Carly and her stalker were peeling away from each other?

Becoming even more anxious as she realised the stalker was obviously not about to follow Carly home, harassing on what to do, it suddenly hit Gemma that by some miracle, he was about to get on the same Tube line she would need to use to get back to Leyton! She took a snap decision.

She would trail him for just a little while longer, then perhaps, she could find out what station he alighted at? Not quite the same as getting a full address but if she was lucky, at least she would have something to make the day — *all those lies* — seem worthwhile.

Stood in the same train carriage as the stalker, though some way down from him, Gemma was hiding behind the broad shoulders of a couple of burly workmen dressed in navy boiler suits. The men enthusiastically talking about some football match they had watched on the TV the previous evening, they appeared to have no sense of her presence.

Three stops later, her deadline to collect the kids fast approaching, Gemma was seriously starting to stress as she observed the stalker looking as though he was readying himself to get off the train. Obsessed with following her mark and unable to bear the thought of giving up too soon, yet knowing she dare not be late for the kids, Gemma hurriedly appraised her options.

The kids attended two difference schools a couple of miles apart and her car, was in Leyton. Used to being collected second, Jessica, she reasoned, was likely to be fine provided she rang ahead to warn her. She could blame the traffic. As for Henry, even if she arrived a bit later than usual, what was the worst that could happen? The playground monitor would never let him leave the school grounds, unaccompanied. Instead, he would be taken back to his form teacher, and she would keep a hold of him until Gemma arrived. What she could not risk though, Gemma reminded herself, was being so late the school ended up ringing Dave or Paul...

Lifting up a shaking arm, pushing back her sodden sleeve, for the third time in as many minutes, Gemma checked her wrist-watch. Hoping she wasn't deluding herself and that she really could get away with it, she would give herself fifteen minutes more to pursue the stalker.

Then no matter what, she would beat it back to Leyton, pick up the car, and collect the kids.

Sweating profusely as she tailed the stalker off the train at the next station — three stops before her own — the anxiety levels again rising, Gemma shoved away the panic. It was not helpful.

Once, almost as though he knew he was being followed, Carly's stalker unnervingly looked back, left Gemma's heart pounding and the blood rushing to her ears as the saliva in her mouth instantly dried. Then he continued on again, strode confidently onto the next platform leaving Gemma unsure, as to what had just happened?

Gemma's phone suddenly springing into life again, vibrating urgently in her pocket and buzzing in her ears whilst she was still in mid-chase, she took no notice other than to quicken her pace. Damn Katie, why couldn't the woman leave her alone? She was meant to be sick, for Christ's sake.

Finding herself going north on the Victoria line, Gemma tried to ride out a mounting panic as she compulsively glanced down at her wrist-watch. Six of her fifteen minutes already gone, and she was getting further and further away from home. She should get off the train at the next stop, and turn back.

Two stops further along, the stalker getting off the Tube at King's Cross, Gemma heaved a sigh of relief as she followed him out of the Underground, across the road, then into St Pancras International station. Five minutes more, and she would turn back.

Hurrying her stride again, Gemma pursued the stalker into the mainline station before she could lose him. The stalker apparently not local, she deduced with surprise, she just had to know where he was going, what train he was catching.

Watching Carly's stalker get on an escalator that would take him to the upper level of the station, Gemma waited for him to nearly reach the top, then cautiously puffed her way up a flight of stairs that ran alongside of them. Her breath ragged, a painful stitch stabbing into her side, like a knife, she reached the second floor just in time to see the stalker slot a ticket into one of the platform barriers. She had got him.

Partially hidden by those milling around waiting for their trains, Gemma pretended to study the LED departure board directly in front of her as she furtively watched him make his way to platform twelve, where there was a waiting train. Registering that this was as far as she could go, that this was it for today, Gemma's relief was almost palpable.

Now she knew what platform he was on, using the LED boards, Gemma could identify where his train was going and then she could beat it back to Leyton, to pick up the kids.

All of a sudden, Gemma's worst fear since starting out that morning was suddenly realised. As he was about to get on the train, the stalker stopped. Turning round, he pointed the index finger of his right hand toward himself, then lifted it up to outside edge of his right eye, and threw it Gemma's way; *I see you.*

Horrified, her eyes widening in shock and incredulity, Gemma's heart leapt into her throat as her breath quickened. His sentiment all too clear as his eyes locked forcefully onto hers, the colour ebbed from Gemma's cheeks. He had seen her!

Cold with fear but unable to break his gaze, the hairs on Gemma's arms stood up.

He smiled, flipped her the finger, then casually boarded the train.

Afraid, very afraid, Gemma shook with fright.

'Oh God, oh God, oh God,' she moaned out loud, her eyes momentarily closing against the awfulness of it all.

A couple of suspicious commuters moving themselves even further away from Gemma, they put themselves well out of her orbit.

Her head shaking from side to side, Gemma looked wildly around for an escape. What if he came after her next? What if he came after her family? Petrified of the actions she had seen him take, of the cruel mockery they implied, she suddenly needed distance. She had to get away.

Running from the upper platforms, sprinting down the stairs, erratically crossing the ground floor concourse, right in front of the main doors, Gemma jerkily stopped. In her panic, she had forgotten to check where his train was going.

All her senses screaming at her, insisting she get away, Gemma shook her head at herself. She had to go back. She could not let this all be for nothing. She had to know.

Ruthlessly shaking off her dread, Gemma hastily returned to the upper level and ejected a sigh of not inconsiderable relief when she saw the train was still in the station.

Quivering as she stood there scanning the LED notice board, Gemma hunted for the information she needed on the platform twelve train. At last finding what she had been looking for, establishing the stalker had boarded one of the High Speed Link trains travelling to Stratford International, Ebbsfleet International, Ashford International, Folkestone west, Folkestone Central, Dover Priory, Martin Mill, Walmer, and Deal, she sighed out with an irritation peppered with anxiety. Never, would she remember all those names.

Agitated and on edge, not thinking to use her phone to take a photo of the board's details, Gemma scrabbled around in the bottom of her handbag, desperately looking for a notebook and pen. Locating what she needed, jotting down a hasty record of each of the station names, she assiduously ensured, there would be no chance of her forgetting a single one of them.

The sound of the train moving off, catching at her attention, it was in that moment, a warning bell went off inside of Gemma's head. *Deal*, she had heard the name recently, she was sure of it. Yet her memory cheated her... Knowing it was of vital importance that she should remember, Gemma ruthlessly interrogated her brain. Then, with stunning clarity, the elusive memory came to her and she gasped out loud.

Deeply distressed, her heart racing all over again and breathing hard as it almost pounded out of her chest, there was no way, Gemma thought fearfully, this could be a coincidence.

CHAPTER EIGHTEEN

Arriving at Henry's school just shy of twenty minutes late, Gemma looked wildly around the nearly empty playground. Her son nowhere to be seen, she picked up her stride and rushed to find his form class. Preparing herself for a couple of awkward questions from Miss Kind, such an innocuous name for a woman who had always managed to put the willies up her, Gemma mentally revisited her excuses. She was so sorry. She would have been there on time had there not been an accident at the end of her road. The traffic hold-up, the diversion, there was nothing she could have done. Listening to herself, Gemma did not feel good about herself.

Marching into Henry's classroom, hoping she appeared far more confident than she actually felt, Gemma was taken aback to find it unoccupied. Concerned but not yet panicked, walking through chilly corridors that smelt of sweat, dust, floor polish and disinfectant, she hurriedly made her way to the school administration office, where she knew, there would be an adult she could talk to.

'Hi,' said Gemma, to the much younger woman sitting behind the glass screen. 'I'm looking for my son, Henry Atkinson, but I can't find him? I've checked his form class but neither he nor his teacher, Miss Kind, are anywhere to be seen?'

Peering out from behind a pair of tortoiseshell glasses, the woman's heavily made-up eyes gave Gemma a considered look as she sighed out her irritation.

Returning a polite, but questioning smile, Gemma gritted her teeth as she silently encouraged the woman to get a move on.

The anaemic-looking woman shoving her glasses to the top of her head, she unhelpfully asked, 'Are you *sure*, he wasn't there?'

Gemma pasted on another pretend smile.

'Yes, I am positive,' she enunciated carefully. She glanced impatiently down at her wrist-watch. 'Look, I don't mean to be rude, but I'm in a hurry. Please can you can you do whatever it is you need to do, to find Miss Kind and my son,' she directed.

Again, the woman sighed out her annoyance before awkwardly slipping off the high stool she had been sat on.

'I won't be a minute.'

The woman heavily pregnant — explained her reticence to move, the dark bags beneath her eyes — Gemma watched with a growing impatience as she waddled out of a door at the back of the office, with what appeared to be, a deliberate slowness.

Restless for the woman to return, Gemma suddenly remembered with an awful start of horror and shame, in her haste to get to Henry's school, she had completely forgotten about Jessica. She had not rung and warned her, she was going to be late!

Sticking a hand into the pocket of her rain soaked coat, Gemma grabbed for her mobile and quickly looking down at the screen was shocked to discover just how many text messages and missed calls she'd received. Her face paling with apprehension. Working out some of the messages had to have been sent when she was riding the Tube — the

Underground having little to no signal — she quickly established that none of them had been received from work as she'd previously thought. Instead, there was one from Carly, two from Henry's school, two from Paul, and three from Dave... And that that could only mean, there had been some sort of trouble with Henry!

Gemma's heart skipping a fearful beat, reading through each of the individual text messages before listening carefully to every one of her voicemails, it appeared Henry had sustained some sort of an injury — fear — a minor injury — relief — and that unable to get a hold of her, the school had called up the next emergency contact on their list, his father. Paul collecting Henry from school, he had also tried to call her a couple of times, followed by Dave. Paul messages initially sounding irritated and then angry, Dave's sounding terribly worried, then irate, and then distraught, Gemma began to sweat. Thinking of what might lay ahead, she gulped. She was in so much trouble!

No longer waiting for the school receptionist to return, turning smartly on her heel, Gemma swiftly exited the building by its main door. Could this day get any worse, she thought dejectedly? Speeding across the puddled playground, rain dripping off the end of her nose, she furiously searched for an answer on what to do next?

Desperate to get to her son, to see for herself that he was okay but aware she had a number of conflicting priorities to work through, Gemma forced herself to think calmly and rationally. Even though Henry had had some sort of a minor injury, he was with Paul, with his father and so fundamentally, he was safe, she reassured herself. Meanwhile, Jessica was on her own and still waiting to be collected from school. Henry's needs as well as her own overridden by Jessica's, Gemma knew she had to call Dave's daughter first. She had to let Jessica know everything was okay and that she was on her way. Then, and only then, she would contact Paul and speak to Henry, followed by Dave.

Walking and dialling, Jessica's phone engaged, Gemma hung up. Redialling, it rang and rang. Picturing Jessica smirking down at her phone as the call went to voicemail, Gemma left an apology and what she hoped, would be a reassuring message.

Back in the car, her palms hotly wet with perspiration, Gemma switched her phone off silent and dropped it into the cup holder between the driver and passenger seat. She would use the car's Bluetooth to call Paul on her way to pick up Jessica. Firing up the ignition, gripping the steering wheel as she jerked the car away from the kerb, her mobile preprogrammed to connect to the car, an incoming call was automatically answered before she could do anything about it. Damn it!

'Hello? Hello?' demanded a male voice. 'Gemma? Is that you? Are you there?'

Hearing Dave's anxious voice booming around the close confines of the car, Gemma started with shock. She was not yet ready to talk.

'Gemma, for Christ's sake! Answer me! What the hell is going on?'

Undoubtably about to be outed as a red-handed liar, abashed and stumbling for words, Gemma's initial response was tentative.

'Hi, yes, sorry, I'm here. It's me.'

An audible sigh from Dave.

Still not ready to talk, wishing she could hang up, Gemma sought to compose herself by concentrating on her driving.

'Thank God, it's you. You're really there,' said Dave.

Unable to miss the uncertainty in Dave's voice, his discernible apprehension. Aware of what Dave had gone through with Sarah and guessing that right at that moment, he was not in a good place, Gemma was beginning to understand just how disconcerting and brutal her actions must have seemed. Disappearing on him, being uncontactable, putting Dave through everything Sarah had put him through the day she had taken her own life, he must have been worried sick.

'Yes,' she replied weakly.

'Right, okay, so where in hell, have you been?' he demanded.

Dave now sounding insistent, a sharp edge of irritation in his almost unrecognisable voice, Gemma flinched. She tried to calm her breathing before she replied.

'Sorry, but I can't hear you very well, I'm in the car. What's up?'

'What's up?' Dave spluttered out his disbelief. 'Your ex has had to collect Henry from school because they couldn't get hold of you. I've had to collect Jessica. And all because we couldn't find you. Where the hell are you? Are you OK? I've been worried sick.'

Dave's questions coming at her thick and fast, anger mixed with a great deal of concern in his voice, Gemma's heart dropped for the second time in under five minutes. She wasn't being fair. She had to say something, anything, to allay his fears.

'I am *so* sorry,' she stressed. 'I can explain everything, really I can. But I'm in the car, Dave. I'm on my way to pick up Jessica. Can we talk later?'

'Didn't you hear me?'

Gemma shook her head as though he could see her.

'No, what?'

'I've already got Jessica,' Dave repeated curtly.

After the day she'd had, the lies she'd told, the things she'd witnessed, the events that had happened whilst she had been playing private detective, not wanting to have to explain herself and no longer able to think straight, Gemma realised she was miserably confused.

'You've already picked her up?'

'Yes, when I couldn't get hold of you, I decided not to leave it to chance. And it's a bloody good job I didn't, because *you* weren't there, were you? Where the *hell* have you been?'

'Look, I know I'm running late but I can't help it. The traffic, it's been abysmal. I promise you, I *was* on my way to pick her up.'

'Funny that, cos the traffic was fine when I went to get her.'

Dave's ice cold sarcasm dripping down the phone at her, Gemma shivered.

'And when I came home earlier, your car was still here and yet for some reason, you weren't? Now, miraculously, it's gone?'

Realising they must have crossed paths within minutes of each other. That Dave must have left work early to look for her, and that she had most definitely been caught in a brazen lie, ashamed all over again, Gemma squirmed in her seat.

Dave emitting another heavy sigh, Gemma braced herself for what more was to come.

'Look, you're driving, and I don't want you having an accident on top of everything else. Wherever you are, you need to turn around and come straight home,' Dave abruptly instructed.

Relief washed over Gemma. No more awkward questions. Well, at least not until she got home.

'OK,' she replied meekly.

'Right, we'll talk when you get home.'

And with that, he abruptly rung off.

Pellets of rain pecking vigorously at the windscreen, on automatic pilot, Gemma drove the car home as slowly as she possibly could, whilst her brain travelled at over a million miles an hour. Obsessing on what to say, on how could she possibly find the words to explain what she had done and why, Gemma was persecuting herself. Yet in the end, it all boiled down to whether she should continue to lie, or choose to tell the truth. Either way, Dave would never forgive her.

Back on their street before she even registered she was there, Gemma carefully parked the car. Her body tense with stress and taut as a bow, freaking out about what lay ahead, she advanced toward the house at tortoise speed.

Approaching the front door, her keys jangling in her shaking hands whilst rain again dripped off the end of her nose, it was flung open long before Gemma got anywhere near the lock.

Dave's usually small frame seeming to fill the doorway and looking like a man who had witnessed an irrevocable loss, Gemma's face blanched. There was no welcoming smile. He said, nothing.

Having to follow Dave through to the living-room as though she were a stranger in her own home, Gemma blinked back a couple of hot tears. She would not allow herself to cry. Everything that was coming to her, she deserved it.

Standing at opposite ends of the coffee table, awkward in each other's presence, Dave looked Gemma up and down as though inspecting her for signs of damage. Gemma's injuries internal and therefore, invisible, he soon nodded his head as though satisfied.

'So, where were you today because you weren't at work?' Dave snapped out tersely and without preamble.

A clammy, sick feeling rising up, almost overwhelming her, Gemma swallowed down hard. Then she coughed, to clear her parched throat.

'Nowhere, I was n-nowhere, in particular,' she stammered.

Dave loosened his tie, unbuttoned his collar and pulled it away from his neck as though he were being strangled. His brow damp with beads of perspiration, his eyes hard chips of brown stone, his mouth was set rigid with disapproval.

'Really? Well, whilst you have been *nowhere in particular*, I've been out of my mind with worry,' he declared with a bitter laugh.

'I really am sorry,' Gemma stressed.

'You're sorry... Is that it? Is that all you've got to say for yourself?'

She would not cry.

'I'm so, so...' she caught herself.

Her brain exploding. Wanting to collapse down on to the floor, to cry out the fear still coursing through her veins from her personal encounter with the stalker, her frustration for how she was feeling about her life in general, her concern for Henry, her bitter regret for all the lies she had told and the secrets she was keeping, Gemma was barely able to hold herself together. Throwing her arms around her body, she held on tight.

'I'm waiting.'

'How did you know? How did you know I wasn't at work,' she stalled, her voice trembling with nervous strain?

He scowled ferociously.

'Work? Is that all you're bothered about?'

'No, of course it isn't. But I can't afford to lose my job as well as you...' she broke off, hung her head.

Dave dispatched Gemma a withering, disbelieving look.

'You weren't answering your mobile, so I rang your office number.'

'Shit!'

Feeling the damned up tears beginning to trickle down her cold face, Gemma angrily swiped them away. She did not deserve his pity, any pity.

'Gemma, the school could *not* get a hold of you. Neither could Paul. And nor could I.'

188

She nodded her head.

'I was worried sick for you. You left me with no choice.'

Gemma tried to swallow away the bitter taste of her betrayal, but couldn't. Feeling physically sick, as though she would throw up at any moment, she gulped.

'I know.'

'And if you're concerned I might have dropped you in it, then you damn well should be.'

Dave's tone clipped, the censure in his face unmistakable, Gemma struggled to return his reproving gaze but still, she wished he had not rung her office. They could ill afford for both of them to lose their jobs.

'I know,' she repeated.

'You can hardly hold me accountable for the consequences of *your* lies?' he emphasised bluntly.

A thick air of tension building around them. Recognising that if ever there was a time to tell Dave the truth, to clear up all the misunderstandings before things got even further out of hand, it was now, irritatingly indecisive, Gemma said nothing. Then, the opportunity passed.

Dave sighed, heavily.

'Look, I told your colleague I'd forgotten you were off sick. I blamed it on a senior moment.'

Gemma emitted an audible sigh of relief.

'I'm *so* sorry Dave. I should never have put you in that position.'

He shook his head vehemently.

'No, you shouldn't have. So why did you?'

Dave's voice flipping from angry to quietly controlled, authoritarian and flavoured with a stern disapproval, Gemma felt like she was a small child all over again, being disciplined by her father.

Embarrassed, the words failing to arrive, Gemma hung her head in humiliation.

'Gemma, what the hell is going on here? You're not a child. Talk to me, for Christ's sake.'

She shook her head. Still, the words would not come.

'Gemma, if you don't talk to me soon, I will leave this...' he broke off.

Despite the unfinished sentence, Dave's threat very real, very imminent, Gemma started. Dave walking out on her, walking out on them, on Henry and her, was not what she wanted, not at all.

'Can't you see, I don't know what to say,' she croaked, struggling to find her voice.

He snorted with disbelief, with disgust.

'How about starting with the truth?'

Gemma forced herself to think, to scrabble for the words, to find some truth in amongst all the unpalatable lies, because it was not going to go away.

'I think I just needed some space. Some time out.'

'Time out? Don't we all?' Dave spat back.

His hands bunching up into fists down the side of his legs, visibly furious again, Gemma inwardly shrank from him, from his contemptuous stare. The exchange between them feeling as though it was on the verge of becoming irretrievably hostile, now she was so close to losing it all, to losing him, suddenly, she so wanted it all, wanted him.

'Two whole days you've been off sick, without telling me,' Dave accused. 'Two whole days you've been lying to me, to the kids, to your boss. How could you?'

Avidly recalling how earlier that morning, Dave had kissed her goodbye before happily wishing her a nice day at work, embarrassment and shame flooded through Gemma all over again, and her cheeks seared.

His jaws clenched.

'Gemma, what is it? What is it about your life that's so bloody awful, you have to have time out? And why haven't you talked to me about it? I thought we were a couple, a partnership? Or have I just been deluding myself, all this time?'

Now certain their relationship was balancing on a knife-edge, for a couple of seconds, Gemma wavered on spilling the truth, on telling Dave everything… But if she did, if she truly opened up, he would be so hurt. Then once he realised just how many secrets she had been holding back from him, that same hurt would turn to anger and he would never trust her again. Damn Henry, why could he not have stayed well, she thought harshly?

'I don't know,' she beseeched him.

'I don't believe you.'

Dave looking distraught, devastated even, Gemma became desperate to settle him.

'I think, everything has moved on so fast these last few weeks, I just needed some time to breath, that's all.'

He lapsed into a frowning silence.

She held it.

'OK,' he broke the quiet. 'I know things have been a bit full on lately, but that doesn't explain why didn't answer your phone today? Or where you were when I came home to find you?'

'I didn't answer the phone because I stupidly put it on to silent.'

'What? Why? You never put your phone on silent,' he insisted, his voice still quivering with tension, with doubt.

'Because I'd lied to work about being ill, and I didn't want Katie chasing me down. I'm sorry, I didn't think.'

'No, you didn't,' he accused grimly.

Gemma shivered. She briefly hugged herself. Seriously cold from being so upset and wet, she could barely prevent her teeth from chattering.

'So *where* have you been these last two days, because you certainly haven't been here?' he pointed out tersely.

'Yesterday, I was here all day,' she answered truthfully.

Gemma's words ejected hastily, maybe a little too hastily, Dave threw her another suspicious look.

'And today?'

'Today, I had to get out of the house.'

He swept his hand toward the living-room window.

'In the pouring rain?'

'Yes, I just needed to get out for a while.'

He snorted again.

'So *where* did you go?'

His voice dripping like ice water down the back of her neck, Gemma paled, then bit the inside of her lip as she prepared to tell, yet another lie.

'I went to the National Portrait Gallery for a few hours.'

'What, on your own?'

'Of course.'

She straightened her spine.

He searched her guilt-ridden face.

'Of your own volition, you used the Underground again? And you used it, all on your own?'

'Yes.'

He looked at her with scepticism.

'Really? What about your phobia?'

At last, she could be truly honest.

'Using the Tube Tuesday night to get to and from Carly's yoga class, well, it seems to have been a make or break moment for me,' she countered earnestly.

For the first time, since she had arrived home, Gemma saw the ghost of a smile flash across Dave's face and she felt a surge of hope. But then he went and spoilt it.

'Gemma, what you said earlier...,' he hesitated, 'about things moving too fast. About you needing time to yourself... is there a bigger problem here, we need to talk about?'

Dave gazing at her steadily, already guessing what he was thinking of asking, Gemma was forced her to look away and fiddle with the hem of her coat. Christ, she could not do this with him now! Dave turning the conversation on to himself, coercing her into dealing with his constant feelings of underlying insecurity, on top of everything else, it would just be too much. For the sanity of her own mind, silently, Gemma begged him not to ask.

He sighed. His shoulders sagged as though all the energy had sapped out of him.

'You and I... do *we* have a problem?' he asked doggedly. 'Would you rather I'd *not* moved in with you? And be honest with me, Gemma.'

Now she was faced with the one question she had been dreading him asking, since the day he *had* moved in, since she'd started receiving those God awful text messages, her emotions confused and all over the place, Gemma hesitated. He saw it.

'Ah,' he nodded his head. 'You *do*, don't you? You wish we'd never moved in together,' he insisted, his voice cracking.

Gemma hated seeing his every emotion — disappointment, mistrust, upset, fear, concern, misery — written all over his face. She could not stand it.

'No, no, of course I don't,' she rushed out.

Looking miserable, Dave slowly shook his head.

'I don't believe you.'

And why should he, Gemma silently berated herself, after all the lies she had told, she had just told yet another one? She loved Dave, had always loved Dave but him moving in with her, it had felt unbearably like the walls were closing in. Swallowing nervously as her heart skipped an extra beat, Gemma clutched on to her clammy hands. It was time she opened up. It was time she told some cold, hard truths before their relationship disappeared entirely.

'Dave, please believe me, when I say I am *not* unhappy that you and Jessica moved in with us. It's just that it all happened so fast, and I don't think I was ready.'

'Too fast?'

'For me, yes, although you seem to have been taking it all in your stride...' she hesitated.

'Go on,' he encouraged.

'Well, I've been feeling overwhelmed. But that doesn't mean I don't *love* you, Dave,' she rushed out sincerely. 'Or that I don't want our relationship to work.'

A look crossed Dave's face, one Gemma was not sure how to interpret. He rapidly blinked a couple of times.

'Overwhelmed?'

Somehow, she had to help him understand.

'Oh, come on, Dave, even you have to admit these last few weeks, they've not exactly been easy for any of us, have they?'

'Does that mean you want us to move back out?'

Gemma shook her head vehemently.

'Absolutely not, you're both here now, and I want to make it work. And I love you.'

'You love me?'

'Yes, I do,' she insisted before hesitating again. 'But…'

'But what?'

Gemma plucked up some more courage from somewhere.

'I'm not even divorced yet, and already you're talking to kids, to our families, about marriage. But I'm not sure, I'll ever want to marry again.'

Looking him straight in the eye, wanting to convey the sincerity of her words, Gemma hoped, she had said enough to help him understand.

Dave returning Gemma's unwavering gaze, he seemed to make his mind up about something as he wiped the misery from his face.

He nodded, sighed.

'Okay, I get it.'

Still, Gemma could see there was an air of sadness about him that lingered, and she felt incredibly sorry for all the pain she had caused.

'And what about tomorrow?' Dave asked.

Confused by the question, by Dave's sudden change of direction, Gemma slowly shook her head.

'Tomorrow?' she asked.

'Work. Your job? I take it you're going in tomorrow?'

She shook her head.

'No, no, I'm not. I self-certified as sick for the rest of the week. I don't go back in until Monday.'

Dave's dark and tired eyes, flashed over with anger.

'Self-certified, so you had it all planned then, your little three day break?'

Guilty as charged and hot with embarrassment all over again, Gemma felt an ugly flush creep up from her neckline to her face as she dropped her eyes and looked away.

Dave exhaled heavily.

'Well, you certainly look like shit,' he pointed out dryly.

Hearing a slight note of jocularity in Dave's voice, lifting her eyes up to his face and seeing the corners of his mouth momentarily twitch up, Gemma seized the moment.

'Thanks, morale, duly boosted,' she snorted self-consciously as she put a hand up to her soaked hair.

'Have you seen yourself, lately?' he asked.

Flicking her eyes toward the pine framed mirror hanging above the fireplace, Gemma saw her unmade face was pinched of colour. Her lips bloodless with anxiety and the cold from outside, her hair unattractively dripping on to her shoulders, not recognising the unsettling reflection looking back at her, she almost had to do a double-take. Never, had she looked so awful. She smiled weakly.

'I've looked better,' she agreed.

'I take it you're desperate to know about Henry,' said Dave.

Finally able to ask the one question that had been uppermost on her mind since arriving home, Gemma felt the boulder in her stomach lurch sickeningly sideways. A terrible mother, she would never forgive herself for not being there when her son needed her most.

'Is he all right?'

Dave sighed, rubbed his hand over the top of his shaven head a couple of times and obviously remembering something unpleasant, he pulled a sour face.

'According to your *ex,* Henry's fine now.'

His words terse again, Gemma guessed Dave's embittered face related to Paul and that their conversation, had not been a pleasant one.

'Good.'

'Oh, and Paul insisted I tell you, he's not happy about being called away from work at such short notice,' Dave stated, his mouth pulling down at the corners.

Gemma didn't suppose Paul was, but it was obviously OK for her to be called away from her job, she thought bitterly.

'So what *is* wrong with him? With Henry, I mean?'

'During PE, one of his fingers got badly bent back. The school were concerned it might have been dislocated or fractured, so they wanted you to take him to A&E. Anyway, Paul took him in and had him checked out, and apart from some obvious bruising, the finger's fine. The doctor's said he can go back to school tomorrow.'

Gemma a sighed out her relief.

'Thanks,' she replied gratefully.

'Paul said not to hurry over. He's going to give Henry his tea.'

She nodded.

Feeling and looking like a ruined mess. Exhaustion kicking in and overriding all shame and embarrassment, Gemma was suddenly keen to get away. She needed a hot shower and to lay on the bed for a few minutes. If she was to deal with Paul next, she had to get some strength back.

'If it's OK with you, I'm going to go upstairs now. I have to get out of these wet clothes.'

'OK, but before you do, you need to know Jessica's in a bit of a strop.'

So what's new, Gemma thought tiredly, but did not say?

'And funnily enough, it has nothing to do with you not being there to collect her from school,' Dave added rather acerbically.

'So what's wrong?' Gemma asked, ignoring Dave's undisguised dig.

'Carly called. She can't have Jessica to stay this weekend.'

Very unlike Carly to pull out of a promise, Gemma thought with a mild panic.

'That's a shame,' she said cautiously.

Dave nodded.

'Yeah, but it's not like Carly can help it. A few of her colleagues have come down with the flu and she's been asked to cover their classes,' Dave explained, his voice sounding tired and sad all over again.

Silently digesting what Dave had said, first chance she got, Gemma determined she would ring Carly, find out what was really going on with her friend. Something had to be up, she was sure of it. Not forgetting, Carly still needed to be briefed on everything that had happened throughout the day, including the fact the stalker had got on a train to Deal...

Dave rubbed a hand backwards and forwards over the top of his shaven head with an ill-disguised irritation as he watched Gemma leave the room. He'd had no idea she could be so secretive, so deceitful. Such a crap end to a crap day, he thought bitterly as he collapsed heavily on to the sofa, tipped his head back and stared at the ceiling.

Exhausted, but unable to let it all go. Feeling so betrayed and angry, so very angry, he could not stop himself from ruminating on the afternoon's events. His nightmare starting with a phone call from Gemma's overbearing ex, implying he should keep her on a tighter leash, then mouthing off about how Henry's school had got him out of work and how inconvenient it was, he had wanted to shove him arm down the phone and rip the supercilious bastard's throat out.

Having to disguise his immediate alarm from Paul as to Gemma's whereabouts, as soon as the arrogant son of bitch had hung up, he had started to panic. Equally unable to get hold of Gemma himself, her number ringing and ringing without being answered until it dropped into voicemail, it had taken all his strength of will to keep it together as a chill had closed around his heart. Frantic but determined, he had immediately called Gemma's office number. The woman on end of the phone confirming that Gemma had been home sick since yesterday morning — news to him — in spite of his understandable shock and feeling such a prick, somehow, he had managed to laugh it off. Telling Gemma's colleague he had stupidly forgotten she was ill at home, apologising for wasting her time, the woman had laughed with him.

Within seconds of ending his call to Gemma's workplace, painful echoes of Sarah surfacing uppermost in his mind and immersing him in a whole host of memories that still smarted to hell, Dave had almost been overwhelmed by them. Sarah's unforeseen suicide and the resulting insecurities associated with that horrendous period of time, crashing down on him, he had been distraught.

Compelled into action. Deeply troubled not only for Gemma's well-being but for her safety, he had dropped everything and rushed home. Hardly the most professional way to behave when one's job was under the precarious threat of redundancy, he thought bitterly.

Arriving home, searching the house from top to bottom, his emotions running high and flipping between fear, relief, and fear again, in spite of what Gemma's workplace had thought, she had not been there. Uncontactable by phone and not at home even though her car was outside, Dave's nerves shredded but trying not to assume the worst, he had repeatedly reminded himself, tougher and stronger, Gemma had a resilience, a strength of character his young and fragile wife, had never had. Gemma, he had told himself firmly, would be fine and there would be a good reason for why, she had chosen to lie to him.

Subsequently establishing Gemma's *good reason* for pulling a sickie, for not sharing her whereabouts with him, for lying to him and everyone else, was at best sketchy, at worst non-existent, he was now struggling to comprehend it all. Whilst he understood she was wrestling with the pace of their relationship, with how quickly they had moved in together, that she loved him but did not want to marry him, what he still could not grasp, was Gemma's weak and reluctant explanation for why she had lied to him about taking some time out. Even now, something about her account felt *off.*

He sighed, heavily.

Powerless to dismiss the niggle of unease still burrowing away at the back of his mind. Again questioning Gemma's blatant mendacity, her selfish irresponsibility, his anger eating him from the inside out, he winced with pain. How could she? How could she do that to him? For two whole days, she had bald-faced lied to him. Anything could have happened to her in that time, and he would have been none the wiser. With her phone off, anything could have happened to one of the children or him, and she would have been none the wiser. He hated liars.

Unsettled, feeling as though he was stumbling around in a fog of bitter disappointment, a vein at the back of Dave's neck began to throb. Embarrassed to find a couple of stray tears falling onto his cheeks, he impatiently swatted them away.

Aware the trust between Gemma and himself had been severely compromised if not broken completely, struggling to see a way forward, he then brutally reminded himself that he was not the only one suffering from trust issues. The vitriolic text messages Gemma had recently received, they had also tested her faith in him. Yet she had given him the benefit of the doubt. Perhaps, he deliberated, that was one of the *unmentioned* reasons she had been so desperate for some time to herself. Perhaps, he thought tiredly, they both needed to work harder at their relationship.

CHAPTER NINETEEN

Later that same evening, driving over to Paul's to collect Henry, Gemma pulled over into the first empty lay-by she came across, stopped the car and switched off the ignition. Retrieving her phone from the plastic cup holder between the driver and passenger seat, she punched in Carly's mobile number. Carly answering her phone on the first ring, Gemma knew she had been right to call.

'Gemma?'

'Yes.'

'Thank God you've called, I've been pulling my bloody hair out.'

Carly's tone urgent, conspiratorial, Gemma sucked in a breath. What now, she thought despondently?

'Why? What's the matter?'

'Someone's been in the house, more specifically, someone's been in my room.'

Recalling the way the stalker had mockingly looked back at her. How he had threatened her with his audacious wave before giving her the finger, Gemma felt the sweat prickling in her armpits.

'A break-in?' she asked hopefully.

'No, whoever it was, they had keys, *my* keys…'

'When?'

'Yesterday, when everyone was out at work.'

A silly question, but she had to ask. 'And you're sure it wasn't one of your housemates?'

'Absolutely, the front door's obviously kept locked. And I always keep the door to my bedroom locked.'

'So they didn't break-in as such and when they left, they locked both doors behind?'

'Yes, all the doors were still locked. It has to be the thief, Gem. The one who took my keys after class, last Tuesday.'

'If they didn't break-in, how do you know they've been in your room? Did they mess it up, or steal something? Leave you another nasty note?'

'No, no notes, and he didn't take anything, either. He tidied the place.'

Gemma's jaw dropped. She must have misheard.

'Sorry?'

'He tidied the place,' Carly repeated. 'I always leave my wardrobe door open, and it had been closed. Clothes I'd left on the bed and on the floor, had been picked up and put in the washing bin. More weirdly, he'd left a load of paperwork, stuff I'd thrown into the bin, neatly lined up across the top of my laptop lid, then he placed a half finished cup of coffee right into the middle of it all. Whoever it was, Gem, it is like he wanted me to know he'd been there.'

Her pulse thundering in her ears, hardly able to believe what she was hearing, Gemma stupidly asked, 'And you're sure, it wasn't you?'

'Yes!'

Hearing the fear behind Carly's angry voice, Gemma held on to her questions for a moment. She needed to let Carly speak.

'I'm scared, Gem. It gives me the creeps to know some pervert with OCD has been in my room, going through all my stuff.'

The break-in happening a full week after the theft, it could definitely have been the stalker, Gemma thought, her belly cavorting up and down like a roller coaster. A week was more than enough time for him to have followed Carly home one day, so he had her address.

'And that's why you've cancelled your weekend with Jessica. You don't want her staying with you, just in case…'

'Yes, but I could hardly say that to Dave, could I? I did try and ring you first, but I couldn't get a hold of you?'

You and everyone else, Gemma thought unhappily as she ignored the barely veiled criticism behind the implied question.

'And you're sure he didn't take anything?'

'Yes, but I'm seriously creeped out, Gem. Whoever he is, I feel like he's playing with me. Weird, right?'

You can say that again, Gemma thought fearfully, but did not say.

'Look Carly, we have to talk. I have some really important information I need to share with you but I can't do it now, as I don't have the time. Can we meet up early tomorrow, tomorrow morning?'

'What information?'

'Not now Carly, I don't have the time,' Gemma insisted.

'Okay, now you're freaking me out,' Carly complained.

'I'm sorry, Carly. I'll explain everything as soon as I see you, I promise.'

'My classes don't start until midday tomorrow, so yeah, I suppose we could, but where?'

Her nerves screwing up, threatening to get the better of her, Gemma made herself think. Was it even safe to have Carly come over to the house? What if she brought him, the stalker, with her, then he would know where she lived. Then again, Dave was going to be none too happy if she went walk about again.

'It'll have to be my place. I'm home sick at the moment.'

'Sick?'

'Yes, but it's a long story and I can't talk now. I'm on my way to collect Henry from Paul's and as usual, I'm late. But it *is* really important, I see you,' she emphasised.

Carly sighed unhappily down the phone.

'OK, what time?'

'I need to drop the kids off at school first. Around nine?'

'OK.'

'Promise me though, you'll make sure you're not left home alone tonight?'

'Don't worry, I've already checked and I won't be.'

'In the meantime, you must get hold of a locksmith. Even if it's only to the change the lock on your bedroom door.'

'Already have. See you tomorrow.'

Eager to get off the phone, Gemma hastily said her goodbyes, then dropping it back into the plastic cup holder, she turned over the car's ignition, slipped it into gear and spun the car on to the main road.

She needed to collect her son, then get home to Dave. Her brain already busily formulating another plan, she had some serious sucking up to do.

Gemma rapped on the door of Paul's flat. Dark outside, almost six-thirty already, she needed to grab Henry and make a move or he would be knackered in the morning. Now she had Carly coming over first thing, it was even more important he be well enough to attend school. No excuses.

Paul's smile tight as he opened the door to her, Gemma pretended not to notice.

'Hi, where is he? Is he ready?'

'Come in,' Paul instructed, his jaw tight.

'No thanks, I need to get Henry home and into bed, so I can't stop,' Gemma explained, not crossing the threshold. Looking down the corridor, surprised not to see her son barrelling toward her like he always did, again she asked, 'Where is he, Paul?'

'Watching TV, I told him to stay put as I thought you and I, should have a quiet chat first.'

Gemma sighed inwardly. The last thing she needed after the day she'd had, was one of Paul's *chats*.

'Sorry, Paul, not tonight, I'm in a hurry. Please, go and get Henry for me.'

On the receiving end of one of Paul's sour looks, Gemma braced herself. He wasn't finished yet.

'Oh, after today's little debacle, I think you can spare me five minutes of your precious time,' he insisted sarcastically.

Paul's tone derisive and quarrelsome, Gemma was startled but unsurprised to find him grip the top of her arm as he more-or-less frogmarched her across the threshold and into his kitchen. She vigorously shook off his restraining hand.

'How dare you?' she hit back.

Stood with her back awkwardly pressed up against the cooker, Gemma deliberately held Paul's gaze and he, standing no more than a couple of paces in front of her, stared confrontationally down into her face.

'What the hell happened to you today?' he demanded to know.

Paul launching straight into what was eating at him whilst ignoring her obvious discomfort, Gemma tried not to show her contempt. Also furious, she had less success controlling her anger.

'Who the hell do you think you are?' she growled out under her breath, not wanting Henry to hear. 'Keep your damn hands off of me.'

'Answer me,' he shot back.

'Paul, we're not married any more. I don't have to answer to you,' Gemma reminded as she stood firm.

'Technically, we *are* still married, but that's not the point...' Paul hissed out, looking more than a little disgruntled.

'Look, I don't have time for this,' she interrupted.

'If you'd just let me finish. Married or not, I am still Henry's father!' he pointed out belligerently. 'And when I get a phone call from my son's school telling me he has been hurt and that they cannot get a hold of his mother, I think I am entitled to an explanation, don't you?'

Paul enunciating every single word. Silently seething, knowing Paul was right to hold her culpable but not liking it, not one little bit, there was a heavy beat of silence as Gemma hastily sought to gather her thoughts.

'You know, if you won't talk to me, there is always the option of having a little chat with Social Services?' he threatened.

Not quite able to believe her ears, the atmosphere between them now cloyingly tense, Gemma came over all hot and claustrophobic. Filled with an intense desire to get her son and leave, to out of his flat, she began to move forward, but Paul blocked her exit.

'I'm waiting,' he said ominously.

Infuriated by him. Finding it unbelievable that she still had to answer to him. Yet also realising, the sooner she got this over with, the sooner she and Henry could get of there, Gemma rapidly pulled herself together.

'I was sick,' she explained begrudgingly.

'Funny, Dave didn't mention a thing about you being ill, when I spoke to him?'

'Really?' she said, feigning surprise.

At that moment, wanting nothing more than to plant a fist right into the middle of Paul's smug face, Gemma gripped her hands tight together. She could not afford to give him the satisfaction.

'So why didn't you answer your phone?'

'I just told you, I was *sick,*' she stressed.

'So? What's that got to do with your phone?'

'I'd gone to bed. Left my phone downstairs, by mistake, and fell asleep.'

He searched her face. 'You look fine to me.'

'Thanks.' Gemma would not be drawn. She had had enough. 'Are we done here, only your son needs his bed? You know, I can always shout for him...'

Looking discomforted all of a sudden, Paul backed away from her.

'No, I'll go and get him.'

His lips compressed into a thin line of displeasure as he turned away to get their son, Gemma wondered, at Paul's sudden compliance?

Henry unusually quiet in the car, Gemma checked on him using the rear-view mirror.

'Hey, little man, you OK?' she asked.

Even though she must have apologised to her son over a dozen times since inspecting and kissing his strapped up finger, Gemma's conscience was still badly pricking. A bad, bad mum, Henry deserved better.

He nodded.

Through the mirror, Gemma stared into her son's expressive eyes.

'You sure?'

He contemplated, frowned, nodded his head again.

'I'm fine.'

Was that a sigh she heard? Henry's response given in such serious tone for a little boy, Gemma had an instant flowering of anxiety somewhere deep inside her chest.

'Henry, I know your finger is sore but you look really sad, baby boy. Are you sure there isn't anything else troubling you?' she probed gently.

Henry's large, blue-grey eyes thoughtfully looking into her own through the rear-view mirror, Gemma could not help but notice how unusually worried he looked. Her heart going out to her little boy, whilst her mother's instincts insisted there was something wrong, she pushed him a little harder.

'Henry, come on, I know there's something worrying you. Tell me,' she insisted.

The frown persisting, Henry bit his quivering bottom lip as a lock of fair hair fell across his pale forehead.

'Daddy,' he said quietly.

Just one word, expressed so sadly, so painfully, Gemma's heart broke. What the hell has Paul been up to now, she thought viciously?

'OK,' she smiled encouragingly. 'What about daddy?'

'I don't want to see him any more.'

Simultaneously shocked and puzzled by what Henry had said, watching a couple of tears fall on to the apples of her son's chubby cheeks, Gemma took pains to hide her true feelings from him. The last thing she wanted to do, was to put Henry off from telling her what was troubling him. Yet not wanting to see his father, it made no sense whatsoever as Henry hero-worshipped his father.

'This is not like you, sweetheart? Don't you like your dad's new flat, your new room?' she asked through the mirror.

'I do, but...' Henry stalled, looked even more upset, if that were possible.

She had had enough. Driving into the first space she saw on the side of the road, Gemma got out of the car and climbed into the back seat so she could sit next to her child. She locked the doors. If there was one thing she had learnt from today's adventure, from chasing around London with Carly and her stalker, it was that you could never be too careful.

'Henry, please, talk to me. You can tell me anything, I won't be cross.'

Using her forefinger, Gemma gently lifted up her son's chin, then pressed a soft kiss to the side of his face. Lightly lifting the fallen lock of hair, pushing it back into place, she could almost see the wheels turning behind his blue-grey eyes, Paul's eyes. Wishing she could wipe away his worry, Gemma stroked her hand reassuringly backwards and forwards across Henry's tightly knitted brow as she patiently waited for him to tell her what was wrong.

At last he spoke.

'Dad keeps asking me loads and loads of questions.'

His bottom lip quivering with emotion, Henry struggled to meet Gemma's concerned gaze.

Her instincts already working overtime, kicking in even more forcefully after what Henry had just said, a prickle of annoyance tickled at the back of Gemma's tightened throat as she picked up on a strong inkling of what might be going on. For her son's sake, Gemma responded as softly as possible, as she tried to find the right words.

'OK, and you don't like these questions?' She kept her voice deliberately calm, reassuring.

Visibly miserable, big fat tears of pain rolling down his cherubic face, Henry passionately shook his head.

Gemma nodded. She gave him a minute, gave herself a minute.

'Henry, can you tell me what the questions are about?' she asked quietly.

'You, mummy, they're always all about you,' Henry discharged, the torrent of words rushing out of him.

Going cold, feeling a shiver run down her body, Gemma knew she had been right. Her instincts bang on, Paul was so predictable, she thought bitterly.

'OK, can you give me an example?'

Henry's face tensing with emotion, he anxiously gazed up at his mother. Gemma's heart gave a little squeeze of pure love for her unfairly troubled son.

'He wants me to tell him stuff all the time.'

She felt a little sick.

'Tell him stuff?'

'Yeah, stuff about you and Dave, like when you get cross with each other.'

Now truly angry with Paul, furious with him, wanting to kill him, Gemma silently warned herself, for Henry's sake, to keep calm.

'OK, anything else?'

Henry started to cry all over again and his little sobs, broke Gemma's heart.

'He asks me so many questions, I don't always know the answers,' he blurted out.

'Like what, sweetheart?'

'He wants to know if you've been out, and who you've been with. I keep telling him I don't know. But he doesn't believe me, mummy.'

Gemma gritted her teeth.

'Anything else?'

'I don't know, I can't remember!' he cried out in a panic.

'Hey, little man, it's OK,' Gemma soothed. 'It doesn't matter if you can't remember. Look, I'll talk to daddy.'

'You can't!' Henry yelled. 'I'm not supposed to tell.'

Gemma flinched from the strain in Henry's voice, from the look of horror on his face.

'Shh, shh,' she comforted him. 'It's OK. Look, listen to me, you are not worry about any of this because *you*,' she stressed, 'have done nothing wrong.'

'But I don't want daddy to be cross with me.'

'He won't be,' Gemma reassured her son as the dark clouds scudded across his troubled little face. 'I promise.'

Even though he was behaving like a creepy lunatic where she was concerned, if there was one thing Gemma was sure of, it was that Paul would never lay a finger on his precious son. He adored Henry. No, whatever was going on here, had nothing to do Henry and everything, she thought resentfully, to do with her.

CHAPTER TWENTY

Perched on one end of Gemma's living-room sofa, a mug of steaming coffee cradled between her hands, for the second time within the last couple of minutes, Carly struggled not to yawn. She had slept badly last night, whether from the bottle of wine she had so readily consumed, or because her eyes had kept being snapped open by an overactive imagination — her brain fooling her into thinking someone was breaking into her room to do God only knows what to her — she could not be certain. Either way, she was supremely tired and oily hung-over.

Gemma also seemingly stuck for words, looking anxious as she fiddled with the hem of her jumper, Carly dispatched her a questioning look.

'Gem, whatever it is, tell me. I won't bite,' she said tiredly.

Gemma got up, started tidying up bits and pieces of stuff scattered across the coffee table.

'Gem, stop it. Stop cleaning.'

'Sorry, it makes me feel better.'

'Well, it makes me nervous.'

Rain unexpectedly rattling against the bay window, Carly jumped as her head swung toward it. She was so on edge. The sooner

Gemma got whatever it was off her chest, she thought moodily, the sooner she could leave, get her day over with and crawl back into bed.

'The reason I haven't said anything yet, is because I'm not sure how you're going to take it,' Gemma preambled?

Gemma's demeanour, her tone, deadly serious as she looked down at her hands in the gloomy half-light, Carly became unsettled all over again. Seeking to steady her apprehension, her increasingly excitable nerves, she took a couple of deep breaths. Whatever it was, it could not be anywhere near as bad, she hoped, as finding out someone had broken into her home and room.

'Christ, Gemma, now you really are making me nervous. Whatever it is, just spit it out.'

'OK, but just to put some context around what I have to say, I think you need to know, this is my third day off work, this week.'

Gemma not looking in the least bit sick, Carly was wondering where she was going with the conversation.

'OK?'

'I told work I'm sick. But that's not the real reason I wanted some time off.'

Still, Carly was none the wiser.

'Right?'

'For all sorts of reasons, I felt I needed some time to myself. But I also needed some time off, to do something for you.'

'For me?'

'Yes, let me explain.'

Intrigued and confused, Carly wished she would.

Hearing everything Gemma had to say, along the way, inspecting a few grainy photos — all bar one of which, gave little to no real evidence of what he looked like — stored on her mobile phone, Carly slowly sunk into disbelief. Feeling sick, her already nauseous stomach churning anxiously as she contemplated the enormity of what Gemma had put herself through, the risks she had taken, the lies she had told. Also astonished, humbled and increasingly worried for her friend, Carly was almost reduced to tears. Even more so, once she found out how much trouble Gemma had got herself into with Dave. Thinking on Dave, about how angry and upset he would be once he found out the full and true extent of what she had been holding back from him, hot tears of shame welled up in Carly's eyes. Not a conversation she was in a hurry to have, it was, nonetheless, one she would have to have and soon, if she wanted to help Gemma and Dave hang on to their shaky relationship.

Reaching out, Carly placed her hand on top of Gemma's and gave it a good hard squeeze.

'Gem, you are an absolute nutter and I love you for it. But I can't have you falling out with Dave, not over me. We have to tell him the truth. No, scratch that, I have to tell him the truth,' she corrected herself.

Gemma flashed Carly a look of exasperation.

'Carly, whilst I get you are worried for me and Dave, don't be. We'll be fine. Right now, you've got bigger things to think about. What was the last thing I mentioned to you?'

Puzzled, Carly raised her eyebrows. Somehow, in amongst everything she had been told, she had obviously missed the crux of the matter. She shook her head.

'I dunno?'

'The train!' Gemma ejected forcefully.

Needing to focus, Carly sat up straighter in her chair as the wheels in her exhausted, wine soaked brain, slowly began to whir and turn.

'Tell me again,' she insisted.

'Your stalker, he boarded a South Eastern train, to *Deal*.'

'Deal?'

Her eyes animated, Gemma nodded her head at Carly.

'Yes, and isn't that...?'

The cogs in Carly's brain finally lining themselves up before snapping painfully into place, she finished Gemma's sentence for her. '... where Steve goes on the weekends.'

Incredulous but nervous at where her thoughts had finally taken her, Carly shivered. He couldn't be, could he?

'You OK?' Gemma asked. 'You've gone as white as a sheet.'

Of course she wasn't OK, Carly thought miserably. The wind sucked out of her by what Gemma had exposed, she had to take a moment.

'Carly?'

'What are you telling me, Gem? Are you saying you think the thief and my stalker, are one and the same person?'

Gemma nodded her head vigorously.

'Yes.'

'And that that person, is Steve?'

Carly held her breath in anticipation.

Gemma shook her head vehemently.

'No, no, of course I don't think it's Steve. He's much too tall.'

'Too tall?' Carly repeated quietly, hopefully.

Gemma nodded her head again.

'Yes, the person I saw following you yesterday, was of medium height and build. Someone about the same size as Paul, I think. So, there's no way, it can have been Steve.'

Though still somewhat confused, Carly sighed out her relief.

'Thank God. But I still don't get it? If Steve isn't the stalker, then who is?'

Gemma gave Carly a keen look. She licked her lips.

'I'm not sure, but I think it might be...'

Gemma seemingly unable to finish her sentence, Carly was left in the awkward position of having to come to her own conclusion until she finally caught on to Gemma's line of thought. Then her earlier relief was short-lived, as once again, she felt sick to the stomach. Swallowing hard to lubricate her throat, Carly shook her head at Gemma.

'No, I don't believe it. It can't be him. It can't be Steve's son. It just can't...'

'Why can't it? Medium height, medium build, your stalker's probably about the same size a teenage boy. He got on train that was going to Deal. Come on, Carly, you've got to admit, it's a pretty strong coincidence, don't you think?'

'But he's just a boy, Gem.'

'A teenage boy with anger issues, according to his father. One who has lost his mother only recently and who has possibly found out, his father's got another girlfriend already. Think about it, Carly. Think about Jessica, all the crappy stuff she's been putting me through. And she lost her mother, four years ago.'

Was that it, Carly asked herself with awful dismay? And yet, Steve and I, we thought we had been so careful, so clever.

'So you think Brian knows about us, about me and Steve?'

Gemma shrugged.

'Obviously, I don't know for sure? But yes, I think he probably knows far more than you realise,' she suggested. 'Either way, it's my best guess for now. And in a weird sort of way, it kind of makes sense, don't you think?'

'But he's just a schoolboy, Gem. Surely he can't just bunk off school without someone noticing and saying something, can he?'

'No idea? For all we know, the school may already be saying something to Steve or to the boy's grandparents. To our knowledge, you've only just begun to be stalked. It's only been, what, eleven days?'

Carly had no idea. It felt like a lifetime.

'Let's face it, even the nasty notes could be interpreted as quite childish,' added Gemma. 'Perhaps, he's been stalking you during an end of term or a half-term break? Without knowing what school he goes to, who knows? But I sure as hell want to find out.'

'Shit!' Carly ejected, unable to stop herself.

Her racing heart now in her mouth, realising everything Gemma had just said did sort of make sense, all of a sudden, Carly had an overwhelming urge to confess her sins, to admit she had lied about the extent and duration of her relationship with Steve, and that Brian could have known about the two of them for far longer than was thought. In a quandary, her loyalty toward Steve getting in the way of her decision, then Gemma interjecting into Carly's thoughts with a question, the moment passed and was gone.

'What's Steve's address, in Deal?'

Carly slowly shook her head.

'I've no idea.'

Gemma looked surprised, then nodded to herself.

'Yeah, well, a new relationship, I suppose it is still early days,' she said more to herself than Carly. 'Can you get a hold of it, his address?'

'Possibly? Why? What are you thinking?'

'I'm thinking we're so close to getting an answer on who your stalker is, we should follow through on what I've started. Make sure you're gonna be safe. Make sure I'm gonna be safe, come to that.' She paused. 'Make sure all the lies I've been telling Dave, actually get to mean something,' she said with feeling.

Carly shook her head. She still didn't understand.

'How, though?'

'What are your plans for tomorrow?'

Carly's thoughts still pinging all over the place, for a couple of seconds, she could not think straight.

'Tomorrow, tomorrow? Saturday, you mean?'

'Yes.'

Gemma's impatience visibly growing as she waited for an answer, Carly marshalled her disorganised thoughts.

'As I was meant to have been spending the weekend with Jessica, I cleared my diary.'

'So, you've got nothing on?'

'Nope.'

'Brilliant, let's pay the seaside a visit.'

Staggered, Carly's mouth dropped open.

'The seaside?'

'Yes, let's go to Deal.'

Appalled at the idea, Carly was almost lost for words.

'Christ, you're serious, aren't you?'

'Damn right I am.'

'You really want to go to Deal?' Carly squeaked with incredulity.

'Yes.'

Spots of colour appeared in Carly's cheeks, Steve would go mad. He would never trust her again.

'But I can't just randomly turn up on his doorstep,' she said, her voice barely above a whisper.

'Why not? You're a couple, aren't you?'

Carly shook her aching head, pushed her hands through the tangled mass of red hair. Somehow, she had to make Gemma understand what she was asking of her.

'But we can't. I can't. His son doesn't know about me yet. Steve will be furious with me.'

'Look Carly, I'm not prepared to hang around waiting for *your* stalker to turn up on *my* doorstep. As far as I'm concerned, I don't think we have a lot of choice. We *have* to know if we're right. And if we are right... well, then perhaps, we can do something about it?'

Despite having strong misgivings, Carly had to concede to Gemma's logic. The sooner they got to the bottom of what was going on and dealt with it, the better. And Steve, always so guarded and intensely private about his *other* life, in truth, she was also intrigued.

'But what do I say to him? How do I explain my being there, you being there?'

Gemma shrugged her shoulders dismissively.

'I don't know? We'll tell him we decided to go down to the seaside for the day, and we took the opportunity to pop in for a cup of tea.'

Carly had gone very white.

'You can't be serious? How does that explain I know where he lives?'

'Look, Carly, I don't know what we'll say, but I'm sure we'll think of something.'

Like it would be that easy, Carly thought with a horrible trepidation.

'Listen, I'm pretty certain your stalker *is* Steve's son,' Gemma added. 'and if I am right, we have to tell him. We have to tell him, what his son has been putting you through, these past few days.'

'But how are you going to prove it? You have no evidence.'

'We get into the house and look for photos.'

'Photos?'

'Yes, everyone has photos of their kids dotted around the house. Then we see if we can spot a resemblance to any of the pictures on my phone.'

With only one of Gemma's photos providing minimal detail on the stalker's facial features — the shape and colour of his eyebrows, the colour of his eyes, the bridge of his nose — Carly seriously doubted they would be able to tell anything. Then again, they could get lucky.

'And if we're still not sure? Or it isn't Brian?'

Gemma shrugged.

'Then we'll have had a nice surprise visit to the seaside. And you'll have a decision to make.'

That simple, Carly thought worriedly, thinking on how Steve would likely finish with her if she showed up unannounced. But if there was any chance of finding out who her stalker was, she had to know. She could not keep putting herself through the stress of worrying about who was following her, what they wanted from her, and what they might do to her.

'A decision?'

Gemma nodded her head firmly.

'Yes, you're gonna have to decide whether you go to the police, or not?'

Carly baulked.

'The police?'

'Look, Carly, after everything you said the other day about what could happen to your job, I don't want to push you into going to the police but this can't continue, you must see that? You could be in serious danger. After everything that's happened, you *have* to consider your continued safety... my safety, now he's seen me. And not forgetting, he was brazen enough to break into your home.'

Even after everything that had happened, without any concrete proof for the police to investigate, still, Carly was reluctant to put her hard-fought career at risk, to go to them empty handed. Conversely, she was not at all keen to put Gemma and her family in danger. Nor could she forever keep looking over her own shoulder, it was too frightening, too exhausting. Gemma was right, Carly decided, it was time for action. Somehow, she needed to get back some semblance of control and if that meant going down to Steve's, to rule Brian in, or out, then so be it.

'OK,' she agreed. 'Deal it is. Then dependent on what we find, I'll take a decision about going to the police. What about your lot, though? What are you going to tell Dave?'

'Henry is at his father's again, this weekend. So it is just Jessica and Dave, I've got to sort out.'

'How, though?'

'Well, Jessica's so disappointed about her weekend with you being cancelled, I had been thinking, it would be a good time for her and her father to spend some quality time together. So later, I'm going to contact Sarah's parents, suggest they invite Jessica and Dave to stay over for the weekend.'

'Bit short notice, isn't it?'

'Don't worry, they never go far. And they haven't seen Jessica in such a long time, they'll love the idea, I'm sure of it.'

'I'm serious, Gem. I don't want you getting into a load more trouble with Dave. From what you said earlier, I'm really scared for you both.'

'And as I said earlier, don't be. We'll be fine,' Gemma insisted.

'You sure?'

'Yes!'

Carly threw Gemma a grateful smile.

'Sorry, Gem, you know I think you're wonderful, don't you?'

Gemma snorted.

'Yeah, what would you do without me, eh?' she teased back.

Carly's stomach churning over and over with a combination of nerves, anticipation, and too much alcohol from the night before, she sincerely hoped what they were about to do would not backfire on them. That they would all, Gemma, Dave, Steve and herself, come out of it unscathed. Somehow, though, she thought it highly unlikely.

Carly furtively looked up and down the corridor of Steve's apartment block. It was empty. With back-to-back classes from lunchtime onwards, the rest of her day following her meeting with Gemma, had flown by. Then almost before she had known it, she was here already, anxiously hoping her plan to break into Steve's flat was going to work.

Nervously swallowing down a sense of impropriety, a feeling she should not be anywhere near the building, never mind in it, Carly took in a couple of deep, steadying breaths. Steve well on his way to Deal by now, she should be safe.

'Come on Carly,' she encouraged herself, 'you can do this.'

Pressing on the bell of the next door neighbour's flat, Carly only hoped the woman was in. She was.

The front door being cautiously opened, Carly quickly pasted on her friendliest smile.

'Oh, hi, Mrs Conway, how are you? It's me, Carly,' she explained.

Beaming and talking the small bird-like woman standing in front of her, like they already knew each other, Carly crossed her fingers behind her back and patiently waited for Mrs Conway to reply.

'Carly?' Mrs Conway queried, a blank look on her face.

Mrs Conway visibly struggling to snag on to her memory, suddenly worried it was not going to go at all well, Carly swiftly tried again.

'Yes, Mrs Conway, you remember me,' she hustled. 'I'm Carly, Steve's girlfriend from next door. You and I, we often say hello to each other in the corridor,' she said with a complete lack of truth.

Mrs Conway peering at Carly, behind her eyes there was almost a glimmer of recognition. Then, there was the ghost of a smile.

'Red hair... Ah, yes, now I remember. Mr Quinnell's young lady,' she said with a hint of desperation.

Mrs Conway's bird-like head nodding slowly up and down as she pecked the information from her brain, Carly reached out a hand, and gently touched the old lady's wrinkled wrist.

'Yes, that's right, I'm so sorry to trouble you, Mrs Conway. And I hope I didn't frighten you?'

Mrs Conway stood straighter as she visibly bridled.

'I don't frighten easily, my dear.' She shook her head. 'Though if you had knocked much later, I would *not* have answered the door.'

'Oh?'

'I never answer my door before nine in the morning, or after seven at night,' Mrs Conway stated firmly.

'You're very sensible, Mrs Conway,' Carly flattered.

Mrs Conway's papery cheeks blushed slightly as she gave a little chirrup of a laugh.

'Well, you can never be too careful these days, can you, m'dear? I see such terrible things on the telly and in the newspapers. It makes one seriously think about becoming a... now, what's the word? Oh yes, I know, an agoraphobic,' she tweeted, her beady little eyes twinkling with merriment.

Ooh, you lovely, lovely, little old lady, Carly thought ruefully as she flicked away a sharp pang of guilt. Mrs Conway was not making this at all easy for her.

'No, you can't,' she agreed.

A vacuous smile beginning to appear on the old lady's face, keen to seize the moment and Mrs Conway's clarity before it disappeared again, Carly smiled broadly as she rushed out, 'I need you help, Mrs Conway?'

'You do, dear?'

'Yes, it seems I'm in a bit of a fix. I thought I had lost my mobile phone. But then when I spoke to Steve earlier, he said I had left it in his flat, and that I could collect it on my way home this evening. But I forgot to bring my spare set of keys, with me. And so I was really hoping, Steve being away and all,' she said wheedlingly, 'you would be kind enough to lend me yours? Obviously, I'll return the keys straight back to you.'

Seeing the hesitation in the old woman's eyes, the purse in her lips, Carly hastily said, 'If you need me to ring Steve so you can talk to him yourself, I would be very happy to do so. But not having my mobile, I would obviously need to borrow your house phone to make the call. Is that OK?'

Having taken a calculated gamble. Guessing Mrs Conway would be reticent to letting *anyone* into her flat, Carly was nervously hoping, she had played her cards, just right.

'Oh, I don't know, should I?'

Watching Mrs Conway dither, Carly held her breath.

Mrs Conway shrugged to herself.

'As you're his girlfriend, I suppose it will be all right. I'll go and get them for you, shall I?'

Carly smiled out her honest relief.

'Oh, yes please, thank you, Mrs Conway. I desperately need my phone for work and the angel that you are, you've just saved my bacon.'

Mrs Conway patted Carly's arm before going back into her flat to find the keys.

Applying pressure to a frail old woman who had to be well into her nineties if she was a day, Carly was finding her behaviour beyond contemptible, but she was desperate.

Swiftly casting her eyes around Steve's meticulously tidy and strangely — without him in it — impersonal flat, feeling like the trespasser she was, Carly guiltily wondered where she should start? Never left alone in his flat before, she had no idea where he might keep his private papers. With no desk or anything similar, just a few drawers and cupboards in the various pieces of furniture dotted around the minimally furnished rooms, she began to sweat a little. Illogically fearful that at any minute, Steve would walk straight in through the front door, she got a wriggle on and began her search.

Nothing found in the pristine kitchen or the well organised living-cum-dining-room, Carly hastily walked through to the cool and shadowed bedroom. For such a small but perfectly formed flat, her shame ridden foray was taking much too long. She needed to find something soon, then leave. Looking under the bed, carefully combing through each of the bedside tables, then a chest of drawers before sifting through a wardrobe full of expensive suits and shirts, she eventually spotted, Steve's leather briefcase sitting on the floor propped up against the bedroom wall.

How in the hell had she missed that? Carly asked herself impatiently.

She snatched up the heavy bag.

Sitting on the end of the Steve's king-sized bed, his grey satin quilt, Carly slid her shaking hands inside the cavernous mouth of his briefcase and very carefully, extracted a couple of plastic wallets bulging with paperwork. Opening each of the wallets in turn, slowly running her eyes over the contents, she eventually found, a plain white envelope.

Sick with nerves, her fingers trembling, Carly turned the unopened envelope the right way over, then almost whooped out with joy as she realised that at last, she had unearthed what she had been looking for.

She had her address.

CHAPTER TWENTY-ONE

Dear reader, my apologies as I think I have been rather remiss, rude even. I have omitted to give you any facts about myself, or my life. So right here, right now, I shall endeavour to correct that little oversight.

Superficially, there is nothing outwardly wrong with my life. The only child of older parents I have been given, what you would likely call, a stable and loving upbringing. Few of us have problem-free childhoods but mine was not excessively difficult, and I do not have an abusive past. I have no history with violence, the law or authority. To any outsider looking in, I have a privileged life. Yet for reasons I cannot explain, I often feel not quite myself and out of sorts?

I have formed attachments to those closest to me, but they are not strong. If you were to ask family and friends how they feel about me, I think they would probably say, I am not as loving or caring as they might have hoped. Emotions — passion, jealousy, desire, anger, hatred — are not beyond or outside my understanding, but they scarcely hold my attention. Although I believe myself to be neither shallow nor heartless, it is true, I have next to no remorse.

If you were to notice me, I look quite normal, even attractive. Dependent on how I present myself, on how much of an effort I make with my appearance, I am the sort of person you might pass on the street and not think twice about.

If I were a person sitting next to you on the Tube and we got talking, I have no doubt you would find me not only charming, but interesting. Yet if we were to chat, I doubt our conversation would be about you as I do not care to hear about the mundane lives of others. Having a natural contempt for humankind, a misanthrope, it is not that I do not comprehend people, it is more that I have a serious aversion to them.

'So why, if your life is so perfect,' I hear you ask, 'do you commit such a heinous crime as murder?'

And I would answer, 'I am not a murderer, but a creator.'

According to some of the philosophers I have read, the way to enlightenment, is to live in insecurity. So by arbitrarily engendering the conditions required for a tragedy to occur, the outcome of which is not predetermined by me but left very much to fate, I obtain a quiet sense of omnipotence, a powerful supremacy that is impossible to resist. Basically, when I embrace risk and uncertainty, I feel alive.

At the end of the day, we all have our urges. It is just that some of us, don't always get to choose what we become.

And yes, before you say it, I guess I am a monster. But I am not crazy. I function perfectly well. And anyway, a monster can be a fabulous creature.

You know, I also read an article that confirmed all of us are somewhere on the   psychopathy spectrum. Consequently, I think its important you remember, there is some of me, in you too...

All of us having inborn temperaments that powerfully shape the personalities of our future, how can it possibly be my fault, if I was delivered from my mother with a brain that is wired somewhat differently to yours?

Oh, is that a train I hear coming?

'Mind the gap.'

CHAPTER TWENTY-TWO

The cool of the pillow against her face, Gemma yawned and stretched. Surprisingly, she had slept well. Feeling rested and keen to prolong the moment, she kept her eyes closed as she put out an exploratory hand. His side of the bed was cold.

Listening, hearing the muffled sound of running water coming from the bathroom and guessing Dave was in the shower, Gemma rubbed the sleep from the corner of her eyes. Reluctantly opening them, she winked at the bedside clock. Already, it was past 8:00 a.m.

Rolling over in bed, a shaft of sunlight streaming in through a crack in the curtains, Gemma judged the incessant rain of the previous week to be finally over. The world hopefully drying out, she was mightily relieved. With the sun out and no rain to consider it would be an excellent day to visit the seaside, she told herself firmly.

Gemma's thoughts naturally turning to the more serious business of the day ahead, a tiny crease appeared in her forehead. Feeling daunted, for the briefest of seconds, she seriously considered cancelling her plans and staying exactly where she was. Whispering in the corridor, the flush of a toilet, the close of a distant bedroom door, Gemma picked up a glass from her beside table, and took a sip of dusty water to steady her tangled nerves. There was no turning back now.

Needing no more sleep but the bed offering warmth and comfort, a temporary safe haven from the pressures of the world outside of her front door, Gemma snuggled back down under the duvet. Five more minutes, and then she would get up.

Seconds later, Dave padding softly into the bedroom wrapped in a towel with water dripping from his hair, Gemma sat up in bed. He stopped mid-stride.

'Sorry, did I wake you?'

'No, no, I was already awake, just putting off the inevitable.'

'That was Henry, he was desperate for the loo so I let him pee, then I told him to go back to bed until you wake him.'

Gemma dispatched Dave a grateful smile.

'Thanks, you ready for your weekend? Need any help packing?'

He returned her smile.

'Yes, to the first question and no, to the second. It's only one night. It'll take me five minutes to pack.'

Dave appearing much calmer today, Gemma felt happily reassured. Talking for some hours into the previous evening, they had eventually arrived at an understanding of sorts and the tension between them, even if not fully resolved, had at least eased.

Sitting on the edge of the bed, Dave discarded his towel to the floor and began to get dressed.

'You sure you don't want to come with us?'

Gemma chuckled. He was so transparent.

'They're not that bad, you know.'

'Yeah, I know.'

She smiled broadly.

'Perhaps you should try saying that again, without contorting your face so much.'

Again, Dave grimaced.

'Hey, look, they were so excited to hear from you. They can't wait to see their granddaughter. It's been too long already.'

He nodded.

'Yeah, I know it'll be good for Jessica to spend the weekend with her grandparents. I'm just not so sure about me?'

'You'll be fine. And the journey up there and back, the visit to her mother's grave, it'll give the two of you some of that father-daughter bonding time I've been nagging you about. It'll also remind her, just how awesome you really are.'

Dave snorted good-naturedly.

'Wow, what a charmer, I can't believe you just said that. I still feel bad about leaving you home alone, though.'

'Yeah, well, there's absolutely no need. After I've dropped Henry off at his father's, I have every intention of spending some quality time on myself. Do some window shopping. Take myself off to Carly's last yoga class of the day. Perhaps, even stay with her tonight?'

Dave now dressed, he issued Gemma a considered stare. Walking round to her side of the bed, leaning over her, his breath smelling of spearmint, his mouth impacted with the corner of her lips. As he pulled away again, she smiled.

'Hmm, that was nice.'

He drew back from the bed and half smiled.

'Welcome. You sure you're gonna be OK?'

'Absolutely.'

'If you need me, you'll call me, yeah?'

'Of course. Oh and before I forget, please don't forget to talk to Jessica about those text messages I saw on her phone, that time.'

Dave's body stiffened slightly.

'Dave, we have no idea how old this Dean is,' Gemma scolded lightly. 'And as I said last night, I've not seen her hanging around with any boys, not at school or at home. She's just a kid, Dave. You have to talk to her.'

He lifted his chin but did not answer.

'Dave?'

'I know I do, and I will. I'm just not sure where to start. I don't want to fall out with her all over again.'

Though outwardly smiling at Dave's visible reluctance, inwardly, Gemma was starting to seethe. They had been through this already. Exhausted by the topic but equally intent on keeping Jessica safe from any unknown predators, she was determined to get to the bottom of the *Dean* conundrum, once and for all. Truth known, she was struggling to understand Dave's continued reticence? If it had been Henry conversing with a stranger on a mobile phone, she would have been all over him, long before now.

'Make sure she knows it was me who saw the text messages, you know, when I took her phone off her that time, so she doesn't think you've been snooping. Then reassure her we're not angry with her. That we simply want to make sure she's safe. See how she responds, then play it by ear.'

'And if it turns out this Dean, is her boyfriend?'

'Then as I said last night, suggest she invite him over here one evening, after school. He could even come for dinner, if that's what she wants.'

'And what if she doesn't want to invite him over? Or she refuses to tell me anything about him?'

Gemma shrugged. They were the sort of questions she had been hoping to avoid.

'I'm hoping, if you handle her sensitively enough, it won't come to that. But if she does become difficult, we'll have to figure it out, won't we? Come on, Dave, you can do this, I know you can.'

Gemma's mobile suddenly buzzing on the bedside table, signalling a text as it conveniently interrupted their conversation, Dave grabbed for the device. Without apology, he read what was on the screen. Then, with an ugly little smile, he flung it none too gently back on top of the quilt.

'It is time these stopped?'

'I know.'

The tension in the room suddenly palpable, Gemma watched Dave close his eyes for a moment.

'Don't be like that?'

'Like what?'

'You're mad again.'

'I'm not mad, just tired,' Dave said over his shoulder as he left the room.

Dunking her head under a hot and soothing shower, beginning to wash her hair, Gemma reflected on the events of the previous evening. The two of them having had a frank discussion about everything that was going wrong in their lives, as well as their relationship, some things had been resolved whilst others, had most definitely not.

Her biggest success of the evening, though, had to be that she had finally got through to Dave where Jessica was concerned. Managing to persuade an incredibly resistant father to take his daughter to see her mother's grave before going up to Nottingham for the weekend so she could visit with her maternal grandparents had, she felt, been a massive breakthrough. Dave initially opposed to her suggestion and stubbornly certain she was overstating the communication problem he had with his daughter, for a while, it had been touch and go. Talking hard, insisting that no matter how much they tried to erase the demarcation lines between their two families, in reality, they were still operating as two separate units, only natural in her opinion, he had eventually come round. In then end, Dave agreeing that blending a family unit was not something either of them could or should force, that they had to find the individual time required to focus on their own children as and when needed, he had finally capitulated. Funny really, Dave older, she had always thought him to be the more experienced, the better equipped parent out of the two of them yet lately, she had begun to wonder? Perhaps, she thought wistfully, she wasn't quite so crap at the parenting game, after all?

A couple of loud raps on the door, a muffled shout of her name, and Gemma's thoughts were brought instantly back to the present. Jessica was waiting to get into the bathroom.

'Just a minute,' Gemma called out over the hiss of the water.

Hurrying to finish the last of her ablutions, Gemma rinsed the conditioner from her hair along with a plunging sense of dismay. Thinking hard on all the additional lies she had told to Dave, about her plans for the weekend, she turned off the shower and firmly reminded herself, needs must. After today, things could only get better, she promised herself.

Stepping out of the tub on to a wet bath mat, Gemma grabbed a damp towel from off the floor, gave her body a quick rub over, then donned a towelling bathrobe. Not enough dry towels, her hair would just have to drip.

She opened the door to Jessica.

'Morning, you looking forward to today?' she asked tentatively.

Her eyes shining, Jessica awarded Gemma with a shy smile, and a precious glimpse of the happy girl she used to be.

'Yeah, I can't wait to see my nana and grandpa. I haven't seen them in such a long time,' she rushed out excitedly.

You know, when it comes right down to it, Gemma thought, Jessica was just like any other teenage girl — awkward, troubled and raging with hormones, she simply wanted a good dose of love and reassurance.

'I bet the feelings mutual,' she replied kindly.

Pulling her bathrobe tighter around her waist, Gemma placed her damp towel over the heated ladder radiator.

'The bathroom's all yours, but you might want to get yourself a couple of fresh towels from the airing cupboard,' she suggested helpfully.

'Thanks, Gemma.'

Bunny ear slippers on her feet Her face unsullied with make-up and blushing like only a bashful child could, Jessica beamed at Gemma through a crop of teenage spots and braces. It took all Gemma's self-control not to sweep the girl into a tight embrace.

'You're welcome.'

Returning to the bedroom, Gemma's heart gave a light skip of pleasure. Wouldn't it be wonderful, she thought hopefully, if all that teenage angst and sulkiness was finally giving way to some sort of normality.

Standing in Paul's apartment block, Henry jiggling nervously by her side as he readied himself to be dropped off with his father for the weekend, Gemma took in a deep, steadying breath. Not at all looking forward to the upcoming conversation, she mentally prepared herself for what she needed to do, and say.

The glossy black door in front of them swinging open, Gemma steeled herself.

Ignoring the usual salutations, 'We need to talk,' she said.

Paul looking puzzled, along with something else, something indefinable that Gemma briefly caught before it flitted away again, he snapped to attention.

Gemma turned her attention to her son.

'Henry, your father and I need to have a little chat, so off you go,' she pressed him gently in the back. 'Go on, go to your room for a while. Have half-an-hour on your Xbox.'

Shamelessly using her son's tightly restricted computer game as her bargaining chip in front of Paul, Gemma gently pushed her son forward. The two of them having already spoken in the car on the way over, Henry needed no further encouragement as he hastily made his way up the corridor toward his bedroom, without a single backward look, comment or complaint.

'Well, aren't you going to invite me in?' she demanded to know.

Sighing before making a show of stepping back, Paul shrugged. Then he gestured her in.

'Whatever.'

Paul now looking for an explanation, he turned to Gemma. Then the sudden sound of a mobile phone ringing from somewhere deep within the flat, he was immediately distracted.

'Shouldn't you get that?' Gemma asked.

Paul seeming confused, then almost sheepish, Gemma watched with a speculative interest as her ex practically bolted away from her. Disappearing into a room up the corridor on the right, she watched him close the door behind him with a firm click. In hot pursuit, Gemma hastened up the corridor, twisted down the handle and pushed open the door. Standing on the threshold of what had to be Paul's bedroom, she found him looking down with disbelief at the screen of a ringing mobile. Drawing her own phone out of her coat pocket, Gemma depressed the big red button on the screen, cancelling the call she had just placed.

Correspondingly, the mobile incessantly ringing in Paul's hand, went dead.

'Very clever,' Paul shot out, his voice dark and heavy.

'Tell me,' Gemma asked, her expression unreadable, her voice calm and under control, 'why I should *not* go straight to the police?'

For a couple of seconds, Paul was unable to look Gemma in the eye. His cheeks colouring up, he stared at the floor.

'I'm waiting.'

'Because I'm your son's father,' Paul hissed back furiously, through gritted teeth.

Gemma snorted.

'Father you say? You actually believe you've been behaving like a responsible father?'

In the tense, almost ominous silence, Paul sent her a vicious look.

'Sending anonymous and malicious text messages to the mother of your child, it's pathetic. Why, Paul? Why would you do something like that? And to me, of all people?'

His mouth working, but nothing coming out, Paul took a couple of seconds as he visibly struggled with his words.

'Because *he's* a stranger. Because you invited *him* into my son's life, into my home. And yet not once,' Paul spat out, 'did you think to ask me what I thought about it all,' he growled pugnaciously.

Control. Always with Paul, it was about control, Gemma thought with a sad disappointment as any feelings of remorse she may have harboured toward their failed marriage, toward him, altogether dispersed.

'*Your* home, don't you mean *my* home?' she challenged.

'You know *exactly* what I mean,' said Paul, pompously referring to his share in the house.

She nodded, then sighed.

'Yes, unfortunately, I do. But when will *you* realise, you do *not* own Henry and you most certainly, do *not* own me? I do *not* need your *permission* to lead *my* life in whatever way I see fit. But then that was always your problem, wasn't it?'

'What was,' he demanded curtly?

Irritation and confusion temporarily replacing the anger on Paul's face, Gemma shook her head at him. Still, he did not get it. He never would get it.

'Your inability to see Henry and I as living, breathing, human beings with minds of our own.'

'You're talking rubbish.'

Blatantly having no interest in pursuing the topic, Paul gave a dismissive shake of his head.

'I'm telling you, Henry doesn't like him. He told me so.'

'Really? And what else has Henry told you?' Gemma asked pointedly.

Paul looked down, concentrated on his feet for a couple of seconds, then lifted his head again.

'For Christ's sake, Gemma, you're talking in riddles.'

'Am I?'

Gemma's implication clear, Paul had the grace to look embarrassed.

'You know what I can't believe,' she pressed on without mercy, 'is that you've been bullying our son into spying on me, on his own mother? How could you, Paul?'

There was a beat of awkward silence as Gemma watched the confusion, the anger, then a flicker of fear chase across Paul's pallid and guilty face.

'I would never bully Henry.'

'So that's why he was crying his eyes out when I took him home the other night, was it?'

'I was only trying to look out for you. To look out for our son.'

'No!' she hissed. 'You don't get to do that. You don't get to defend your actions. Because what you've done to me, what you've done to our poor innocent baby boy, is reprehensible.'

'But…' he stalled.

'Do you have any idea what you've done to him, how scared and anxious you've made him of you, of his own dad? You know what, no matter how you try and dress this up to yourself, you're a bully.'

For the first time since she had arrived, Paul looked genuinely concerned and upset. At last, she was getting somewhere.

'Scared?'

'Yes, he's so worried about making you angry when he can't answer all your idiotic questions, he's stopped wanting to see you. I really had to persuade him to come here today. And I'm not doing it again.'

The silence stretching, Gemma decided it was time to push home her point.

'Whatever this craziness is Paul, it has to stop and it has to stop now. It's insane of you to use our son in such an awful way. And it's insane of you to send me such vicious text messages. You hear me?'

He murmured something unintelligible.

'What did you say?'

'I said, OK.'

'Look, I know you love Henry. And that you would never normally do anything to hurt him. But if this behaviour doesn't stop, right now, I *will* go to the police,' she insisted threateningly. 'Then I will take you back to the custody court and I will make sure you never see your son, or me, ever again.'

CHAPTER TWENTY-THREE

By the time the train pulled out of the station, Carly was practically gagging to talk. Meeting up with Gemma no more than a few minutes ago, diving straight in to get their tickets then running to catch the train, they had barely had enough time to say hello and she had so much to say and ask.

Divesting herself of her outing clothing, Carly dropped into her seat on the opposite side of the table to Gemma. She sent her friend a beaming smile.

'So how are you?' she asked.

'Fine,' Gemma responded.

No return smile, Gemma noticeably distracted, Carly was instantly concerned.

'You sure?'

'I said, I'm fine,' Gemma snapped.

Gemma turning her head to look out of the window even though they were travelling through a pitch black tunnel, it was obvious she was preoccupied with something and that she did not want to talk about it. Not taking offence at Gemma's rudeness, Carly wondered if a change of subject would help to open her up.

'I didn't have a chance to check the departures board before we left, do you know how long the journey will take?' she asked.

Turning her head with a sudden and jerky movement as though she had been interrupted in mid-thought, Gemma blinked rapidly a couple of times. Then she pointed up to the air above Carly's head.

'According to that thing, it's going to take us an hour and twenty-one minutes.'

Twisting round in her seat, Carly tipped her gaze upwards and saw an LED board hanging from the ceiling of the train. Watching the display scroll through each of the stations the train would stop at in turn, she noted they would arrive at their destination right before one p.m. She turned back to face Gemma.

'Oops, sorry, I hadn't noticed the board.' She looked up and down the carriage. 'Not a particularly busy train, is it?'

Vacantly looking around, saying nothing, Gemma nodded her head in agreement.

Time to try again, Carly thought.

'Gem, you're miles away. You sure you're OK?'

Gemma ejected a heavy sigh.

'Sorry, I don't mean to be rude.'

Carly looked her inquiringly.

'Is it today? Is that what's worrying you?'

Gemma shook her head.

'No, no, it's got nothing to do with today.'

'OK, that's it, if you don't start telling me what's wrong, I'm gonna kick you under the table, until you do?'

For the first time since boarding the train, Gemma dispatched Carly a weak smile.

'Sorry.'

Carly's foot delivered Gemma a light tap on the ankle.

'Hey.'

'Tell me,' Carly demanded.

Gemma drew in a deep breath.

'I had to have a strong talk with Henry's father, this morning.' She sighed out again. 'And now I can't stop thinking about it.'

'I'm listening,' Carly prompted.

Gemma ran her eyes over Carly's face as though deliberating the wisdom of telling her something.

'Let's just say, I've found out who's been sending me those God awful text messages.'

Carly started.

'What? Really? Hang on a minute, you're not going to tell me it was Paul, are you?'

Gemma slowly moved her head up and down.

Stunned by Gemma's unexpected revelation, for a couple of seconds, Carly was lost for words.

'Paul?'

'Yep.'

'You can't be serious, Gem?'

'Well, I am. But that's not the worst of it… He's also been asking Henry to spy on me. Go figure?'

'Dear God, I can't believe it. You must be livid?'

Gemma laughed, but just a little.

'I was to start with, but now I'm just relieved it's all over.'

Carly frowned.

'Hang on a sec, how on earth did you work out it was Paul?'

'When I collected Henry from Paul's the other night, he had a meltdown in the car. Told me his dad has been asking him loads and loads of questions about me and my personal life. And on hearing that, I started to put two and two together.'

Gemma's tone was brisk and ordinary.

'Still... Paul?'

'He's always been the jealous type. And he's a control freak. Quite scary when he gets going.'

Shocked all over again, Carly's eyes widened with incredulity.

'But you never said?'

'Yeah, I know. But believe me, he's always had major trust issues.'

Puzzled, Carly shook her head.

'Sorry?'

'Paul always *has* to be the one in charge. The one slap bang in the middle of everything, controlling everything. Thinks it will all go wrong if he isn't. And by everything, I especially mean me.'

Carly shivered a little.

'I had no idea.'

'No one did. I didn't until after we married.'

'So he wasn't like that before you married him?'

'No, came as quite a surprise, I can tell you.'

'Must have done.'

'You know, I always thought, with time and reassurance he would change, that he would learn to trust me. I hoped, I suppose, he would grow out of his fear that I would one day leave him.' She shook her head. 'But he never did. Once we married, I couldn't move without him checking up on me — on where I'd been, on who I had been with. It was embarrassing and suffocating. And it got to the point where I couldn't live like that anymore, I just couldn't. Ironic really, cos in the end, I proved him right, didn't I?' She gave a wry smile.

Upset for Gemma, realising how lonely she must have felt in her marriage, Carly reached across the table and gently squeezed her hand. She had to ask.

'He never physically hurt you though, did he?'

Gemma thought. She shrugged.

'He grabbed me a few times, though more out of frustration than anything else, I think. But he's never actually hit me in anger, if that's what you mean?'

'Christ, Gem.'

'Yeah, so now you know the real reason I left him. Well, that and the fact I was bored out of my brains, of course.' She smiled weakly.

Gemma reminding Carly of her thoughtless comment the night of the dinner, she felt a terrible prick of conscience.

'I'm so sorry, Gem. I wish I'd known.'

Gemma shrugged her shoulders.

'Nothing you could have done. Nothing anyone could have done. It was my marriage.'

Gemma sinking into silence, Carly let her be for a couple of minutes. Then she ventured to put a question.

'Going back to the text messages, how did you trace them to Paul? Weren't they being sent from a withheld number?'

Gemma flashed Carly a brief smile.

'Oh, in the end, it was easy. I went on to the internet, bought an identification service that allows you to reveal restricted numbers. Then when I dropped Henry off at Paul's this morning, I rang the number of phone that's been sending the text messages, and hey presto.'

'Crikey, I never realised you were quite so smart.'

'I can be when I need to be.'

'So how did Paul take it?'

Gemma shrugged her shoulders.

'Pretty much as I'd expected. He's upset about what he's done to Henry, knows he has some making up to do. But he's also furious at being found out. You know what, I don't think he's in the least bit bothered about all the stress and anguish he's caused for Dave and myself?'

'So how did you leave it with him?'

'I threatened him with the police… and the custody court.'

'Christ!'

'Yep, he won't be pulling a stunt like that again.'

'Smart and tough,' said Carly, with a renewed respect.

For the first time since meeting up at St Pancras station, Gemma gave Carly a hearty smile.

'You'd better believe it, sister.'

'Does Dave know?'

Gemma nodded her head.

'Yeah, I told him of my suspicions, last night. But only after I had made him promise, he would let me deal with Paul.'

'And he was OK with that?'

'Are you kidding me? Of course he wasn't. He was so mad, he wanted to go straight to the police. But how would that help Henry?'

Carly nodded. She could not agree more. Little Henry having to deal with a father in trouble with police, it did not bear thinking about.

'Well, as least that's one mystery solved,' said Carly with feeling.

'Yeah.'

'Talking of Dave, that reminds me, what have you done with him and Jessica today?'

'They're visiting her mother's grave. Then they're going up to Nottingham to spend the rest of the weekend with Sarah's parents.'

Carly threw her head back in surprise.

'Wow, how did you manage that one?'

Gemma flashed Carly a tight smile.

'Amazing what you can achieve when the pressure's on. After another *chat*, shall we say, Dave eventually rang them yesterday evening and fortunately for me, they were tickled pink at the thought of spending some time with their granddaughter.'

'Good, I'm pleased for Jessica. I bet Dave's a bit nervous though?'

'Yeah, he is a bit. But Jessica hasn't seen her grandparents in such a long time and she told me this morning, she's really looking forward to it.'

Watching Gemma happily smiling to herself as she visibly reflected on her conversation with Jessica that morning, Carly felt relieved and pleased for them both. At last, things appeared to be moving in the right direction.

'Sounds great. Also sounds like Dave and Jessica are going to get some of that father-daughter bonding time, you were so keen on the pair of them having?'

'That's certainly what I'm hoping for.'

'And what about you? What did you tell Dave you were doing today?'

'I told him I was going to do some shopping, attend your last yoga class of the day, then stay overnight with you.'

'Christ, and he believed you? Cos you're bloody awful at yoga.' Carly said, lightly laughing at Gemma's instant look of pained indignation.

'Yes, he did, but as you already know, I'm not exactly happy about telling him even more lies,' Gemma scolded. 'It doesn't sit well.'

'Sorry,' said Carly, feeling duly chastened. 'I'm an idiot.'

Now was her chance, Carly thought as she spotted the opportunity she had been waiting for since boarding the train.

'Talking of telling a few white lies…' Carly launched in, the need to unburden herself too overwhelming to ignore. 'There *is* something else I need to talk to you about. Um…' she broke off, all of a sudden unable to go on. Carly's insides weakening, it seemed now she had opened up the conversation to where she had so badly wanted it to go, she no longer knew what to say or how to say it. Noticing the confusion and concern flitting across Gemma's face, Carly felt a sudden prick of tears and she had to look away for a minute.

The city of London, the urban stations of Stratford International and Ebbsfleet International already far behind them, for a couple of precious moments, Carly immersed herself in watching the pastoral scene whizzing past outside the window. Observing an azure sky ribboned with white clouds, brilliant sunshine bathing everything in its glory, verdant green fields with grazing sheep and the occasional picture book farmhouse, whipping past, it was as though she was stepping out of black and white, and into colour. The train swiftly sliding her into a different place and time, Carly tried to kid herself that what she had to say, could wait until later. But Gemma had other ideas.

'Carly, what lies?' Gemma demanded to know as she ruthlessly broke into Carly's make-believe world.

Carly took a deep breath. It was now or never.

'Please, don't be angry with me Gem but that night at dinner, I wasn't wholly honest with you…' Once again, the words failed her.

Gemma nodded.

'Go on,' she prompted.

Wishing she had some water, Carly cleared her parched throat.

'Steve and I, we've known each other much longer than you think,' she admitted in a rush.

Saying nothing, Gemma shifted in her seat. She cast Carly an intent look.

Carly blinked back the tears again, but now she had started the words she had been waiting to say for so long, suddenly exploded from her mouth. 'We've been together for almost a year. And yes, before you ask, he was still married when we first met but I assure you, it was in name only. And I'm so sorry. I hate that I've been lying to you and Dave, all this time.'

Gemma seemingly needing to digest what she had been told, she turned her uncompromising gaze from Carly, to the train window again.

Fingers gripping on to the table that separated them, nervously awaiting her friend's response to her inarticulate confession, Carly anxiously wondered how Gemma was feeling? Was she angry, sad, disappointed or all three of them? Gemma's face inscrutable, it was hard to tell. A fly buzzed between them, smacked itself hard against the window a couple of times, fell on to the table and legs in the air, spun crazily round on its back. Then it died.

A couple of minutes later, Gemma returned her attention to Carly. Gemma looking straight at her as though she were considering her for a moment, Carly braced herself for the angry disappointment, she was sure would come.

'So why *didn't* you tell me? And please Carly, be honest with me as I don't think I could take any more lies,' said Gemma, sounding surprisingly calm, with no hint of disapproval.

Keen to give Gemma the honest answer she had asked for, but also desperate for her not to think ill of Steve, Carly was circumspect.

'Because I felt so guilty about him still being married, albeit in name only,' she reinforced.

Gemma's return smile was tightly controlled.

'So tell me how you really met him?'

'On the Underground, like I said that night at dinner. We used to get on the same train and one day, we simply got talking.'

Gemma raised an eyebrow.

'And the marriage thing?'

Carly gulped.

'For the first few weeks or so, I had no idea Steve was married. He never wore a wedding ring. He was readily contactable and he was always available. Then a couple of months in, there was this one weekend where I could not get a hold of him and obviously, I wanted to know why?' Carly sighed at the difficult memory. 'And that was when he told me he was married, and that he had a son.'

'So you were tricked into having an affair with him?' Gemma asked sharply.

Carly shook her head vigorously. Somehow, Gemma had got hold of completely the wrong end of the stick. She needed to set the record straight, and fast.

'No, no, that's a bit harsh, what do you take him for? Of course he didn't trick me. As I said to you that night of the dinner, he and his wife hadn't been getting on for some time, years in fact. And when I first met him, he was already in the process of leaving her.'

Gemma slowly shook her head.

'Carly, no matter what you say, you've been conned.'

Carly bit back her anger.

'No, I haven't,' she insisted.

'Really? He was a married man when you first met him. He had a wife and son at home and yet for some weeks, he didn't see fit to tell you that fact? And let me guess, he didn't say anything until after you had started sleeping with him?'

Carly squirmed in her seat. All of a sudden, she felt incredibly naive and gullible.

'Can't you see,' Gemma added, 'if he cared about you, if not his wife, he would have told you he was married *before* he asked you to go out with him? And definitely before he asked you to sleep with him.'

Even though Carly hated hearing what Gemma had to say, she was having a hard time disagreeing with her. Yet still she defended Steve.

'Come on, Gem, he's not a monster.'

Gemma gave Carly a hard stare.

'If you had known he was married, right from the start, would you have gone anywhere near him?'

Carly slowly shook her head.

'No.'

'Exactly,' Gemma pointed out ruthlessly.

Feeling horribly uncomfortable with what Gemma was forcing her to face. Needing time for the words to sink in, Carly flicked a miserable look her friend's way.

'I don't know what to say?' she admitted reluctantly.

'Well, I do. His behaviour toward you, toward his family, pretty unscrupulous, don't you think?' Gemma persisted.

On the defence all over again, Carly bristled.

'I'm not sure I would describe it quite like that.'

'Okay, so how would you describe it?' Gemma asked, eerily calm.

Wanting to disappear into herself, hardly able to bear what she was hearing, yet not really able to argue with Gemma's quiet but firm take on Steve's approach to the start of their relationship, Carly tried not to feel like she was being flayed alive. And the look on Gemma's face, Carly had the distinct feeling her friend was not yet done.

'So at the time of his wife's suicide, you two were already a couple?' Gemma dropped almost casually, into the silence.

Carly sucked in a sharp intake of breath. Instantly catching on to what Gemma was inferring but not saying, she was suddenly so ashamed and embarrassed, she did not know where to look. She took a moment.

'Yes, but she didn't kill herself because of us, Gem,' said Carly, red in the face. 'She had no idea I was on the scene. None of the family did, or do,' she tried to justify.

Gemma nodded.

'Odd,' she mused. 'If Steve was so intent on leaving his wife long before you came along, then why all the secrecy?' she asked, her tone conversational.

Without success, Carly willed the blood not to rise up her face again.

'Because of Brian,' she said simply.

'Meaning?'

Carly traced an invisible pattern on the table top, flicked the dead fly away. Intensely unhappy with herself and her choices, she was starting to think she should have kept her big mouth shut. Steve insisting their relationship was their business and their business alone, he had warned her not to be so honest and now, she was wishing she had listened to him.

'Steve never wanted Brian to think he was leaving his mother, for another woman. He also said, if Helen ever got wind of me being around, she would be mean and spiteful about it. He said she would use his relationship with me, to poison Brian against him and I couldn't let that happen, could I?' Trying not to sound as though she was pleading but unable to help herself, Carly inwardly cringed. She so wanted Gemma to understand, to not think so badly of Steve and herself.

Gemma studied Carly for a moment.

'OK, so help me out here. On the one hand you say Steve was always going to leave his wife and yet on the other, you say he could never leave her because of his son?' Gemma paraphrased back to Carly. 'Have I got that right?'

Having all her random errors of judgement unambiguously laid out before her. Gemma making it impossible for her to escape from realising what she had become, a cliché, Carly felt an unwelcome surge of bitter anger rise toward Steve.

'Carly?' Gemma prompted.

She shrugged miserably.

'Honestly, I don't know any more? We talked about him leaving his wife so many times… But right from the beginning, there was always something going on with Brian that would get in way. You know how it is, Gem. Like Jessica, Brian's at a difficult age.'

Aware she was effectively grabbing at straws and ashamed of herself, Carly hated that she had become a mistress, another woman's nightmare.

Saying nothing, Gemma simply lifted a well arched eyebrow.

Carly felt a hard lump at the back of her throat as her eyes watered all over again.

'Then his wife died,' she gabbled on, 'and we felt we had no choice. We felt we had to wait until after everything had settled down again. Give it time for the dust to settle before we talked to Brian, to our families. You know how it is, Gem.'

Gemma moved her head up and down very slowly, a careful, deliberate nod.

Not for one minute was Carly fooled. There was no way Gemma believed she had no choice in the matter. It was written all over her face.

The train slid to a gentle halt at Ashford International station. Both of them lost to their own thoughts for a couple of minutes, neither woman noticed as the seats around them quickly vacated, then sparsely filled again.

'So to summarise, your relationship with Steve started on a lie and has continued on a lie. You…'

Carly cut Gemma off.

'Please, Gem, where are you going with this?' she pleaded bitterly.

Gemma let out a deep, long, sigh, one that seemed to express tenderness and pity.

'Relax, Carly. I'm not angry with you for lying to me. After everything I have done of late, it would only be hypocritical. All I want to do…' She paused, sighed again as she looked for the words. 'Is to help you to see the facts of your relationship with Steve, from a different point of view.'

Carly about to argue, Gemma interrupted.

'Carly, you are like a sister to me. Just let me speak, eh?'

Feeling like an insect pinned under a microscope, Carly briefly closed her eyes against the excruciating, piercing pain of it all.

'Please,' she murmured, 'be kind.'

Reaching out, Gemma gently touched Carly's lightly trembling hand across the table.

'You know, I wish I could, but I'm not sure that's possible.'

Pausing for a moment, Gemma took a deep breath. Carly held the silence.

'Right, here goes. I think, Steve knowingly tricked you into having an affair with him. A man with scruples, would have told you the truth about his marital situation right away, so you could have taken an informed decision before you dived right in. But he didn't give you that choice, or at least not until you were already up to your neck in it. An honest and responsible man, would also never ask you to keep your relationship a secret from all those who love and care about you.' Gemma shook her head at Carly. 'No, he would want to celebrate his relationship with you, not hide it away like some dirty secret. And as for his relationship with his wife, regardless of any marital problems they might have had, a principled man, would never cheat. He would either fix his marriage, or leave. And although he's told you on numerous occasions he could not leave his wife because there's a *troubled* teenager in the mix, if he truly cares about you, he would have found a way. Don't you think?'

A couple of tears squeezed themselves from Carly's glittering green eyes. She hated Gemma's point of view.

'But it's not like he hasn't met any of my family. He's met you and Dave. And he fully intends to tell his son about us soon, really soon. And once that conversation's been had, well…'

'You think? After all this time, you really think he'll get around to telling his son all about you?'

Carly bit her bottom lip. Confused, instinctively agreeing with Gemma yet still unable to shake off her feelings of disloyalty toward Steve regardless of how angry she was with him, she had no idea what to say next.

'I know you think because he's met us, he'll get around to telling Brian and his family all about you but I guarantee you, there'll always be another teenage crisis for him to hang his excuses off of. I think, meeting us, was probably more to scratch an itch or to keep you happy whilst he works out what to do with you next.'

There was a beat of silence.

'You think he's going to dump me, don't you?' said Carly miserably

'Look, I probably shouldn't have said that. Not my place,' Gemma apologised.

The way she and Steve had been fighting recently, Gemma probably had a point, Carly thought. God she had been such a fool.

'I've seriously messed up again, haven't I?'

Gemma smiled gently back at Carly.

'Yeah, well, you're not exactly on your own there. I've not exactly been getting a lot right lately, either.'

'What do you think I should do, Gem?'

A further beat of silence.

'That's not a question I can answer,' replied Gemma in that calm placid way of hers. 'Only you know how you feel about Steve but after this weekend...' she hesitated, 'I'm going to have to come clean with Dave. I really need to be honest with him about everything that's been going on, Carly. And that, I'm afraid, includes me having to tell him about you and Steve.'

Worriedly thinking of Dave, of how disappointed he was going to be in her, Carly chewed her bottom lip again. She made it quite sore.

'Carly, I'm seriously worried I might lose him, if I don't,' Gemma added, her soft brown eyes asking for understanding.

'I know, I know. It's OK. I get it. Really I do. It's all my fault you're in this mess in the first place, I got you into it. And I don't want you losing Dave because of me and all my crap. Let me know when you've spoken to him and I'll come round, talk to him myself.'

'Thanks, I... we, would appreciate that,' Gemma whispered, her eyes glittering wetly in the bright sunlight streaming through the carriage window.

'You watch, it'll all be OK between you two,' said Carly, resolved to making it so.

Both women tormented by their guilt and shame, what little remained of the journey, passed in total silence.

CHAPTER TWENTY-FOUR

The roads and streets of Deal pleasingly wide and self-confident, the town's jewel in the crown had to be a yawning horizon that looked straight out across the English Channel to what had to be, Calais in France, thought Gemma. White horses breaking on the distant Goodwin Sands, a spectacular vista, it would have been so easy to rest a while and soak up the ambiance. But the address they were looking for — according to *Google maps* — still a good twenty minute hike away, she was keen to push on. Tired of living with all the uncertainty, the constant worry and anxiety, she wanted the next bit of their journey over and done with as soon as possible.

'We can stop later. Perhaps, even have something to eat and drink before we head back to London. You agree?' she asked Carly.

Still feeling dejected from everything said on the train, Carly really could not care less and Gemma's suggestion put to her in such a way that brooked little argument, she had very little choice anyway.

'Sure,' she agreed readily.

The sun shining down on them as they walked, becoming warm, Carly unzipped her coat and breathed in the not unpleasant smell of the sea. Gulls circling overhead, emitting their melancholic cries, the delightful seaside town had a very different vibe to the narrow and harried streets of London. Thinking on how privileged it must feel to live by the coast, she had a sudden and unwelcome spurt of envy. Lucky for some, she thought resentfully.

Some time later, the two women arriving alongside a long, broad, boulevard that ran parallel to the seafront promenade on which they had been walking, they stopped to check their progress. *Google* showing them they had meandered from Deal into Walmer — the two towns seamlessly merging into each other — and that they were within a few metres of their final destination, feeling very exposed all of a sudden, Carly did up her coat and anxiously pulled up the hood in order to hide her telltale red-hair.

Gemma walking on a little further, locating the actual house and pointing it out to her, Carly's earlier need to disguise herself abruptly disappeared as she clocked the imposing Georgian villa. Unable to believe what she was seeing, her mouth dropped open. Surely, they had to have the wrong address, didn't they?

The ginormous detached house having unrestricted views across the English Channel, and sporting a gravelled driveway big enough for at least three or four cars, it had sage green masonry, a decorative wrought-iron balcony running the full width the upper storey, brilliant white plantation shutters on the outside of every window and a grey, slate, mansard roof. The grand property having an almost French feel about it, Carly struggled to take it all in.

'Wow, now that is what I call, some place,' Gemma remarked, giving a low whistle of appreciation as she eyed the place acquisitively.

Wow indeed, thought Carly, her mouth still hanging open with astonishment.

'Are you sure you've got the right address?' she whispered.

'Of course I am. How come you never told me how rich Steve is?'

'Uh, because I never knew.'

'You never knew?'

Carly slowly shook her head.

'Nope.'

Although she and Steve had never talked about their respective finances, from the way his London flat was so expensively decorated, its rather prestigious location, she had often wondered as to his wealth but had never presumed to ask. Yet this, she thought as she continued to marvel at the house in front of her, this was on a whole other level entirely.

'Don't forget, it isn't owned by Steve, it belongs to his in-laws,' Carly reminded Gemma.

'Yeah, well, looks as though someone's in,' said Gemma, her finger pointing to the smoke curling up from the multiple chimney stacks. 'You ready?'

A balloon of fear swelling inside of her, nowhere near ready, she's got to be joking, Carly thought. She swallowed down the rising bile.

'Gem, what if we're wrong?' she whispered hoarsely. 'What if the stalker has *nothing* to do with Brian?'

'Carly, we've been through this already,' Gemma confronted impatiently as she crunched her way up the gravel driveway. 'Come on, we're here now. Let's get this over with.'

Panicking, her stomach somersaulting over and over like an overexcited gymnast, Carly was starting to feel physically sick.

'Carly, come on, get a wriggle on,' Gemma instructed over her shoulder as she headed for the front door.

After another heart-flipping moment of hesitation, a white-faced Carly squared her shoulders and willed herself to move forward as she put one reluctant foot in front of the other. Gem's right, she encouraged herself, they had not come all this way for nothing.

Gemma depressing the front door bell, Carly found herself suddenly dragged forward.

'Over to you,' she was told as Gemma abruptly stepping behind her, she was left facing the formidable front door, all on her own.

The front door opened by a *young* woman with soulful dark eyes, a heart-shaped face and long brown hair that almost reached her waist, expecting someone older, a lot, lot, older, Carly assumed all over again, they had to have the wrong house. Trust Gem, she thought with relief.

'Can I help you?' the young woman asked.

The woman well spoken with a voice like velvet, Carly found herself uncomfortably on the end of a speculative look. Ill-prepared, she searched for what to say.

'Oh, I'm so s-sorry to trouble you,' she stammered. 'We're looking for someone, but I think we might have the wrong address?'

The woman's curious gaze flicking from Carly to Gemma, then back again, she gave a light incongruous chuckle.

'Right. So who *are* you looking for?'

God, this was awkward, awful, Carly thought, feeling the colour drain from her face as she found herself suddenly wanting to vomit. She should not be here. She should not be anywhere near here. No possible good could come of it.

'S-Steve, Steve Quinnell?' Carly just about managed to get out.

'Okay?'

The woman coolly appraised Carly for a moment.

'You've gone quite pale. Are you feeling OK? Do you need to sit down for a moment?'

Flinching from the woman's overtly chilly gaze, for a second or two, Carly lost all her ability to speak. The woman finely dressed from head to toe in chic and expensive clothes, her glamour confidently understated, she was so very unexpected. More importantly, Carly thought almost tearfully, it was obvious she knew Steve.

Picking up on Carly's visible distress, Gemma hurriedly stepped out of her stricken friend's shadow and swiftly intervened.

'If it would be no trouble, perhaps a glass of water?'

Grateful that Gemma had taken charge, no longer able to stand the woman's unflinching gaze, Carly awkwardly hung her head.

Hesitating, albeit for a fraction of a second, the woman slowly pulled the front door wide open.

'By all means. Do come on in,' she said, stepping slowly backwards.

Though the words were inviting, the woman's manner cold and almost imperious, she was not in the least bit welcoming, Carly thought as she looked to Gemma for guidance.

Gemma nodding, she placed a hand into the small of Carly's back then give her friend a good firm shove from behind.

Carly thrust forward, almost tripping over her own feet as she stumbled across the threshold and loudly knocking the heavy front door hard against the doorstop behind it, everyone instantly stopped, mid-stride. Gemma sighing with impatience, the woman looking back to see what had caused all the commotion, embarrassed by her clumsiness, Carly felt such a klutz.

'Sorry,' she called out with a forced cheerfulness.

The adrenaline of the last couple of hours long since dissipated, leaving her feeling drained and dazed as she moved deeper and deeper into the intimidating foyer of the house, Carly had to take a number of intense breaths. Her impression of her surroundings merely fleeting — black and white chequerboard tiles on the floor, lots of cold blue on the walls — fighting off a spell of dizziness, she nervously continued to follow in the now beckoning woman's footsteps.

In spite of her own nerves, Gemma purposely nudged and manoeuvred Carly forward. Now they were here, in Steve's surprisingly opulent weekend domain, she was even more determined to finish what they had started. Curiously taking in her surroundings as they moved through a hallway that was possibly as big as the total footprint of her own house, Gemma observed a soothing and tasteful decorating scheme of cool blues, thick creams and crisp whites. An ornate floor to ceiling gilded mirror hanging on the end wall, highlighting dust motes as it caught an occasional shaft of sunlight, she picked up the pleasing smells of beeswax and lavender. A soaring ceiling embellished with plaster mouldings, and festooned with two, high-wattage, balloon shaped crystal chandeliers. A wide and sweeping mahogany staircase curling up from the centre of the gargantuan hallway, antique furniture adorned the edges of the walls. The space and house unmistakably grand, everything about it screamed, thought Gemma, *Do Not Touch!*

'Please, go on in. Take a seat,' the woman instructed on opening an oak panelled door. 'I'll fetch you something to drink.'

Gemma dragged a reluctant Carly over to one of two gold tapestried sofas in the middle of the formal drawing-room, as soon as the door closed behind the woman with a soft whispering sigh and then a click. Her chosen sofa positioned directly facing a lit fire that provided a drop of much needed warmth in an otherwise sophisticated but coolly decorated room, Carly did not argue.

'Christ Carly, you've gone quite green,' said Gemma her face creased with concern and worry as she urgently pressed Carly down on to one of the plushly cushioned seats.

Gulping, unable to speak, Carly opened and closed her mouth like a dying fish.

'Carly?'

Cradling her roiling stomach, Carly felt a fine film of sweat break out along her upper lip.

'Christ, Gem, I think I'm gonna be sick.'

'Sick?'

Nodding her head with an exaggerated slowness, Carly tried to get a grip on her turbulent stomach. There was no way she could vomit, not here, not on the floor of this strange woman's mansion.

'Right,' Gemma said, swinging into action as she pushed Carly's head down toward her knees. 'Take a couple of deep breaths. That's it, come on, in, out, in, out.'

Her head hanging between her knees, knowing she had to keep it there until the bright spots stopped dancing in front of her eyes, as instructed, Carly opened her mouth and breathed deep for a few seconds.

'Better?' Gemma asked.

Lifting her head from between her knees, still feeling miserably weak, Carly gave Gemma a tiny nod.

'I think so. Christ, Gem, what the hell is wrong with me?' she asked, a choke of emotion constricting throat.

Gemma surveyed Carly's red and sweaty face, then nodded to herself as though satisfied.

'You're in shock, I think. But at least you're no longer green.'

'Shock?'

Gemma sat next to Carly.

'Yes, I was expecting to be greeted by Steve or one of his in-laws, not that young woman. And I think you were too.'

'Yeah,' Carly agreed. 'I think I was. So who is she, Gem? And why is she being so nice to us? For all she knows, we could be her friendly neighbourhood axe murderers,' she gabbled out.

'I have no idea. But I have every intention of finding out.'

'Can't we just leave?'

'No.'

'Gem, I really think we should leave,' Carly tried to insist.

'Absolutely not, we haven't come all this way for nothing. Look, you stay put. I'm gonna have a quick poke around before she gets back.'

Carly groaning out her disappointment, Gemma ignored her as she keenly flicked her eyes around the sumptuously decorated Wedgwood blue room. Searching for clues amongst the sea-green floor-to-ceiling silk curtains, the dark, oak floorboards covered in strategically placed silk rugs that effectively zoned the room, the Louis XIV style furniture, the antiques dotted around the room and against the perimeter walls, for anything really that would help them understand who they were dealing with, Gemma's inquisitive eyes eventually alighted on a sideboard located at the back of the room. Discovering a number of silver framed photographs spread out across the top of the highly polished piece, taking her courage in her hands, Gemma was up and off the sofa in a flash but before she could get anywhere near close enough, there was the unwelcome sound of lightly tapping footsteps travelling across a tiled floor. The footfall only getting louder and louder, coming closer, Gemma had no choice but to beat a rapid retreat. She did not want to have to explain herself.

Retracing her steps, taking up the empty seat next to Carly on the sofa right before the door began to swing inwards, feeling absurdly guilty, Gemma folded her sweating hands neatly in her lap, then feigned an air of innocence.

The woman setting a silver salver with two full glasses down on to the coffee table in front of them, without a word, she turned her back and retreated from them. Stood to one end of the crackling fireplace, she rested her forearm on the marble mantle shelf and leant easily against it.

'Please,' she said, signalling for them to help themselves. 'It's homemade lemonade. Very sweet, so it should do the trick.'

Doing as instructed, Gemma and Carly each picked up a glass, then dutifully took some sample sips of a drink that was indeed so sweet, they could almost feel their teeth loosening in their sockets. Each of them slowly drinking their difficult drinks, neither of them quite sure what to say, the silence lengthened.

'Thank you, you're very kind,' said Gemma, stretching her mouth into a wide smile.

'Am I?' The woman shrugged.

Taken aback by the woman's odd comment, her strange tone, Gemma looked at her curiously. The woman's return gaze openly hostile, Gemma was unsettled even further. For a few dragged out seconds, Gemma and the woman circling each other like a couple of recently introduced dogs, they eyed each other apprehensively. In the end, it was Gemma who broke the silence.

'Sorry, we forgot to introduce ourselves,' she said as confidently as she could. 'I'm Gemma, Gemma Atkinson and this is my friend Carly, Carly Rogers.'

The woman's gaze steady and unflinching as she poked a stray lock of long brown hair behind her ear, she nodded in acknowledgement. Yet still, she offered no clarification as to who she was.

'And you are?' asked Gemma, determined not to be beaten.

Served with a look of disdain, Gemma held fast to her growing impatience, her trepidation, as she waited for the woman's slow and grudging answer.

'Helen.'

Stunned to hear *that* name, Gemma felt an awful trickle of anxiety. For Carly's sake, she had to be certain.

'Helen?'

The woman eyed Gemma coldly.

'Yes.'

'Helen, who?'

'Helen Quinnell.'

Both of them swearing in unison, next to Gemma, Carly gasped. The crystal water glass in Carly's hand dropping to the floor with a thud, Gemma started with surprise. Sticky lemonade spraying everywhere before soaking into the silk rug, she immediately felt sick with embarrassment for her visibly distraught friend. Carly close to collapse, desperately wanting to help her friend but in shock herself, Gemma had absolutely no idea on how to do so.

A huge dark stain appearing in the rug, thin rivulets of lemonade running down her jeans, for a couple of terrible seconds, Carly could feel the woman's eyes boring right into her, judging her. Humiliated and horror stricken by what she had done, by what the woman had said, she clapped a hand to her mouth.

Sighing heavily, her lips pressed tight together as her unblemished brows knitted, the woman pushed herself off the fireplace, strode over to the rug and looked down on the spreading mess.

'I suppose I had better see to that,' she said.

Helen's words relayed to no one in particular, she approached the drawing-room door.

'Oh, and by the way, that rug is silk. So, please, don't even attempt to deal with it yourselves,' she commanded over her shoulder before she left the room.

'My God, did you hear her? Did you hear what she said?' Carly moaned out miserably to Gemma as soon as the door had closed.

Gemma nodded.

'What the hell is happening here, Gem, I don't understand?'

Disregarding Carly for a moment, grasping her opportunity, Gemma shot up off the sofa and sprinted across the vast room. At the sideboard, a faint frown on her forehead, her eyes swiftly scanned each of the silver photo frames, in turn. A number of them of Steve with the woman, their mouths smiling reservedly into the camera, his long arm loosely draped over her slim shoulder or around her ultra-slim waist, it was obvious they were a couple. It was also clear their host, was exactly who she had said she was... she *was* Helen, Helen Quinnell. And that could only mean, Gemma realised with a fresh stab of foreboding, they were not in Steve's in-law's house but in his marital home, and the woman who had introduced herself to them as Helen Quinnell was indeed, his *dead* wife.

Knowing what she now knew, anxiety trickled from Gemma's breastbone to her belly. She squeezed it away. She needed to concentrate, to keep looking.

In the remaining photographs, the couple were joined by a dark eyed and dark-haired boy at different stages of his development. Staring down at a more recent photo taken of a fourteen or fifteen year old Brian, the resemblance to his mother extremely strong, studying the medium height, medium build, boy-man smiling politely back at her, for a moment, Gemma had to wonder, if she had truly found Carly's stalker?

Steve's wife's footsteps again travelling along the tiled hallway, for a split second, Gemma froze. Then gathering her wits, she flew swiftly to the sofa and landed next to Carly. With insufficient time to update a still visibly shocked and horrified Carly, for now, Gemma had no choice but to hold on to her findings.

Spraying some sort of cleaning solution on to the wet patch, Helen dropped a fluffy white towel on to the rug, trod it in then twisted her foot a couple of times as without mercy, she ground the cloth in.

'There, that should do it for now,' she said.

Helen's air haughty and superior, she looked pointedly over at Carly for a couple of seconds before needlessly, and cruelly saying, 'You know, this rug has been in my family for over two generations. I'll have to get a specialist cleaner in to fix the stain.'

'I'm so sorry,' Carly blurted out.

So ashamed, blushing to the tips of her ears as she readily apologised, Carly's face was an embarrassed, deep cherry red. Gemma's face, meanwhile, was as pale as skimmed milk. Helen looking from one to the other of them, like a teacher surveying her errant pupils, there was nothing kindly in her examination.

'Don't worry about it,' said Helen, her voice dry and insincere.

A lengthening silence.

'Now, where were we? Oh yes, I remember, we were introducing ourselves. But if I remember rightly, weren't you looking for my husband?'

Helen disseminating a tight little smile, one that did not reach her cold eyes, her speculative gaze immediately locked onto Carly.

Carly feeling sick to the stomach again as she discernibly avoided the woman's cold and penetrating stare, she concentrated on her hands, watched the way her white fingers knotted and unknotted.

'So, *Ms* Rogers, how do you know my husband?' Helen asked casually.

Fighting her nerves, uncertain and feeling incredibly guilty all over again, there was no way Carly could answer Helen's question, or even lift her head as she continued to focus on her hands.

Helen swung her head toward Gemma.

'Your friend seems a little indisposed. Perhaps, you could answer for her?'

Guardedly on her toes, whilst completely unnerved by the direction the conversation was suddenly going, all Gemma could do, was slap a smile to her face as she too, struggled to find her words.

An awkward, condemning silence.

In the end, it was Helen who filled the gap.

'Well, if you were looking for Steve, you're out of luck,' said Helen, looking at Carly with a long and thoughtful gaze. 'He's out with our son and they won't be back until,' she paused, glanced down at a dainty gold watch sitting above her wrist, 'after seven, this evening.'

Helen's eyes betraying nothing, yet saying everything, she stared impassively at each of them in turn.

Right, stalker or no stalker, we're getting the hell out of here, Gemma decided as every bone in her body, tingled with panic. She found her voice.

'Okay, well thanks for the lemonade. We'll leave you in peace.'

'Really?' said Helen, sounding surprised as she took up a seat in an armchair adjacent to the fireplace, made herself comfortable. 'But you haven't yet told me, why it is, you want to see my husband?'

The woman's eyes again resting thoughtfully on Carly, the constant prickle of unease gnawing away at her stomach began to spread and grow as the anxiety in her throat rose like a sickness.

'And there I was, thinking we were only just getting started,' the woman added calmly, ominously.

Carly's head swam.

Patches of sweat bloomed under Gemma's arms.

The woman looked past both of them as she glanced toward the window for a moment. Then with a small flick of her head, her gaze moving disdainfully from one to the other, she looked right at them.

'Come on you two. I think we've had enough of the fun and games. Why don't you tell me what you're really here for?'

The blood in Carly's veins freezing as the nausea rose, she swivelled her pained eyes toward Gemma, silently pleaded with her to say something because she could not.

Gemma, her mouth gaping open with astonishment, her eyes out on stalks and also at a loss for words, she could do nothing more than slowly shake her head at Carly.

The silence had become menacing.

'You know, I've been expecting you for weeks now,' Helen said almost conversationally to Carly. 'In fact, I would go so far as to say, you are marginally overdue.'

Having to acknowledge Helen already knew of her, Carly's face suffused to a hot red all over again. She sucked in a breath as her toes curled up with embarrassment.

'What did you say?' Gemma forced herself to ask, in spite of being equally as mortified as Carly.

The woman's eyes swivelled from Carly, to Gemma.

'I said, I am well aware your friend and my husband are… *acquainted*,' she emphasised.

Seeming on the point of collapse, a terrible shudder shook Carly.

Gemma gulped. Had she heard right?

'Sorry?' Gemma whispered.

'Your friend, she *is* my husband's mistress, isn't she?'

Both of them distraught and dumbstruck, Carly had her head in her hands, whilst Gemma was on the verge of getting to her feet and running.

'Oh, please, don't look so shocked. Of course I know all about you,' Helen confirmed with a pitiless smile. 'I know all about you, and *all* my husband's *other* women,' she added just as ruthlessly. 'You,' she directed her head toward Carly, 'are hardly the first. And I can assure you, you won't be the last.'

Carly released a small moan.

'Are you saying he's a serial cheat?' said Gemma, sharply.

As though deliberating on how to answer, Helen seemed to think for a second or two. She released a faint grin.

'Oh, I think, I would rather say my husband has... poor impulse controls?'

Gemma stared at the woman in astonishment.

'Poor impulse controls? What the hell is that supposed to mean,' she ejected without thinking.

'Yes, has had, since he was a very young man.'

Gemma shook head. With no real explanation forthcoming, she was struggling to understand.

'And that's a good thing?' Gemma queried, not even trying to hide the incredulity from her voice.

Helen looked into the distance for a moment. Her manner calm, almost relaxed, eventually, she shrugged.

'Who knows? But I can assure you, he's not like you and me.'

Gemma gasped, what a woman. The woman's statements as perplexing as her body language, she was becoming more and more infuriated by the minute. It was time for some answers.

'You know he's had a number of affairs and yet still, you stay with him?'

Helen coolly smiled.

'Of course, we're married.'

Gemma gawped. To say she was shocked at the woman's seemingly nonchalant attitude toward her husband's flagrant disregard for their marriage vows, would be an understatement.

'Again, you're shocked,' said Helen, addressing her comment to Gemma. 'But my husband and I, we've always had a very open and honest relationship. Consequently, I have always known about all his little... hmm... what does he call them? Oh yes, I remember now, his silly little conquests... Because he tells me about them. The type of person he is, he has always had a predilection for screwing any woman stupid enough to make it easy for him...' She switched her attention from Gemma to Carly. 'And, unfortunately, *Ms* Rogers, that now includes you. So you see, in Steve's world and in our marriage, you are nothing special.'

So close to vomiting she had to hold her fist to her mouth, Carly's heartbeat quickened as she struggled for breath.

Silence.

'He told me you were dead,' Carly was eventually able to whisper.

Helen shook her head slowly, disappointedly.

'My, my, not that old chestnut again?'

Carly dropping her head into her hands again, Gemma rubbed her friend's back in what she hoped was a soothing manner. The woman was a complete and utter bitch, she thought aggressively.

Helen chuckled lightly, nastily.

'Oh dear, you poor thing,' she addressed Carly. 'I'm afraid my husband's not very original. Whenever he starts to run out of believable excuses for why he can't *possibly* leave me, he does tend to kill me off.'

A deathly silence.

'Oh, come, come, *Ms* Rogers. Isn't it time you lost that look of astonishment, of hurt? After all, who really is the injured party here?'

'But you were meant to be dead,' Carly repeated uselessly, her voice barely audible.

'Er, no, as you can see, I am still *very* much alive,' Helen said with an unpleasant little smile. 'And if there is one certainty in this life, it is that I will do everything in my power to outlive my husband.'

Carly shook her head slowly. Shock vying with disbelief and horror, she revisited Steve haltingly telling her about his wife's unexpected death, her tragic suicide, the tears glistening in the corner of his eyes, running down his face. She should have checked out his story, been far more thorough and a lot less trusting. If everything this woman had said was true, she had been such a fool and he had played her, for all she was worth. Her thoughts veered suddenly on to how Steve had encouraged her to lie about their relationship, on how he had been so determined to keep her away from his son, from his life in Deal. No wonder, she thought bitterly.

'No matter what you *thought* my husband felt for you or what he told you he felt for you, he will have lied, *Ms* Rogers,' said Helen as she crashed rudely into Carly's thoughts. 'My husband, *Ms* Rogers, is damaged goods. He does not have it in him to love you or anyone else, for that matter. You are simply one more casualty in a long line of indiscretions. Surely you can see that?' she said, her voice flatly monotone as she stuck in the knife.

Filled with a guilty self-reproach, yet still unable to fully convince herself of Steve's duplicity, Carly whispered, 'I don't believe it.'

Carly's statement said more to herself than to the seated woman watching her every move, her every facial gesture, she swiped away her tears.

'He loves me,' she stressed. 'I know he does.'

Almost imperceptibly, Gemma shook her head. Whilst she had the greatest of sympathy for Carly, for what she was going through, what the hell was she thinking? A serial cheat and liar, the man was obviously the lowest of the low, an immoral scumbag. Yet still, Carly was looking to defend him, to defend her relationship with him. What more would it take for Carly to realise, Gemma asked herself, her perfect boyfriend was not to be trusted?

'Tell me, did my husband ever enlighten you as to his background?' Helen asked, her tone expressionless, her face immutable.

Being thrown yet another curveball, the question unexpected and not all sure how to answer, the colour drained from Carly's tear-stained cheeks.

The room growing darker and cooler as a cloud hovered over the sun, the silence lengthened.

The tension too much, Gemma threw a protective arm over Carly's shoulders and gave her a good hard squeeze.

'Come on,' she cajoled. 'Let's go. We've heard all we need to hear.'

But Carly shook Gemma off. Wanting very much to leave but already hooked into what *other* secrets the woman had hinted at, she sat perfectly still.

The woman smirked at Gemma.

'It seems your *friend*,' she enunciated the word like it was a dirty one, 'is keen to stay. But if *you* want to leave, by all means,' she taunted, motioning her hand toward the door.

Though seething with indignation, Gemma stayed put. Her anger kicking in, she could quite easily have wiped the smug grin from the woman's face. She firmly sat on her hands.

'Not going?' The woman derided.

Gemma mutely shook her head.

'OK, so I'm guessing, from your lack of response earlier,' she addressed Carly, 'he somehow forgot to mention that his parents and younger brother... were all murdered?'

Carly and Gemma shared an aghast look.

'All three of them were stabbed to death. Apparently, his father and mother were dispatched with first, then the younger brother met his grisly end. And yes,' she continued on almost chattily, though her eyes were dead, 'it was my husband and your lover, who was found to be the guilty culprit.'

Silent tears ran freely down Carly's cheeks, followed by a swallowed sob.

Gemma lifted a hand to her jaw, and forcibly had to close her gaping mouth.

'Steve was only ten at the time of the murders. All three of them killed in their sleep, he was found guilty of manslaughter on the grounds of diminished responsibility. Placed into a specialist secure unit, at Her Majesty's pleasure, he stayed there for the next thirteen years. Thirteen years, it's a long time for a youngster to be locked up. Must have felt like an eternity. But then the attack, was *frenzied*. In a way,' Helen mused, 'I suppose Steve is one of the lucky ones. Still just a child when he was incarcerated, he was allowed and encouraged to pursue his education to degree level. And he was also given access to all the medical and psychological support the prison system could throw at him. Then after years of therapy, he was rehabilitated and at the age of twenty-three, deemed *safe*. Released from detention with a protected lifelong anonymity, he was granted a whole new identity. As I said, one of the lucky ones really.'

Turning her inscrutable gaze from one to the other of them, Helen stopped on Carly's distraught face. She shook her head and tut-tutted.

'Oh, please, *Ms* Rogers, don't look so upset. You know what, I'll be honest with you. At first, I never knew about my husband's terrible little secret, either. It took me some years and an awful lot of money to wheedle out his past.' She paused for a moment, pondered on something, then began again. 'You know, I was so young when we married, barely twenty-one. So I think I can be forgiven for not recognising how much of a difference, the family money made to my eligibility. Funnily enough, my parents did try and warn me. You see, they thought there was something a little *odd* about his lack of a family, about him actually. But then I always have been strong-willed.' She snorted unattractively. 'You know, if he had managed to keep it in his pants or even been a bit more discrete, I might never have found it necessary to delve quite so closely into his shitty past. Still, as they say, *knowledge is power.*'

Carly softly groaning as she rocked backwards and forwards in her seat, she could not take it all in. Steve was a murderer, a *monster*. Yet, of her own free will, she had invited him into her life, given him access to all areas, her mind, body, and spirit. She must be mad!

Equally struggling, the blood draining from her face, Gemma tightly gripped her hands as she pointedly reminded herself, Steve's wife, could well be lying. By delivering such a horrendous story, about such a heinous crime, what better way for the woman to ensure Carly was put off from continuing the affair?

'If you don't believe me,' Helen said as though reading Gemma's mind, 'I can always show you some of the newspaper clippings dug up by the private detective, I hired.'

The woman's cold and unflinching gaze completely unnerving, Gemma blushed. Seriously tempted to ask for the documents but even more desperate to leave, in the end, it was easier not to. She shook her head at Helen. What did it matter, anyway? After today, there was no way Carly would ever be seeing Steve again, she was sure of it.

'OK, well now I've given you some background information on *my* husband perhaps, *Ms* Rogers, we can get down to the real reason you're here. Time, I think, for a little quid pro quo,' she said ominously.

CHAPTER TWENTY-FIVE

Sat in Steve's palatial seaside home, having a more-or-less one-sided conversation with his *dead* wife, Carly felt sure she was going mad. Enlightened to the fact her boyfriend was a liar, a serial cheat and a money grabbing, three time convicted murderer, she wanted nothing more than to jump up from her seat, tear at her hair and run away screaming. Yet somehow, she had become frozen to the sofa.

The woman now asking her a direct question, something about why they were *really* here, Carly tried to snap herself out her nightmare. In the end, her nemesis appearing to like the sound of her own voice and on an unstoppable roll, she got away with just having to listen.

'I'll tell you why you're here, shall I?' said Helen, her words dripping like acid into the toxic silence as she rigidly stared across at them. 'I would suggest, *Ms* Rogers, you being under the misapprehension that I am dead, having ruled out Steve on the basis of his height, you've been unwisely wondering if your stalker, is my son?'

Both of them unbalanced again, Carly and Gemma looked at each other with horror.

'Oh dear, I can see I've shocked you again?'

She sniggered unpleasantly.

'How do you know about Carly's stalker?' Gemma cried.

'Well, let me reassure you, my son is *not* a stalker,' said Helen, with an edge.

Carly listening but no longer hearing a word, she had to leave it to Gemma to get to the bottom of whatever was going on.

'You didn't answer my question,' said Gemma indignantly.

'Brian is an exceptionally gifted and studious young man who is doing extremely well at school and hasn't missed a day, in months. He has a bright, bright, future ahead of him. So, no, *Ms* Rogers,' she insisted in a deprecating voice, 'my son, is *not* your stalker.'

All Gemma's previous anxiety and fear eclipsed by her need to know how this woman even knew about Carly's stalker, she tried again.

'How do you know about Carly's stalker?' She demanded.

Helen ignored Gemma. Her studied gaze focused only on Carly, there was a strange and terrible glint to her eyes.

Shocked at the coldness radiating out of the woman, Gemma reeled back in her seat. There was something about this woman, Gemma thought as she surreptitiously watched the tightly controlled face, the unnaturally still hands, the tightly crossed legs, that was seriously *off*. Admittedly, she was the wronged spouse so she had every right to be angry, perhaps even cruel and vindictive but there was something else, something more. Suddenly feeling contaminated, like she had been exposed to some sort of unholy disease, it slowly began to dawn on Gemma that there was something about the woman's expression, the blankness behind her eyes that *seriously* creeped her out.

'Nothing to say?' Helen demanded of Carly.

That's it, Gemma thought. Whatever was wrong with the woman, she was not going to allow her bully or frighten Carly, or herself, any longer. It was time they turned the tables and came out fighting.

'So, who is Carly's stalker?' she challenged robustly. 'The way you're talking, you obviously know.'

The woman's return smile was one of pure, malicious scorn.

'Do I?' She shrugged.

The answer not given outright but left clearly hanging in the air, it was unsaid but implicit. Gemma nodded her head at herself.

'Oh, I get it, now. You hired someone, didn't you? The same private detective you used to find out about Steve?'

The woman raised her eyebrows.

'Maybe I did, maybe I didn't?' she teased maliciously.

'God, you are such a *bitch*,' Gemma spat out, unable to stop herself and no longer caring. 'No wonder your husband cheats on you.'

Unshakeably unfazed, the woman smiled condescendingly.

'Your friend has the nerve to cavort with *my* husband. You turn up unannounced at *my* house. Then you accuse *my* son of being a stalker, and I am the bitch?' she retorted.

Gemma shook her head. She placed protective hand over that of her friend.

'I don't get you. You know what type of a person your husband is. You know what he does to other women's lives, not to mention your own, yet still, you do *nothing* to stop him?' Gemma paused for thought, then had a lightbulb moment. 'Christ, that's it, isn't it? You do his dirty work for him. You pick up the pieces when he makes a mess. You're an enabler, aren't you?'

The woman's eyes narrowed as she looked curiously at Gemma.

'Ooh, feistier than you look.'

Two can play at that game, Gemma thought as she shifted in her seat. She pasted on a smile.

'If I find any evidence to show that you *are* the person responsible for hiring someone to stalk my friend, I promise you, we will go straight to the police. Let them deal with you and that sick bastard of a husband, of yours. And as he already has a *past* to reckon with, well…'

The woman sighing, like a person who had seen worse, done worse, her lips curled back with scorn.

'You can go screaming to world about what you think I've done, but you have no proof.'

Even though she was on tricky ground, Gemma had to retaliate.

'If it doesn't stop, right here, right now, I'll get the damn proof. You just watch me!'

'Really?' Helen taunted.

'I'm not sure how much you know but the person you hired to stalk my friend also broke into her home? He defiled her privacy. How sick is that?'

The woman's lip curled up in a half laugh, half sneer. Her eyes narrowed as her voice became more threatening.

'How awful, I can only *imagine* how distressing it must be to have some *stranger* interfering with your most intimate things, your most personal possessions.'

Unable to miss the irony in what the woman was saying, the implied subtext. Knowing that for now, she was beaten, Gemma shivered suddenly, with the horror of it all.

'You *bitch*!' she shouted. 'You and your psycho husband are well suited!'

Throwing her head back, the woman burst out laughing, a high musical laugh that jarred every bone in Gemma's body.

Helen wiped a couple of stray tears of amusement from the corner of her eyes.

'My, my, your tongue is sharper than a guillotine, watch it doesn't cut you.'

Before Gemma could respond or react further, the woman's eyes took on a vicious glint as she stood up from her chair and gestured to the drawing-room door.

'We're done here. You know the way out,' she commanded imperiously. She swivelled her steely eyes to Carly. 'Oh, and you can leave it to me to update *my* husband, *Ms* Rogers. As soon as he gets home, I will let him know he won't be hearing from you again.'

The train leaving Deal station, experiencing a sudden sense of déjà vu as it slid rapidly through the countryside on its way back to the grime of the city, Gemma cast Carly a weak smile across the barrier of the grey metal table in front of them. Met with a frozen stare in return, the tense silence that had dogged them all the way from the woman's house to the station still there, and now unbearable, she lightly addressed her friend.

'Seems like we only just got off this thing.'

Dry eyed, yet apparently still beyond speech, another quiet moment passed as Carly remained unresponsive and reflective.

Giving up for now, Gemma tuned back in to her own thoughts.

On leaving the woman's house, they had not stopped, not anywhere and not for anything. Unable to get away from the picturesque seaside town fast enough, Deal unsurprisingly having lost all its earlier charm, they had hurried straight for the station and boarded the first High Speed Link leaving for London. After all that had happened, both of them miserable and doing a good deal of thinking, they had barely conversed. Now though, they needed to talk. They needed to clear the air.

Determined to get a conversation going, Gemma pointed to Carly's hands.

'You're poor hands, Carly, they're still shaking.'

Carly fumbled for a tissue. She dabbed at the corner of her shining eyes. She shook her head.

'Hadn't noticed.'

Carly's smile wan, in the intensity of her haunted look there was still a touch of horror that tugged at Gemma's heartstrings. Across the table, she placed her own hand over one of Carly's.

'Thanks, Gem.'

'For what?'

'For having my back, for taking care of me in that awful woman's house.'

Touched, Gemma inclined her head toward Carly.

'You know I don't scare easily, Gem, but that woman,' Carly shook her head at the recollection. 'She seriously got to me.'

Gemma felt the exact same way.

'Yeah, there was something really weird about her, don't you think?'

Carly nodded her head thoughtfully. She took a minute.

'Yeah, disturbed, right? Crazy?'

It was a sobering thought. Gemma pulled a wry face as she visibly shivered.

'No idea, but she certainly left me with a lasting impression. The awful thing is, she was right about everything. We still can't prove you've been stalked or that your room was broken into. We can't even prove that's she's the one responsible for hiring the bastard who's been following you.'

Carly bit her sore lip.

'Do you think it'll stop now? The stalking?'

Gemma contemplated. She nodded.

'Yeah, now we've met her, faced her out, I think it has to.'

'You sure?'

Gemma shook her head.

'Can't be a hundred percent, but we know who she is now. And as your affair with Steve is obviously over, what more could she possibly have to gain?'

Carly slowly nodded her head. Then she thought for a moment.

'And you definitely think the stalker was someone she hired, not Brian?'

'I'm not sure it matters anymore? Either way, I suspect she's the one in control.'

'Even though you thought differently before?' Carly pushed.

'I was never sure, I simply suspected it might be Brian. Now though, I'm pretty certain your stalker was someone *she* hired to investigate her husband. He's probably someone she uses regularly, you know, to frighten off the competition when they get too close.' Gemma paused for second. 'Bearing in mind Steve's background and the fact she can't trust him, I reckon she probably has someone permanently keeping an eye on him and reporting back. If I had the money and was married to someone like him, I know I would.'

Carly's tears started to fall again.

'I feel such a fool, Gem. I trusted him. I thought we were in love,' she said wretchedly. 'Everything that's happened today, these last few days, it all seems so incredulous, so unreal.'

Gemma's head swam with the enormity of everything Carly had been through, with everything she had been through. Reflecting back on the dinner with Steve, recalling how charming he had been and how easily he had lied, it helped her to understand how dangerous he really was. Truth known, Carly had had a lucky escape, they all had.

She nodded.

'Yeah, I know what you mean.'

'Nothing about him was real, was it?'

Gemma sadly shook her head.

'No.'

'If his…,' she stalled, 'if his wife was telling the truth and he is a psycho, what if he decides to come after me, after you? Don't forget, he knows where we both live.'

'Something tells me, no matter how sick or twisted he might be, that woman has him well under her control.'

'You think?'

Slowly, Gemma nodded her head.

'Yeah, definitely and if it suited, I don't think she would have the slightest hesitation in getting him banged up again.'

'Begs the question, why hasn't she already? Steve cheating on her all the time, how on earth does she put up with it?'

'No idea?' Gemma mused. 'Perhaps, it has something to do with the boy?'

'Brian?'

'Yeah, I reckon, she's trying to protect him from finding out about his father's past. Not really the sort of thing you want your child having to deal with when they're growing up, is it?'

'No, but she could just divorce him, couldn't she? She said Steve's got protected anonymity, so there's no way Brian would find out. Unless of course, she told him herself.'

'Perhaps, it's Steve? Perhaps, he's the one threatening to tell Brian if she divorces him? She'd also have her family to contend with, don't forget. And for all we know, her parents might be the ones holding the purse strings? Especially if they don't trust Steve,' Gemma added meditatively.

'Christ, if you're right about any of that, what an unholy alliance the two of them are in. In fact, I could almost feel sorry for her, right now.'

Gemma shook her head.

'After today, there's no way I could.'

Carly looked suddenly distraught again.

'Christ, Gem, I've been sleeping with a maniac, a convicted murderer,' she whispered, looking wildly round the almost empty carriage as she checked for anyone within earshot. 'Whatever I do, wherever I go, whoever I go out with next, I'm never going to get over that one, am I?'

Gemma issued her friend a hard stare.

'Yes, you *will*,' she emphasised kindly. 'This will pass. In a short time, this will be a long time ago and *he* will fade into the dim and distant past. I promise you.'

Carly shook her head as the tears welled.

'I've been so silly, ridiculous.'

'Naive.'

'Stupid, stupid, stupid.'

'No, not stupid, you were just in love.'

'Where I'm concerned, it's the same thing.'

'Carly, stop, stop beating yourself up. Focus on the fact, you've had a lucky escape.'

Carly allowed herself a small smile.

'Only you could find the upside to this mess.'

Gemma threw Carly a wicked smile.

'You know what?'

'What?'

'I wouldn't want to be in Steve's shoes tonight. I dread to think how he's gonna feel when that woman tackles him about what's happened today.'

'Steve can shove his thoughts and feelings right up his own arse.' Carly spat out with feeling.

Attagirl, Gemma thought, pleased to see some of Carly's natural feistiness starting to return.

'Carly, I'm sorry. The craziness of these last few days. My almost bullying you into coming down here today. On top of everything else you've been going through, it's all been a bit much, hasn't it?'

'No, no,' Carly protested. 'I'm the one who's sorry. I won't have you blaming yourself for my mess. If I hadn't have been so bloody gullible in the first place, you would never have had to get involved.' She paused, thought. 'I think I need to get me some serious therapy, Gem. Go and see someone qualified to give me some techniques on how to select the right man, or at least avoid the wrong ones.' She grimaced.

Hearing Carly's words, Gemma felt a kind of relief wash over her. Carly seemingly serious about what she was saying and not at all a good judge of character where men where concerned, Gemma was positive it would be good for her friend to get some much needed professional support before she even dared to start dating again.

'I think that's a great idea,' she encouraged.

Carly grinned weakly as she swiped away a solitary tear.

'Yeah, I though you might.'

'So, what now?' Gemma asked.

'I need a drink.'

'Yeah, we'll pick up a bottle of wine on the way home, shall we?'

Carly nodded her head vigorously.

'Two bottles. You're staying at mine, then?'

'Yep.'

'One thing, are you still going to talk to Dave? Tell him about everything that's happened?' Carly asked, looking worried all over again.

Gemma thought through the likely repercussions of updating Dave. On the one hand she wanted to be totally honest with him but on the other, she was wondering about the wisdom of doing so? Obviously, she had to update him on how things had gone with Paul. Reassure him the anonymous text messages had been dealt with. But now the urgent threat of Carly's stalker had been removed from their lives, was there really any gain to be had from telling Dave, everything?

'What would *you* prefer me to do,' she asked?

Carly nervously bit her bottom lip.

'Honestly, I want you to do whatever is right for you and Dave.'

'But?'

'But, we still don't have any evidence for the police to act on.' She paused. 'And now the stalker is out of the picture, is it really worth upsetting Dave? If you do tell him and he forces us to go to the police regardless of the lack of evidence, my career would be ruined.'

'And that would mean, in a roundabout way, Steve and that bitch will have won.'

Carly sighed, thought some more.

'You know what, in truth, all I really want to do is lick my wounds. Put all this behind me and get on with my life.'

'Hmm,' Gemma nodded. 'I feel the exact same way.' She came to a decision. 'OK, that's it then, I won't mention anything to Dave, provided you keep well away from Steve?'

Carly picked up her phone from off the table. She unlocked the device, then passed it over to Gemma.

'Here, delete his contact details for me, will you?'

Scrolling through Carly's contacts, doing as she had been asked, Gemma sighed out with relief as she allowed herself to enjoy a much needed feeling of pleasure, and closure.

CHAPTER TWENTY-SIX

Later that same evening, around nine o'clock, Steve was comfortably ensconced in the drawing-room of his marital home. Wearing pressed navy cords, a perfectly ironed white shirt that was open at the neck and slip-on leather mules, he was sat in a wing chair — his chair — placed adjacent to the righthand side of a hissing, spitting fire. A crystal tumbler with an amber liquid in his left hand, a pen in his right, he was pretending to concentrate on solving the cryptic crossword lying across the arm of the seat. He had always been terrible at crosswords, but he liked to boast otherwise.

After an enjoyable day taking Brian bowling then on to the cinema before dining out at his son's favourite pizzeria — Helen's suggestion — Steve was feeling smugly complacent. His whole objective in life to be throughly comfortable, having replaced his inauspicious beginnings with multiple homes, plenty of money, guilt-free access to other women whenever he wanted them, a clever son, and an organised wife who understood him like no other, who knew life could be so sweet, he thought. If only he didn't have to be gainfully employed but even that, he was working on. A few more embarrassing cock-ups to seriously annoy the wife, the interfering father in-law — not enough to jeopardise the family firm as there was no point in biting off the hand that fed him — he knew they would see sense and rethink the situation.

Helen unexpectedly entering the drawing-room, Steve's pleasant train of thought was instantly compromised. Rarely, did she seek out his company.

His wife taking up the end of the sofa that faced him, Helen kicked off her black ballet pumps, brought her legs up off the floor and stretched them out in front of her as she put a pillow behind her head. Steve looking at her inquiringly, she snapped closed her eyes and ignored him completely. Brian staying overnight at a friend's, the house sat quietly around them as the silence lengthened.

Some minutes later, Steve felt Helen studying him.

Still no acknowledgement and curiosity getting the better of him, Steve looked up from his crossword.

'Good day?' he asked genially.

Steve's eyes sweeping all over Helen's form, he took in every little detail from the scarlet painted toenails, the three-quarter-length black trousers, the grey cashmere jumper, the long hair tidily caught back with a sliver Alice band from a subtly made-up face, the small gold watch on her wrist, the diamond studs in her ears, to the large diamond solitaire on the third finger of her left hand sparkling in the firelight. As always, his wife looked effortlessly and sublimely perfect, thought Steve, with a keen sense of self-gratification.

Helen's face blank and dispassionate as she looked across at him, she comfortably held his penetrating gaze.

'Different,' she replied.

Helen's response perplexing and beginning to feel a niggle of apprehension, Steve bestowed on her a winsome smile. Unsurprisingly, it was not returned. His charm offensive snubbed as usual, Steve returned to his crossword and they both fell quiet. If he had to wait, then so could she.

'Aren't you going to ask me *how* my day was different?'

Steve grinned to himself. Whatever it was that was eating at her, she was dying to tell him. Yet her tone cool, her voice indifferent as he found himself on the end of a very sweet smile, one of the falsest he had ever seen, he was instantly suspicious.

'OK, I'll bite. Tell me, my darling, how was your day so different?' he urged her on, his curiosity whetted in spite of himself.

She closed her eyes, took her time again.

Sensing Helen was leading up to something unexpected, something likely to unsettle his equilibrium, that she was trying to play with him, Steve shifted in his seat and got a little more comfortable as he prepared himself for the ensuing game.

'Tell me, is living here agreeable to you?' Helen asked in a tone that crackled with ice.

Steve exhaled loudly, as if the question was so loaded he had no idea where to begin. He took a swig of brandy, bought himself a little more time as he searched for a reason as to why his wife would be baiting him so ruthlessly. Nothing obvious sprang to mind.

'Well, is it?' she prompted.

His wife sounding unusually impatient, Steve arched his eyebrow at her. He loved to wind her up.

'You know it is.'

'Really? You do surprise me,' she said obscurely.

Starting to lose his own patience, Steve frowned. His wife's atypical behaviour tiresomely mirroring the complexity of his crossword, he wished she would stop giving him only cryptic clues and get to some of the solutions.

'Is something the matter, my dear?'

'Tell me,' she paused for effect, 'what do you know about a woman called, Carly Rogers?'

Straightening in his seat, Steve's crossword dropped from the arm of his chair and into his lap. Now that was a question and answer, he had not expected. Helen sounding more than a little annoyed and not in any hurry to incriminate himself, Steve took another sip of brandy as he sought to gather his thoughts.

'Well?'

'The fact you feel so compelled to ask me about her, obviously means, you already know I do,' he replied with a sudden irritation.

'Yes, I suppose it does,' she conceded.

'So why ask?'

'I ask... because she came by the house today.'

'The house?'

'Yes, and she wasn't looking for me,' Helen said quite casually.

Taken aback by his wife's rather surprising news, Steve tried not to grimace. Their Deal home sacrosanct, he knew he was on dodgy ground as he scoured his brain for a plausible reason as to why the stupid girl would dare to turn up on his doorstep, as to how she even knew where he lived? But he came up empty. He shook his head at himself. He thought he had had her under better control.

'She came here?' was all he could find to say.

With eyes that were dark and empty, Helen shot him a good hard look.

'Yes, and why do you think that might be?'

A long silence.

His back stiffening, Steve loosened his shoulders. Helen obviously prepared to wait it out, he decided, there was little point in not answering. So he shrugged, then batted the ball back to her.

'How should I know? I wasn't here,' he protested, grinning from ear to ear.

Unamused, Helen looked him straight in the eye. Her voice low, there was a rigid, underlying cold edge of steel to it.

'Because of your laziness, your stupidity, or both, you've obviously let this affair continue on for far too long and she's got curious.'

Irritated, and even a little fazed to realise he had somehow dropped the ball, Steve continued to try and make light of the matter.

'Ouch, now that hurt,' he complained wryly.

Helen twisted round her right foot, held it up for a moment as though she was inspecting the bright red polish on her toenails. Then she flashed him another steely look.

'For years, I have put up with your petty indiscretions. I've them hidden from my family, and our son. But if there is one thing I will *not* tolerate, it is your *tarts* turning up at this house. I may be liberal enough to allow you to use *my* London flat as your private whorehouse but this,' she expressively waved her hands around the room, 'is *my* home. It's our son's home.'

In spite of himself, anger never far from the surface and the real reason he *never* drank to excess, Steve bridled.

'Hey, I'm not the villain here,' he spat out nastily. 'I didn't ask the stupid bitch to turn up, did I?'

'And yet she did, though, didn't she?' Helen pointed out coolly. 'And at the risk of repeating myself,' she said, her demeanour aloof and patronising, 'I really don't care about your *women*, your *whores,* or whatever you want to call them? But I do care about our son and my family. And so should you.'

'I do,' Steve said succinctly.

'If that's true, then perhaps you'd care to explain how *Ms* Rogers and that fat friend of hers, know this address?'

This was getting tricky, really tricky, Steve thought warily.

'Her fat friend?' he delayed.

'A woman called Gemma.'

Steve nodded to himself.

'Gemma Atkinson, she's Carly's best friend and her partner, Dave, is Carly's brother. Gemma and Dave have a couple of kids between them. One each, from different partners. They live together, in Leyton. I met them the other…'

Thinking out loud, too late, Steve realised he had divulged too much information. Helen raised her eyebrows as a thunderous look flashed all too briefly, across her pale face.

'All very cosy, I thought we had an understanding?'

Saint Helen getting all high and mighty, when in fairness, all he had done was bend the rules a little, Steve sighed.

'We do.'

'So how did you meet them?'

There was no point in lying now, Steve thought. If there was one thing Helen was exceptionally good at, it was that she read him like a book.

'A couple of weeks ago, we went to their place for dinner.'

Steve's smile drippy and fake as he sought to sweeten the sour news, Helen visibly recoiled from him.

'Christ, really? Where?'

Steve reeled off Gemma's address.

Helen filed it away for another day.

'You are *such* a fool! What the hell did you think you were you playing at? We agreed, no more than three months, per tart. And you certainly do *not* get to socialise with their family and friends.'

Helen regarding him like a disappointed parent, or in his case, a dispirited probation officer, Steve could not be less bothered.

'Yeah, well, I was getting bored. It was simply a bit of harmless fun.'

'Bored? Harmless? You are such a schmuck. And if you were so bored, why haven't you got rid of her already?'

'You really want to know?' He leered suggestively.

'Always so charming,' she bit back.

Again, Steve shrugged. Finding Helen seriously tedious, her flagrant lack of respect and total disregard toward him starting to really bite, he was almost at the end of his tether.

'What can I say, I'm a *bad* man?'

Feeling an unexpected prick of regret as it suddenly dawned on him his relationship with Carly was now well and truly over, Steve immediately consoled himself with the thought, there were plenty more where she came from. Shame though. Naive and uncomplicated, a sucker for romance, Carly had been so easy to manipulate, and she was fun.

'Well, your *bit of fun*, has got out of hand. Tell me, how did your *Ms* Rogers come by this address?' Helen asked coldly, her glacial eyes narrowing and flashing dangerously.

No matter what he said, this was not going to go away, Steve thought as he took another distracting sip of brandy. His eyes met hers.

'How should I know,' he snapped out, tired of all her questions, her accusations?

'Well, she didn't conjure up our address from out of thin air, did she?'

Helen's words cutting, Steve took a deep breath. The sooner he thought this through and got to the bottom of how the stupid girl had found out where he lived, the sooner his wife would leave him in peace.

Putting his hands together, as if he were in a church, he concentrated, hard.

For a minute or two, there was an eerie silence.

'The spare key,' he muttered.

'What?'

Steve slugged back the last drop of brandy with a rattle of ice. He stared defiantly back at his wife. Well, here goes nothing, he thought.

'Months ago, I gave a spare flat key to the old biddy next door, for deliveries and such like. Carly was there when I did it. She must have tapped up the demented old bird and borrowed it from her?'

Shrugging his shoulders, Steve slid the responsibility from them.

'So? How does that equate to her getting our address?'

'My briefcase, with my mail in it, it's in the flat. I forgot to bring it home with me.'

Helen issued Steve a withering look.

'You are such a brainless imbecile,' she said brutally.

He stared at her impassively, said arrogantly, 'I don't know what you're so worried about? I take it you've sent her packing?'

Helen pulled herself up off the couch, slipped on her ballet pumps, smoothed down her clothes and walked over to the windows. Closing the heavy silk drapes against a pitch black night sky, the oily sea, she slowly turned to face him.

'Never again, will I clear up your mess,' she snapped harshly.

Feeling unexpectedly uncomfortable under the gaze of his wife's all too hostile stare, Steve got up out of his chair. Turning his back to her, he walked toward the sideboard and refilled his glass with a slim finger of brandy, added ice. He hated that she had unnerved him. Glaring at his glass with ball-bearing eyes, anger boiling inside him, he knew he had to get a hold of himself before he did something he, and his wife, would ultimately regret.

In the glow of the firelight, the amber liquid glittering like tarnished bronze as Steve swilled it round and round the glass, he turned to face her.

'Whatever,' he said pugnaciously.

Without warning, Helen's relatively composed guard abruptly dropped. Her face coming suddenly alive, it flickered with disgust and fury as her eyes flashed dangerously.

Steve having to acknowledge to himself that his wife had never looked more savage or attractive. That it was this other, more menacing and usually hidden side of Helen that had first allured him to her all those years ago — that and the money of course — he could almost wish she was not frigid. Such a complex character his wife, how hidden her depths were, he mused.

Helen pointing a finger at him as she spoke, she stabbed it toward his chest as though it was a knife. 'You are a loathsome, self-centred, self-satisfied creature, a moral abomination. And although I accept you are unable to help the more *base* of your urges, I *refuse* to live with the consequences of them. Not forgetting, I own *everything* you hold dear and enjoy, including our son,' she said savagely.

Steve pasted on a grin as the hair on his arms and the back of his neck, electrified. It wasn't like they hadn't been here before. Under no silly illusions as to what was expected of him, he sighed. At that point where she would accept nothing less, the time had come, he knew, for him to grovel. Still it stung.

Made to think on the unvarnished truth, on how his wife did, indeed, own everything, Steve inwardly winced. Helen's parents signing over the family business — ably run by a board of directors and trustees so Helen had no need to work herself — to his wife a few years back, she was also the sole owner of all three of their properties — Deal, London and Italy. She also owned the cars, the boat, their stock and shares, their bank and savings accounts, everything. Even her will was made out in entirely in favour of their son. He also knew, because she had told him, should anything untoward happen to her, there was a handwritten and signed letter lodged with her solicitor that provided information, in detail, on his disadvantageous background. Having to concede to himself, just how clever and devious his wife was, feeling simultaneously infuriated and turned on, the sudden and unwelcome thought he might not know his glorious wife quite as well as he thought he did, irked Steve, immensely.

Toasting his glass in Helen's direction, Steve took up his seat again. 'Yes, you most certainly do.' He nodded sagely

Helen was not finished with him yet.

'In three years time, our son will be eighteen and going away to university and at which point, his need for you...' she threatened.

Steve held his wife's glare for only a second before looking away. Silently acknowledging that for now, she had him completely by the balls, he sighed out dramatically.

'I'm sorry about today,' he grovelled, 'but it's all sorted now, so no real harm done. And I know I've said it before, but I'll say it again, I am so lucky to have such a beautiful and capable wife,' he flattered.

Was that a smirk of satisfaction he saw cross her face? He grinned.

'You're insane.'

He nodded, gave a mirthless chuckle.

'Yes, I most certainly am but then, my dear, so are you. You and I, we are so alike, we deserve each other.'

The slightest flicker in one eyelid, her guard restored, no other emotion crossed Helen's face as she quietly but warningly stated, 'Be careful, husband dear. You have no idea who I really am, or what I am capable of.'

298

Yeah, nor you, I, Steve thought with a real twist of loathing.

CHAPTER TWENTY-SEVEN

Six weeks later, the days have come and gone, and are palpably shortening now in the run up to Christmas. The house chaotic with the sound of a family readying itself to leave for the day's challenges, Gemma checked her reflection for the hundredth time that morning as she anxiously chewed her bottom lip.

'You look beautiful,' Dave reassured, nuzzling a kiss into the side of her neck as he came up behind her. 'Perfect, in fact.'

Gemma smiled back at him through the dressing table mirror. She spritzed some perfume on her wrists, the base of her throat, then pulled at the spikes of her brand new pixie cut, made them stand proud.

'You think?'

'Stunning.'

Dave leering at her through the mirror, Gemma returned a self-conscious smile. He really was incorrigible.

'What about the kids, are they ready for school?'

'Almost.'

'You?'

'Gemma, I've got this. All you have to do, is focus on getting to your interview on time.'

She nodded and smiled as brightly as she could.

Patting down the dressing table top, Gemma looked around its scattered contents.

'I know it's silly,' she said to Dave through the mirror, 'and I'm getting wound up about nothing, but I can't find my new glasses anywhere?'

Having to wear glasses was a new phenomenon for Gemma and she had yet to get used to having them. To vain to wear them on a chain, she was always misplacing the damn things.

'Are they in any way, like the ones on top of your head?' Dave teased as he pointed to the glasses she had only just buried in amongst the spiked tips of her hair.

Gemma giggled.

'Honestly, I've been looking for them for ages. What a Wally? I'm losing it, Dave, I'm definitely losing it,' she said nervously.

Before Dave could reply, there was a light knock on the bedroom door. A muffled, 'Mum, Dave, can we come in, please?' from Henry.

Dave striding across the room, he opened the bedroom door wide as their answer. With Jessica directly behind him, Henry hesitantly moved into the threshold.

'C'mon you two, come on in,' said Dave, ushering in both children.

'This is for you, mum,' said Henry, proudly. 'It's from all of us.'

Her son's chubby little cheeks pinking up adorably as he hastily shoved the package he had been so gingerly carrying out in front of him, Gemma pushed away her nerves and smiled broadly. Taking the tissue wrapped parcel out of Henry's hands, she gave it an exploratory squish, then beamed at the three of them.

'A present? You bought a present, for me?'

'Yes, it's to wish you luck,' Henry explained earnestly.

All three of them smiling back at her, they all looked happy and excited for her. So different to how things were a few weeks ago, Gemma mused, with a contented silly grin.

'Come on then, open it up,' Dave encouraged.

Needing no further persuasion, Gemma ripped off the tissue paper and extracted a bright red scarf. The silk garment slipping luxuriously through her fingers, she exclaimed with awe and surprise.

'Gosh, it's beautiful, exquisite. And simply perfect for what I'm wearing today.'

Gemma motioned to the dark navy skirt suit that had cost her and Dave a small fortune. An investment in her future and therefore, *an upfront expense that just had to be borne*, Dave had insisted after watching her try it on.

'Henry and I chose it,' Jessica piped up shyly.

Gemma got up from her dressing table stool. Artfully draping the silk scarf around her neck, now in a mood of boisterous excitement, she went over to the children and gave each of them a massive squeeze followed by a peck on the cheek.

'I love it. It makes me feel really special. But you know what's best of all, it means I get to take the three of you into the interview room with me. And having you three there, will give me all the confidence I need,' she enthused.

'Right you two, go and get all your school things together. Five minutes and we're leaving,' Dave insisted as he chivvied the kids along. 'Love you,' he whispered over his shoulder as he left the room, taking the kids with him.

What a long way we've all come, Gemma mused happily to herself as she went on the hunt for a brand new pair of leather pumps bought at the same time as her suit. Such an awful, shaky start to them living together, yet somehow, they had got through it all — the nightmare of Jessica's disruptive behaviour, the nastiness of Paul's horrendous text messages, the loss of Dave's job, the polarising fear caused by Carly's stalker.

Following that horrendous day in Deal, it hadn't taken Gemma long to realise just how fortunate she was to have a Dave in her life. Finally appreciating just how much she loved and respected her partner's agreeable and conscientious personality traits, his easy sense of humour, his generous and loving heart, his quiet strength, suddenly desperate not to lose him and unable to believe that someone like *him* loved *her*, she had got her act together. From that point forward, the pair of them pulling together, they had been determined to make their relationship work and not just for the sake of the kids. Out of adversity, she smiled, had come strength.

With Gemma's blessing, Dave had used the bulk of his redundancy money as a springboard to set up his own accountancy business. Whether Dave's new business venture would become a success or not, Gemma had no idea as it was still too early to tell. But feeling as though she was at one with life again, she was not worried. Dave's change in circumstance also allowing them to reassess their stereotypical roles, with him now working from home, he had willingly taken over the running of the household and the kids. 'Relish the challenge,' he had said easily.

At last realising, she could totally depend on Dave and that she could respect his judgement, Gemma had listened carefully when he had encouraged her to reclaim her career. Leaving university at twenty-one with a degree in Business Administration, Gemma's ultimate goal had always been to make Senior Manager by the age of thirty. Just like Katie, she had aspired to having a secretary, an assistant, an expense account and a designer wardrobe, but she had also planned on being a whole lot nicer. Her future carefully mapped out and tantalisingly within her reach, after a boozy night out with Paul and one unplanned pregnancy later, it had all been snatched away.

Once she had got over the shock of being 'knocked-up' as Paul had so politely put it, even though Gemma had been the higher salary earner out of the two of them, the old-fashioned type, he had refused to even consider he might be the one to put his fledgling career on hold after their baby was born. She then struggling to leave their vulnerable son in the hands of strangers and unable to juggle the needs of a baby alongside a demanding career, it had not worked out. By the time Henry was six months old, she had handed in her notice. Now, though, with Henry reassuringly deposited into the safe care of Dave's guiding hands, the years of penny pinching, of putting up with a monstrous boss, would soon be over. On the cusp of launching her career again, she was so excited, she could hardly wait.

Lifting her gaze from the floor, where she had been avidly hunting for the new shoes, catching an unexpected glimpse of herself in the full length mirror on the front of the wardrobe, Gemma was briefly stopped in her search for a moment. Shyly admiring her slightly trimmer form, she smiled happily. Dave cooking healthy meals for the four of them, she keeping up a weekly yoga class with Carly and walking everywhere now she was actively using the Tube again, the combined effect was beginning to make a noticeable difference not only to her figure, but also her confidence.

'Gemma, we're leaving now!' Dave yelled up the stairs. 'See you later! When you get a minute, don't forget to give me a ring! Let me know how you got on!'

'I will! But don't forget I'm catching up with Carly straight after the interview!'

'Got it! Give her my love!'

Gemma nodded to herself as she heard the front door crash closed behind Dave and the kids.

The elusive shoebox at last found at the bottom of the wardrobe — of course — and shoes slipped on, Gemma took one last look at herself in the full length mirror and decided, she would do.

Exiting from the modern glass and steel building in which her interview had just taken place, Gemma breathed out a grateful sigh of relief. In spite of the nerves, the tricky questions, she was quietly optimistic she had done well. Her potential new employer promising to call her with their decision within the next couple of days, she was feeling simultaneously excited and terrified. Liking what she had researched on the company's ethics, their place in the market, her interview with them confirming she was keen to get the role as well as the opportunities it would bring, the benefits and salary it promised, Gemma had the distinct feeling it was going to be a long and uncomfortable forty-eight hours.

Upbeat, sure that even if she was unlucky enough not to get *this* job she would get another, even better one, Gemma stepped out cheerfully. Equally relieved to know it was only a matter of time before she would be freed from a boss she despised and a role that left her feeling bored and unfulfilled, what little fear remained, came only from wondering if she still had what it took to survive in the dog-eat-dog world of Advertising & Marketing. Whatever the end result, Gemma comforted herself in the knowledge that there had to be a much better place to work, and an even better way to make a living.

Still electrified by her interview and enjoying her solitary walk, Gemma had to physically prevent herself from skipping along the pavement like a delighted child. Feeling liberated and wonderfully unburdened, she could shout to the rooftops.

The sudden hiss of air breaks from a London bus pulling up alongside a bus stop, Gemma broke out of her reverie. For the first time since she had left home that morning, it being the second week of December, she began to notice she was surrounded by all the sights, sounds, and smells of Christmas spilling out of the shops. Twinkling lights and decorations hanging and swaying on light posts above the streets, Yuletide was most definitely in the air and the entire city, blatantly getting into the spirit.

Gemma loved *Crimbo* as her father called it and this year, she was particularly looking forward to it. Their first Christmas together as a unified family, it should be fun. The kids also excited, already wanting to decorate the house and their bedrooms, she and Dave had encouraged them put up the Christmas tree far earlier in the month than either of them would normally allow. The season of goodwill to all men, and all that, who the hell cared, she thought jauntily?

Striding nonchalantly into an expensive food market famed for its organic but expensive produce, Gemma picked up a pack of smoked salmon, six eggs and a bottle of champagne for Dave and herself, a disgustingly rich chocolate fudge cake for the kids to share, and a skinny soy latte to go. Tonight, the job interview having gone well, her hopes high, she intended to treat them all to a celebratory feast and for once, hang the cost.

Met by a wall of sound, the Underground manic with people, Gemma tucked herself into a cramped but free corner of the main concourse. Stood not far from the entrance-exit steps, she sipped at her drink and avidly scanned the crowd. Carly already riding around on the Tube somewhere, Gemma knew she would appear from one of the station's connecting tunnels anytime soon but so far, she could see no sign of her friend's tell-tale red hair dancing up and down between the pirouetting throng.

The December wind flinging the last leaves of autumn down the Underground steps,   from somewhere up top, Gemma occasionally caught muffled wisps of piped Christmas music filtering out from a shop's sound system. Lunchtime Christmas revellers everywhere, the noise levels in the station were raucous. One woman wearing gold tinsel threaded through her platinum blonde hair unknowingly trod on Gemma's toes. Whilst another, leeringly drunk, his Santa hat lolling crazily to one side, looked as though he was after groping the gold tinsel lady as he lurched hotly in her wake. Smiling at the antics, enjoying that it was the season of good cheer, Gemma liked everything about today.

Her coffee finished, Gemma glanced at her wristwatch, Carly was late. Checking the LED boards for any line closure notices, she saw nothing untoward but still, she was getting twitchy. She agitatedly scanned the crowd. Where was she?

'Come on, Carly,' she whispered under her breath?

Ten more minutes later, Carly still nowhere to seen and now twenty minutes late, Gemma wondered if she should try and call her. But Carly down in the Underground somewhere, realising there would be no reception, there seemed little point.

A cold draught blew Gemma's hair from her cheeks and for some inexplicable reason, she felt an inner chill, along with a sudden foreboding. Another rush of icy air swirled around her stocking clad legs and this time, the chill sliced through her.

Shivering with uneasiness, a horrid feeling of fear, Gemma suddenly had to fight off an all to familiar and unwelcome feeling of panic, God help her!

CHAPTER TWENTY-EIGHT

So now you know who I am. Or at least you think you do. I bet you also thought this story was all about her, didn't you? Yet you could not be more wrong because always, it was only ever about me.

I have decided to kill her, Ms Rogers, but not, you understand, through jealousy as that is an emotion I have always deplored. No, what drives me, is anger and resentment. Who is she to assume she can so randomly infiltrate the life of another, without consequence? Caught red-handed, exposed, and yet not once did she apologise for her clumsy intrusion into my life. Her audacity, it is astonishing. Her presumption, her conceit, her concern for her own welfare rather than her wrongdoing, all of that along with the unspoken insults she and that fat friend of hers levelled at my intelligence, no, that is what I can never forgive. And now, I will destroy her.

Unlike my other, opportunistic accident-suicides, this time, I have made my plans carefully. Determined to encourage a false sense of security, for six tedious weeks, I have kept my distance and patiently waited. Now though, I am done with all the subterfuge and I have every intention, of watching her gasp her last breath.

Arriving at her address under the cover of darkness early this morning — her daily teaching schedule deleted from her website — no-one saw me. She never saw me. Now following her down into the Underground, which at this time of the day and at this time of year, is heaving, I pursue boldly behind her knowing my presence will never be noticed — not by her, not by any cameras, not by anyone. Barely important enough to kill, she is certainly not important enough to go to jail for.

Measuring my tread to hers, her stride full of momentum as she purposely advances through the subterranean tunnels, I automatically lower my head as I hunch down into my jacket and blend in with the cavorting crowd.

Dressed in bright, vibrant clothes, the Underground her catwalk as she parades through, like a fashion model, she seems unaware that all eyes are on her and that striking red hair. I admire her nonchalance.

Soon, I promise myself, soon.

Suddenly, I spot the other one. The redhead approaching her fat friend, it starts me wondering... two, for the price of one? If the opportunity presents, why not? No matter what, today, I will have my pound of flesh.

They greet each other — sickening air kisses, a brief hug, a look of utter relief on the fat one's face as she extends a wagging finger of admonishment toward the redhead. Tut-tut, Ms Rogers, you must be late, I think. The pair now pushing their way through the horde that seeks to constrain them, I watch them follow the signs for the Central Line tunnel.

Perfect.

Down on the heaving platform, the next train due in three minutes, the redhead and her fat friend squeeze through the crush in single-file as they manage to inch themselves closer and closer, to the edge.

Even better.

Sensing how near I am to achieving my goal and tantalised by the thought, I find a few precious seconds to savour the moment. Slowly, I lick my lips.

The friends standing side by side and right on the cusp of the dull yellow line, both of them hemmed in at the sides but not a soul between them and the platform's edge, I push myself forward. Tucking myself in right behind the redhead, I am so close I can suddenly smell her perfume, an overpowering stench that now has the power to bring back memories.

My heart pumping with adrenaline, getting ready, I catch my excited breath.

A muffled ringing, a mobile phone extracted from her cheap imitation leather handbag, she clasps it to her ear. Smiling animatedly at the unseen caller, turning her head, she briefly looks straight at me with zero appreciation for who I really am. Having experienced a moment of qualm, with this last glimpse of complacency, it vanishes.

A puff of warm air sighs down the blackened tunnel, the muffled roar of a rapidly approaching train.

The crowd pulsating in response, it expands its swelling form, outward and forward.

Distracted by her phone, she has moved well beyond the yellow line. Within centimetres of the platform's edge, she has no awareness of who is behind her.

I too step forward.

The pit of my stomach tingling in anticipation, with excitement, the train drawing nearer and nearer, becoming louder and louder, it is now or never!

Feigning a shove from behind, I stumble and allow the full force of my weight to slam into her back.

At first, there is a grunt of surprise, then as she instantly drops from sight, there is an agonised shriek of pure terror followed by a muted scream of pain as something thuds heavily on to the train tracks below.

Barely able to contain my rapture, I hold fast to my glee as not wanting to be evident, I unify myself with the confused and staggered crowd.

The other one also on the extreme edge of the platform as she peers down into the void, I weigh up the possibility… But I am too far back. And she is too plain to see.

This time, she has got away with it but next time, she won't.

Reminding myself there is no need for haste, let her grieve, I console myself. Let her suffer!

Side-stepping round the those rubber-necking to see what has happened, I take a moment. Looking down on to the train track, I see she has missed the live rail. Her body writhing and convulsing, visibly broken, she wears a look of indescribable terror. Tortured by her mortal injuries and beyond speech, her head flails around like a dying fish as silently, she pleads for help. Her audience almost motionless with stupefaction, her friend screaming for someone to do something, suddenly, her terrified eyes lock on to mine. A flash of puzzlement followed by an instant recognition, this time, she has plainly seen me. Dispatching a surreptitious wink, a small smile and look that says, yes, I am exactly, who you think I am, she emits an agonised wail.

Whoosh and there it is. There is that sense of immediate gratification, of overwhelming omnipotence as I immerse myself in her all too visible distress, her helplessness and pain, so satisfying.

Indecision and panic all around me, a few hardened individuals spring into action as they begin to push their way through the melee. Others, peel away from the horror that is about to unfold. A few even hold their phones aloft, their arms rising into the air to ghoulishly video or take pictures of the scene that is about to play out before them.

Mental note to self, I remind myself, check YouTube later.

Acknowledging there are a lot of onlookers, numerous amateur photographers and film makers plus a number of CCTV cameras, I have to ask myself, what has anyone actually captured or seen? Time elapsed — under three minutes. Potential perpetrator — Caucasian, short blonde hair, average build and height, and wearing nondescript everyday clothes, the sort that would have been bought from the main high street shops and that could be worn by anyone, of any age, of any sex. Out of the station, I will dive into one of the many store bathrooms and change my appearance, in under five minutes. Congratulating myself on how well I am developing, on how well I am evolving my method of working, my undetectable modus operandi, I get an instant buzz of gratification. My ability to transform so easily from who I am into who I am becoming and ultimately, into who I want to be, evidently second nature, it is all within my control.

Reassured I am safe from detection, I award myself a tad more time to look back. To have a last little linger as I relish the results of my accomplishments.

Shouting, a cacophony of competing voices, a woman's shriek.

The train, it is coming.

The familiar screech of the train, of metal squealing against metal as it applies its breaks.

The friend lying down at the platform's edge, she screams. Just in time, she pulls back her outstretched head and hands.

You dare to hurt me, I'll hurt you worse, I think, smiling to myself.

Reluctant to leave but my objective met, I force myself to casually turn away.

Out of the corner of my eye, I catch sight of a strip of bright red fabric, hovering in the air.

End of our story? No, not quite...

Just when you think you've forgotten me, when you are mindlessly interrogating your phone, reading your book — this book — remember, I will be watching and waiting...

Everywhere, yet nowhere, I will be right behind you...

You are never safe.

'MIND THE GAP!'

45135844R00186

Printed in Poland
by Amazon Fulfillment
Poland Sp. z o.o., Wrocław